WHEN YOU GET TO THE OTHER SIDE

WHEN YOU GET TO THE OTHER SIDE

MARIANA OSORIO GUMÁ
translated by CECILIA WEDDELL

CINCO PUNTOS PRESS
an imprint of Lee & Low Books Inc.
New York, NY

CINCO PUNTOS PRESS
an imprint of LEE & LOW BOOKS Inc.
95 Madison Avenue, New York, NY 10016
leeandlow.com

Edited by Stephanie Frescas Macías
Cover design by Grace Han
Production by The Kids at Our House
Manufactured in the United States of America
by Lakeside Book Company
PB 10 9 8 7 6 5 4 3 2 1
First Edition

Cataloging-in-Publication Data on file with the Library of Congress
PB ISBN 978-1-94762-761-1
EBK ISBN 978-1-94762-766-6

¡Vivan los pájaros de El Chuco!

In memory of Marcel and Edmond Sanquer, travelers, friends, the best hosts in the world. With profound gratitude.

"El verdadero anfitrión es el que invita a cenar."
–Molière

"Yo no crucé la frontera, la frontera me cruzó."
"I didn't cross the border, the border crossed me."
–Los Tigres del Norte

The morning they left Amatlán in the bed of a pickup truck, in the hours between darkness and daybreak, the world became immense and noisy. Emilia Ventura shut her eyes and inhaled deeply, bringing in the fresh air of her homeland. She wanted to hold onto it. Let it go down into the depths of her soul, wrapped securely in the mist of daybreak. All it would take was a search through the corners of her mind for the mountain to return, all at once, complete with its colors, its crickets and chachalacas, and its smell of rain. At twelve years old, she already sensed the unbridgeable measure of time that would have to pass before she could recover even a piece of the world she'd grown up in.

As the truck passed, dogs from the nearby villages ran and barked after it. They wanted to catch up to the monster with ten heads and four wide, round feet that traveled down the road. Heads of silent and preoccupied travelers, immersed in their sense of loss and longing. The leaves of the jocote trees were already behind them when Emilia and Gregorio Ventura felt the eyes full of questions, advice, and warnings on them. Wondering if the boy, with his crooked foot, would be able to handle the relentless marching that lay ahead. If the girl, so young and green, could escape all the vermin lurking along the way. One of the men piped up and asked if someone was meeting them before the crossing. If anyone was waiting for them on the other side. If they knew how to take care of themselves. If this, if that.

"Yes, sir," Gregorio jumped in, exasperated. "They're waiting for us right up ahead. Right, Calandria?" And he threw his sister a conspiratorial glance.

A row of adobe houses gave way to cinder block constructions—soulless grays with the debris of old junk and trash gathered wherever you looked. The truck shook as it crept forward. And even still, Emilia Ventura dozed off for a couple hours, until the sun beat down on the back of her neck. They finally stopped in a village populated by busted-up sheet metal structures, dirt, and balding trees in pastures drier than a dead animal's loin.

"I'll be back right now—gonna look for the guy takin' you through the next part," said their driver, a sour-faced young man named Darío, and he disappeared down a path.

The travelers stepped down. The men went off to pee. The women did what they could farther off, out of sight, covering for each other. Then they all stood next to the car, just off to the side since nobody dared to go more than a couple steps away. Half a dozen houses made from sheet metal and concrete formed a line a few meters further. Another truck arrived a while later, carrying about twenty people. A coming and going of people at wait. They wandered back and forth with their backpacks still on, or they splayed out on the dry and dusty grass, chewing, drinking, talking.

An abrupt wind brought in a dust storm: wrappers, litter, dry leaves. Straw hats and baseball caps went flying, thoughts got scrambled in the air. It felt like a whirlwind that brought with it a secret message from a parallel universe. Emilia looked at her brother.

"What're you lookin' at me for, Calandria," he asked, then felt a tenderness as he inspected the bright and questioning eyes of his little sister. The freshness of her curiosity. He, too, recognized there was an omen in the dust storm.

"Nothin', Caco," Emilia said with a shake of her head as she followed the dust with her eyes.

Caco, Goyo, Gregorio. Emilia, Calandria.

The strong winds of her hometown swirled into Emilia's thoughts—the way they came during the dry season, lifting dust and dirt and whatever else they found in their path. So strong that the trees' branches would crackle and the electric cables would swing from side to side until they broke free of their posts and left the town in darkness. The wind would whir through the spaces between rocks and produce a whimper like a suffering animal, making even the toughest people's skin crawl. Emilia remembered how, after all that, something unexpected would happen. They'd find money or hear of the sudden death of an acquaintance or get news of someone falling off a cliff or someone else drowning in the deepest part of the river. Or it could be an unannounced circus, or a fair, or a bullring popping up in the central plaza. And then their father, who almost never spent time with them, would hurry them to get dolled up in their nicest rags and take them to see the animals and the acrobats at the circus or to stroll through the fair and go on the rides. Or he'd buy tickets to get a glimpse of the brave riders who managed to stay on a bucking bull. There was no way to know if the dust storm would bring something good or bad. They just knew that there was no mistaking it: The windstorms always announced the arrival of something new.

The dust devil surrounding them didn't last longer than a minute. Gregorio lowered his head and drew circles in the dirt with the toe of his sneaker—that's what he did whenever the disorder of his soul overwhelmed him.

Finally they saw Darío on his way back. He was talking to an obese man who had a scar on one cheek. The man's eyes, dark as a capulín cherry, looked over each traveler one by one. He paused when they landed on Emilia, and she turned her face the other way.

"You're lucky," Darío announced. "Chato here tells me that the group is almost all set to go right to the crossing. You'll pay him the half we agreed on, and the rest you'll pay over there where he leaves you."

Emilia and her brother exchanged looks. They had already given part of the money to Darío and now they only had enough to pay at the crossing. He had promised them they wouldn't have to let go of another peso until they reached the border.

Some of the men were haggling when Gregorio went up to Darío.

"We already gave you the money. Didn't you say we wouldn't have to pay out until the crossing? If we give this guy our money right now, we won't have jack to pay with over there."

Darío considered him silently. Then he threw a glance at Emilia.

"Don't forget that I gave you two a special deal . . . only because your abuela did what she did. Gimme what you have now and lemme see what I can do."

"But we already gave you some. . . ."

"Yeah, but that was just for starters. I told you that."

"No, you didn't."

"Listen, if you wanna go, go, and if not, well, don't. It's on you."

Gregorio and Emilia looked at each other.

"Get the money out, then," he said to his sister.

She didn't take her eyes off him. Then she extracted some of the cash in her sneaker. They counted it and handed it over to Darío. With his back to them, he counted and stuck a couple of the bills in his pocket.

"Son of a . . ." Emilia heard Goyo murmur.

Darío approached Chato, who was arguing with the rest: "I already told you. If we get at least ten more in the next batch, I'll lower the price a little."

Darío whispered something in his ear and gestured toward the brother and sister. Chato chewed on a toothpick and kept glancing over at them. They negotiated for a while until Darío handed him the cash.

"All right, then," Chato said at last, and spit. "It's a deal." His dry capulín eyes shook lightly as they settled upon the brother and sister.

Darío came up to them. "All set. You'll give 'em the rest over there." And he clapped Gregorio on the back before walking away.

"Fuck. I hope he doesn't screw us over," Goyo burst out, his voice shaky. His sister looked at him from the corner of her eye and asked herself what kind of omen the dust storm had brought along. For the first time in her life it wasn't clear to her.

Another group of people arrived at last. There were ten of them and everyone rushed to clamber into the truck that would take them to the border.

After getting in, Gregorio was silent—he had a thorn stabbing at his thoughts. He was worried by how the driver looked at them through the rearview mirror.

"Stay right by me," he murmured to his sister. "Just in case. So nothin' happens. Put on your cap and lower your face whenever they look at you—let them think you're a boy. And don't be a chismosa sticking your nose places it doesn't belong. Got it?"

A singing traveler's voice rang out, like a sad bird's song. The sounds of the motor and the tires grinding over the asphalt flooded the air for the rest of the way.

Mamá Lochi was a brave woman, even though she was afraid of lightning bolts. She said they were sent by an ancient god to remind men how teeny they were and show them who runs the universe. She also said that a soul could only be tempered beneath the flash of lightning. And she was brave because, even though she was afraid, she never stopped doing what she had to do when a storm started to get real strong. She'd lost count of the times she'd seen, in the middle of one of those downpours that knocks the bottom out of the summer sky, an electric serpent wiggling through a crack in a door or a fissure in the ceiling, looking for somewhere to let itself free. They'd chased after her since she was a little chamaca. When the rain crashed down, she would order us to stay still, to feel the strength of the heavens, of the earth— but, she'd say, we'd better put on our rubber-soled sandals if we didn't want the lightning to fry us to a crisp. She'd tell us about the times she saw those thin ropes of fire dragging themselves across the ground, never at peace, always setting everything in their path aflame. The palm bed mats were the first to singe, then the dry firewood, then it'd get to the little clothing she had. That's why I thought it was strange that when I turned seven she gave me a burlap sack and said:

"C'mon, chamaca, we're goin' up the mountain."

That wasn't what was strange, as I often went with her on her trips through the mountain to look for herbs, fungi, bark, animals, or whatever else she needed for her salves and incenses. What was new was that she had never before given me a bag of my own to carry. And it was especially strange for her to say we were going out on a day with the sky all dyed black like that. She never let my brother and me walk out in the rain, out of fear that we'd be hit by lightning.

"But it's gonna rain, mamita," I told her, knowing how her skin prickled whenever she heard distant thunder making its way closer to us.

"Doesn't matter. It's about time to temper your blood," she responded. "Hurry up, put on your rubber sandals. You're old enough to learn what can only be appreciated under the rain."

I'd heard that when she was a chamaca like me a lightning bolt had gotten her. I heard someone say it in passing, to one of my uncles or to my father—the way kids learn about things in life. It took me a while to connect it to that scar, like a fern with little red branches that crisscrossed her left arm from shoulder to elbow. That was the trace the lightning left when it passed through her body. When the power went out at night and we were left in the shadows, Mamá Lochi would take a few steps away from us and uncover her arm: In the darkness, the fern's little branches shone with their own light. She'd walk around the house and we would follow, seeking out her luminosity, wanting to see the branches of her little tree, as she called it, enthralled by the wonder that she carried on her body.

That wasn't the only souvenir the lightning left her. People said that it was also responsible for her power of vision and her ability to cure people. Back then, there was no way for us to ask questions—we had no right to, we were just kids. But we'd try to figure it all out anyway: My brother, Caco, and I collected phrases, words heard here and there, and put them together, reconstructing and telling each other the stories in secret, huddled in a corner of the house, even though our tales ended up being miles away from the original.

We called my abuela Mamá Lochi. Even though her name was Eloísa Blanca del Carmen Molina Trueba. She had a long name, like they did back in the day, and she always told me, "You have one name because havin' just one name will make you stronger."

I don't know why she thought that. The truth is that she was very strong even though she had a lot of names. Everyone respected her, and she was Mamá Lochi to everyone. Mamá Lochi to her children, to her grandchildren—the two of us she met—to her curaditos, which is what she called the people she rubbed with her herbs and treated with her incenses. Mamá Lochi this, Mamá Lochi that. Lots of people asked her for help, especially when she went to sell her herbs and liniments at the Santiatepec market.

To be honest, when it came to my name, she didn't even follow her own belief because she liked to call me lots of different things. Calandria, Mila, Alondra, Emilia, Chaparra. I made her laugh because ever since I was a little girl, when I got excited or scared, I'd lose my speech and all that came out of my mouth was that whistle, like a bird's trill, instead of words. She said she'd noticed it as soon as I was born—when my mother nursed me, I would pull away from her chichi every once in a while, look around, and let out that little bird's whistle that started out soft and went on gaining volume over time.

"A woman has to be strong, Calandrita, and especially when she's poor," she'd tell me as she warmed tortillas on the comal.

Ever since I can remember, I'd go up the mountain with her to look for the ingredients for her salves. We would reach the tops of the ridges by climbing the tangled paths up the mountainside until we got to the oak forests, so pretty when the fall hit. Streams of light splashed through the orange, red, and yellow leaves. These luminescences seemed like they came from another world, their shine gliding like waterfalls down the tree branches, creating spots of light in the shadows, highlighting the green-and-white moss growing on the tree trunks. When the heat came, the ocote and pine spread their scent all over. I'd take a deep breath, filling my body with the delicious perfume of the bark, the plants, the earth. And when the oak leaves, as big as mule-drivers' hands, carpeted the ground and created rivers at my feet, I loved crunching them with my steps. Mamá Lochi walked through it all with ease, through the grasslands and through the crowded sugarcane at the mountaintops, guiding herself by the paths made of light and shadows. Always singing. Now and then she would name the plants, the leaves and roots that she tossed into her sack, and she'd explain to me what each thing was good for. She never missed an opportunity to tell me a story, to teach me a song, to share a secret.

"The *beyond* isn't beyond, Emilia. It's right here. There's more to this world than what we can see with our eyes. Even what we see isn't what it seems. You'll know it for yourself someday. You're my blood. You see up ahead, where those two rocks are touching? There's a spirit 'round there. If you stay still and really look at it, you'll see its shadow pass by."

Sometimes she'd send me to hunt insects, especially grasshoppers when there were so many they filled the mountains or the farmlands. Afterward, when I got home, we'd toast them on the comal and devour them with chile and lime. She'd set aside a full bag because sometimes she'd use them for salves.

"These are good for when you want someone to jump far. Rub 'em on their feet and right on the top of their head, and that'll do it. They can also help with varicose veins if you boil the grasshoppers' feet with some squash blossom in a big pot. Give it to the person to drink every night, then rub their legs with what's left at the bottom of the pot—in a few days the veins disappear."

One time, she was looking at me so intently that I even got goose bumps, and she told me something I'd remember years later: "You, kid—you have grasshoppers in your feet. You'll jump far from here. And then, you won't stay still for a long time."

That's all she said and I found it really strange. I had no desire to go anywhere. Though the idea of traveling, of getting to know other places, did excite me. I tried to get her to say something more about this prediction. But there was no way. I couldn't squeeze another word out of her.

What I liked least about going to the mountain with my abuela was hunting snakes. Even if they were just rat snakes. They grossed me out, so Mamá Lochi would pick up a live one and make me hold it to get over the twisting in my stomach. She'd say who-knows-what to it in that language that she sometimes spoke and I didn't understand. But it seemed like the snake did. She'd whistle to it, sing to it, and then kill it with a twist of the neck or a blow from the machete she carried in her sack. Before she killed it, I could feel in my fingers how the animal's skin hardened as soon as it heard her voice, and its little head turned toward Mamá Lochi so it wouldn't miss a word. I held back a *yuck* but couldn't help but twist my face with disgust. She'd watch me very seriously, waiting for my scowl, and then she'd let loose a burst of laughter.

"Don't be squeamish, Calandria. I already asked her permission and she gave it to me: She knows her flesh will return to the earth. From the earth, for the earth," she'd say as she raised the snake's languid body into the air. "We need to take off the skin while the body's still warm"—and she'd pull it off right there in one tug, then put the skin in her sack and the meat in a plastic bag. Back at home she'd put it to boil and, once it cooled off, crush and grind it in her molcajete along with some seeds. She'd take the paste it made and leave it out in the sun for a week.

"Everything has a heart, even if it doesn't seem like it. If you look for it and know how to hear it, you'll realize even stones have real strong heartbeats. As still as they are. They're the secrets of the world, crushed to dust and packed together. Just feel 'em. When you eat the little mushrooms that grow over there, by that big pile of rocks, you'll understand the real truth. You can put a little pebble in the palm of your hand and feel its warmth, just like it's a newborn. And butterflies. If you pay close attention, you'll see they're tiny women in disguise. And they're tricky little bitches. You need to be careful with them: If you ignore them or get on their bad side, they get pissed, their sharp fangs come out, and they swarm at you and bite you all over. You have to admire them so they don't get jealous. I knew an herbalist in San Nicolás who screwed with them so much that one night, they took out one of her eyes with their little teeth and nobody could help her fix it. Poor Hilaria, they left her with just one eye."

After telling me these stories, Mamá Lochi could go quiet for the rest of the way. I almost snapped my head off my neck looking around to see what I could not see. Even the shadows seemed to crackle. And worse: There were tons of butterflies. Especially in the spring. And even though it was hard to believe they could take out someone's eye, much less with their little bites, I still buttered them up in a low voice, just in case—so I could rest assured they wouldn't turn on me. I stared at them so hard that eventually I felt like I could see a girl's little head, her eyes wide, right there between the wings. Her tiny fangs flashed bright. I'd stay very still, just moving my lips as little as possible to tell them how pretty they were, how totally precious their beautiful little wings were, or whatever else my tongue came up with to keep them happy. I didn't want them to get mad and tear out pieces of my skin or leave poor me with just one eye.

Whenever a hummingbird came near it was Mamá Lochi who turned to stone. She wouldn't even breathe. She only moved her eyes: She'd let it pause near her, sometimes next to her ear, and the clear hum of its wings buzzed in the air. When it flew away, she followed its flight with her eyes until it disappeared into the trees.

"They're messengers," she'd tell me, "and you have to be real still and silent to understand the message they bring."

"What did that one that just left tell you, Mamá Lochi?"

"You can't just go tellin' everyone, chamaca." And the reverberation of her laugh traveled through the gullies. "When one comes up to you with a message, then you'll know."

At other times she would become very serious.

"Listen here, Emilia. Everything in the world is born from ripping and tearing," she told me. And there I stood, hearing her words but not understanding them. "Tear after tear after tear. The prettier, the more powerful things are, the more brutal things got."

She would take a breath, light her reed pipe, and study me as though sizing me up.

"After the tearing something new comes together, unites, and takes form. So nothing is exactly like any other thing. And there's nothing—if it's real and true—that has a double anywhere, no matter how hard you look for it."

Who knows where my grandmother got these ideas. Maybe from eating her mushrooms. Or from wandering her mountain since she was a girl. Or from the magic she carried in her soul. I just know that it all started after the day the lightning struck her. They say she was seven. I think that's why, one evening after I turned seven myself, she made me go up into the mountain with her during a storm.

"Wake up, Calandria. We're here."

Goyo had been shaking her for a while. Sunken into her jacket, Emilia wasn't easy to wake up. When she awoke, she felt her skeleton crackling. Her guts grinding. And her mouth was a dry sponge.

Chato hurried them along. They got out of the truck one after another, as quickly as their numb bodies could manage. The sun hit them like a cudgel until it beat out whatever humidity remained inside them.

"Fuck this fuckin' heat," Gregorio murmured.

"C'mon, assholes, I don't have all the time in the world," Chato yelled, herding the group toward a path that led up an arid mountain. A few steps ahead they were met with a stake bed truck and clambered into the back. Behind the wheel there was a man with a dense mustache and wide-brimmed hat. Another man sat beside him, one-eyed and wearing a baseball cap, a golden earring gleaming from his ear. Both men's eyes shone capulín-dark. As they climbed into the truck, the man in the driver's seat watched them in the rearview mirror. Chato leaned on the driver's door and downed a beer they opened for him in one gulp. They spoke in low voices punctuated by explosive, loud laughter.

"You're with these guys now—they'll tell you what to do and what it costs," Chato told everyone sitting in the back of the truck. And he set off back the way they'd come.

"I'm really fuckin' thirsty, Goyo," Emilia mumbled, not expecting a response. She couldn't even make her mouth water with her imagination. Her lips burned from sucking on them so much. Her tongue stung and tasted like rotten egg. Her own breath disgusted her.

Then the bouncing of their feet began, as the tires passed over the gravel road.

"Hold on, Emilia. We're almost there." It was Goyo, whispering, late to answer.

"Where's there?"

"You'll see in a little bit."

"Don't act like that. You don't know either."

He threw her one of his looks.

"So then why the fuck are you askin' questions if you already know that I don't know?" And then, without another word, he turned his gaze back out to the desert, which was an open mouth of infinite extension.

The road was straight but full of potholes and bumps. Cacti appeared like exhausted specters in the middle of the nothingness. Emilia Ventura kept her pupils fixed on the landscape. It was like it wasn't real. She didn't recognize a thing. She'd carried the belief that all landscapes were just like the ones back where she'd grown up—she was waiting for her mountains, her trees, her wild brush to appear, for the sky to be framed by the branches and leaves of jocote trees. She waited to see them sprout forth from all that desolation, but not even a small hill or a miniature tree emerged along the way. Just dry earth, arid as a crazed person's gaze. *So where do the spirits of this desert hide*, she asked herself in silence.

"I'm thirsty, Caco."

"Don't fuckin' start, Emilia. Me too. Just hold on. We're almost there."

"But where are we goin',"

"Just wherever they take us, Calandria. Wherever they take us. Don't be a crybaby. We have to go with these guys if we're gonna cross."

"I'm not being a crybaby, fuckin' Caco. Stop being an asshole."

"Okay, fine." Goyo thought it was better to stop. He didn't want her to fly off the handle, like she did sometimes when she was pissed off.

Demetria, a woman from their town, was listening to them all the while. She took a bottle of water out of her backpack.

"Here, have some, chamaca. Your lips are cracked already." And she passed her the bottle.

Emilia drank like it was the last thing she would ever do in her life.

"Just a little, niña, we have to save it." The woman snatched the bottle back before it was empty. She offered it to Emilia's brother, who took two long gulps and gave it back.

"Thank you, doña."

"You have to take it easy with water. One sip at a time," Demetria said, as if they didn't know. "Whenever we can, we'll refill it. You can't know how much time will pass before you can." She lifted the bottle to see how much was left.

The truck carried on for a stretch, bouncing over the dirt road. The saguaros and open-armed yuccas seemed like they were throwing prayers out to the heavens. Emilia thought maybe those were the desert's lost spirits.

Evening was falling over the earth when the silhouette of a distant building appeared on the horizon.

The truck took a path headed that way, until it reached a run-down warehouse, which in some other time had been a chicken coop. Fifty meters away, there were three sheds scattered about in disorder, poorly made of cinder blocks and sheet metal. All that was left of the chickens were feathers and a soulless smell of rot.

"Who would raise chickens in bumfuck nowhere," they heard one man say.

"Wouldn't you call this a chicken run, though?" A couple muffled laughs rang out one by one.

Farther away, mounds of garbage piled up against the remains of a ramshackle old car. Behind the chicken coop, out of sight of anyone who arrived by the path, there was a parked, military-green Jeep. A muscular woman with a hard shadowy face and bleached hair pulled into a ponytail, leaned against a doorframe through which a stove and table were half-visible. She chewed gum with her mouth open.

"Güerita! Wassup, cutie," the one-eyed guy yelled, lowering the window as they arrived.

An apron, stained with grease and soot, hugged her body, and her hands were tucked into the front pockets.

They called the man driving the truck Vaquero because of his wide-brimmed cowboy hat. When he laughed, sounding just like a barking dog, his eyes leaped off his yellowing face and his mustache trembled over a mouth missing most of its teeth. The other man, the one with one eye and a baseball cap, they called Donojo. Vaquero hurried them—his barking voice boomed as the group jumped down from the truck and entered the chicken coop.

"C'mon, hurry it up."

Donojo lit a cigarette and pointed his steel-toed boots toward the woman, who gestured for him to come closer. As he entered the cinder block room he closed the door, but first he yelled to Vaquero that he wouldn't be long, to watch the group, that he was going to rest for a bit.

Emilia felt a misplaced joy leap around inside her. They were close to crossing the line, everyone was saying it. It wouldn't be long before she found her father and her uncles. Life would be like it was before. So what if she was thirsty and hungry—their scattered journey was almost over. She soon discovered what about that joy was misplaced. The travelers whispered, saying this and that, that now the difficult part was really coming. Anxiety lurked nearby, and Emilia erased that slim shred of happiness from her memory.

Once they were all inside the chicken coop, Demetria set herself up next to the brother and sister. She gave them advice, predictions: If they were lucky, they might even get a taco soon.

"Water," muttered Goyo, "at least a sip."

"At least," Demetria agreed. After this, they wouldn't find anything. And it was important to build up energy for what was coming.

Donojo brought over two buckets of water, and they drank and refilled their bottles from them. They distracted themselves by poking around the insides of the room, and it wasn't until the evening was well underway that the smell of greasy food reminded them of their hunger. Güera spread out tortillas and spooned a glob of beans and lumpy rice onto them. Ten pesos each taco. Vaquero charged people while the woman served the food.

Goyo paid for three tacos, one for the road.

"It looks like the scraps they give pigs," Emilia whispered, her gaze fixed on the scrambled mass inside the tortilla.

"Don't whine, Calandria. You heard Demetria: We don't know when we'll eat again."

The girl brought the greasy blob up to her nose. The rancid, oily smell didn't remind her of anything she'd ever tasted before. She'd never had to force down slop like this, not even in her worst moments of hunger.

Demetria's eyes lingered on her. "Eat it, chamaca. It's not good, but you're gonna need energy for the journey. Ándale, eat. And save something for later," she suggested when she noticed Goyo eating voraciously, already wishing he could start in on the third taco. He was never fussy about wolfing anything down, no matter what it was. "Later you'll be glad you thought ahead."

Without hiding her disgust, Emilia chewed the sticky goop and swallowed quickly. She was hungry. Gregorio set aside a portion, stored it in a plastic bag, and put it in the backpack. He refilled their water bottles and drank. That's when he noticed that Donojo, standing at the entrance to the chicken coop, wouldn't take his eye off him. His lone pupil a familiar shade of dry capulín.

"You need to watch out for your sister. And yourself. Stick together," Demetria warned him, between bites, in a hidden whisper, after throwing a look toward the door. "Like clockwork, the youngest ones disappear. The girls more than anyone.

"This is the third time I've tried," she continued, like they'd asked her. "First try, they got me right after crossing. They even set dogs on us. I wanted to make it to the mountains, at least. Second try, they got my husband and who knows what happened to him. I trust in God that he's waitin' for me on the other side."

"God?"

"No, niña . . . Chepe, my husband. May God be with us." And there she stopped speaking. The thought had pushed her up against the edge of a cliff.

Emilia looked at Demetria—she wanted to delve into her thoughts. She let her mind run with the hazy evening light entering the warehouse. The night's shadows and the distant murmurs of tired faces and scattered bodies slowly took over the space. A pale light blinked from an oily and dusty lightbulb. Donojo and Vaquero left after announcing that they needed to wait for another group that would arrive in a couple hours. They'd try to cross before daybreak. Now and then their figures were projected onto the ground from where they stood at the entrance to the chicken coop.

A thankless calm reigned, heavy with uncertainties.

As we started up the path to the mountaintop, the downpour broke out. Big, big drops, the kind that hurt. Thunder and lightning broke out across the sky and the echoes and booms resounded deep into the ravine. Soon we were soaked. Mamá Lochi's slip stuck to her body and the water came down her dark and leathery legs in streams. Water slid down my face and mud seeped into my sandals.

My father had tried in vain to stop us from going. "But, mamita," he said, his voice a thin thread, "don't you see it's gonna be coming down real hard? You know what can happen when there's lightning. . . ." And he stayed silent for a moment, like he wasn't sure if he should or shouldn't mention what everyone was thinking.

"You know how it is with you and lightning, mamita. . . ." he attempted. Mamá Lochi threw him one of those hard and cutting glares that petrified even the wildest spirits.

"Don't you worry, mijo. We'll be back real soon, the two of us, bushy-tailed and singin' like the calandrias tuneras in the spring, no doubt about it—" And then, as though she was reconsidering what she was about to add, she stopped and looked firmly at my father. "Besides, don't you see that this chamaca is cut from the same cloth as me? If lightning hits her, nothing will happen to her that hasn't happened to me."

My father stood with his mouth half-open. It looked like words were whirling about inside him, but they lacked the strength to make themselves heard.

"Ay, my sweet mamita," he managed, finally, in a whisper. "If the lightning takes her from me . . . I'm telling you . . ."

Mamá Lochi didn't respond anymore. And even though grasshoppers were leaping in my stomach, I snapped my beak shut and walked after my abuela. There was no way to go against her. If she got an idea in her head, it was best to obey and not say a word. Once we'd turned the corner I looked back. There they were, my father, my uncles Beno and Isidro, and Goyo—they were arguing among themselves, without taking their eyes off us, not a single one of them daring to stand up to Mamá Lochi.

We'd already climbed partway up the mountainside when the rain started to come down harder. It went from those fat, spaced out drops to bucketfuls falling from the sky. Mamá Lochi walked in silence. Even if she had been saying something, I wouldn't have heard her, because the roaring rain, the wind that picked up as we went along, and the echoing thunderclaps wouldn't have let me. We climbed for a while until we arrived at a ridge that ran up against a pile of boulders carpeted with lichens and ferns. The moss covering them made the dimples and pointy edges of the rock phosphoresce like they were illuminated by a secret inner light. In the deep black sky, electric serpents spread like branches and leaves and cast light through the shadows.

The thunder sounded again and again without rest, and right when I was going to tell Mamá Lochi that maybe we should go back, a bolt struck nearby, leaving me momentarily blinded, deaf, and trembling like a leaf caught in a strong gust of wind. She stopped in her tracks and grabbed my hand without looking at me.

"Let's go, chamaca, don't be a wimp! We're going to tempt the heavens themselves today, to see if they really want you up there, too, just like they wanted me!" she shouted, pulling me along harshly as we continued up the mountainside. I wanted to burst out in tears, to start chirping like a calandria so that the fear could get out from inside me. I wanted to tell her that we shouldn't keep going, that the lightning was going to split us right in half like it had so many people from our town, but I stayed quiet. I didn't want to make her mad or make her think I was a scaredy-cat.

"A woman has to be strong, Emilia," she always told me, "and she has to know how to give herself fully, body and soul, to whatever destiny has planned for her."

We walked in silence for a good while. And once we'd climbed up high, grabbing tight to the ridges of boulders, roots, and branches, she turned and shouted so I could hear her over the pouring rain that had us both incapable of hearing anything else:

"I know destiny has something for you, Calandrita. And today we're going to discover if it's what I think it is."

I couldn't bear for Mamá Lochi to think I was weak. For her to give me crap about being a wimp. That was the worst insult that she or anyone could use on me. I didn't want her to pull back on her affection, on the care she gave me, and to stop sharing her wisdom with me. If she said that we had to test me under a storm of lightning bolts to see if one would hit me, well, I couldn't complain. It was a huge honor that my abuela had chosen me to test in the downpour. Neither my brother, who was older and who she thought was so great, nor my father nor my uncles, who she loved so much, had been given a test like this. So we continued through the storm.

We climbed without stopping for more than an hour until we reached the mountain's peak. From there, at a distance, you could see the lightning strike the trees and the distant towns. The bolts filled the sky with light, and their electric branches lit up like a foliage of embers, spreading over the mountain to nourish the earth with their unbridled energy. A fierce wind blew, freezing the water on my skin. We kept walking until we came to a crevice where we could only fit by going one at a time. We walked down it, one behind the other, our feet slipping on mud streams, careful not to fall over the steep edge. She went first. She walked with sure steps despite her age. I stumbled along, falling on my butt every time my foot slipped on a loose rock or my sandal slid down the moss. I could already count a half dozen scratches and bumps all over me. It was a long and narrow way that I had never walked before. I focused, alert to each step so I wouldn't fall and splatter all over the rocks. I glanced up at the sky, monitoring the lightning bolts as if I could avoid the moment one would strike me. When I looked forward, Mamá Lochi had disappeared from my sight. I stopped, grabbing onto the edges of the cascade of boulders we were descending, and saw that the path ahead opened into a curving downhill slope. And Mamá Lochi? My heart stopped to think that she might have fallen over the precipice.

"Mamá Lochi! Mamá Lochi!" I wanted to yell, but all that came out was the chirp of a bewildered calandria.

Soon the calandria sounded like a hog in a slaughterhouse. My voice broke, like it did whenever I was washed over by panic, and I was left without speech, completely wordless. I didn't know if I should move, keep walking forward to look for her, or keep screaming. *Now I'm really fucked*, I thought. What was I going to do, alone on the mountain, in the middle of a storm, with Mamá Lochi splattered at the bottom of the gully. Who was going to take care of me—if my papá had lost his mind when Mamita Estela died, and it was still missing. And my uncles, well, they only paid attention to their own problems. Who was going to teach me about herbs and incenses. Who was going to make cures for Goyo and me, who was going to tell me stories about apparitions. Who was going to show me the mountain's secrets. Who, who.

"C'mon, chamaca, before you catch a cold." First I heard my abuela's hoarse voice and then I saw her looking out from a wide crevice, up ahead, next to a forest of oak trees growing up against a tall cliff.

I'm comin', mamita, I thought, but not even a choked whistle came out of me. I tried to shout to her so she could hear me over the thunder that was starting to fade away. Little by little, I regained speech by the grace of the relief that washed over me.

Mamá Lochi was sitting inside a deep cave at the end of the wide crevice in the rock, on the edge of the trail. Against the rock wall, there was a pile of dry firewood, and I could make out the remains of a campfire. I also spotted a big basket with a bunch of herbs, dry mushrooms, a box of matches, a clay bowl, a gourd capped with a piece of ocote bark, a chunk of piloncillo, a little dish of honey, and a colorful old blanket.

"Ándale, Emilia. Get undressed and dry yourself off with the blanket, and I'll make you a mint tea right now so you don't get a cough."

I ended up in my undies, trembling with cold under the mildewy blanket draped over my shoulders. I felt an immense happiness leaking from my pores. It didn't matter to me anymore if the world fell apart in the storm. The thunder and rain fell with less urgency. The joy of having Mamá Lochi at my side, protecting me with her powerful warmth, her strong and sweet caress, made me forget every possible danger. The joy that neither one of us was hit by lightning, that we hadn't fallen down into the gully, filled me with gratitude.

And despite all of that, Mamá Lochi looked discouraged and wasn't trying to hide it.

"Well, seems like this isn't your destiny. I must've made a mistake. But to be real honest, it seems strange to me that I made a mistake, with that calandria flutterin' around inside you. . . ."

She passed me a tea, and I sat next to her with the blanket on my back. It unsettled me so much to see her disappointed that I even felt ashamed that I hadn't been struck by lightning.

"Don't worry, mamita. Tomorrow, when the thunder starts, we can go out again, to see if I'll get hit by lightning this time."

Mamá Lochi gave me a surprised look that I still remember now, and suddenly burst out laughing so hard that she got tears in her eyes.

"Don't be stupid, niña," she said, finally composing herself. "You've got guts, chamaca. You were very brave today." I must have blushed, thinking that she had no idea of the terror I felt. "Someday or another, we'll see the gift the voices say you have. We'll see." And she sipped from her mug, looking me over with her wise eyes, like she was trying to understand something about me that wasn't clear to her.

"You have to promise me something, Calandrita: Not a word to anyone about this place. It's gonna be our secret." And she flashed me her smile, shining with perfectly aligned teeth.

We spent the rest of the evening by the fire, drinking herbal tea and watching the rain slide off the entrance to the shelter. Mamá Lochi didn't say another word until the darkness of the sky cleared away and we got ready to return. I bit my tongue to stop myself from asking what gift she wanted to find in me, who was telling her about it and what they were saying—what this place she'd brought me to was, why she'd never mentioned it before, and why I had to keep it secret.

Close to midnight, they turned off the lights in the warehouse. Irregular snores crashed through the air. Emilia felt Goyo's measured breath at her side—he'd sunk into a deep sleep, and she wanted to go to the bathroom. She wasn't going to wake him, she'd go nearby. She got up and stepped around the scattered bodies, moving through shadows, whispered conversations, interrupted exhalations, and one snore after another until she managed to exit the barracks.

She was surprised by a wide, open sky overflowing with stars. She'd never seen so many bright spots of light. The mountains that surrounded her town shrunk the celestial landscape and only allowed a few twinkles to appear at night. Under this new immensity she felt like the universe was watching her, wide and unmasked. She started to walk, dodging spiny plants, gazing up to continue her marveling. Mamá Lochi always said that stars were the hearts of the departed. When Emilia had a tantrum about something and ended up climbing onto the roof, or up the avocado tree with its wide trunk and comforting branches, she calmed herself down by counting stars. The firmament's radiance soothed her—on the other side of that darkness full of shining polka-dots, there must exist other girls just like her, up in trees with begging branches, looking up at different skies and imagining that even more girls were doing the same thing through the long and wide universe.

"Where's the center of everything, mamita?" she asked Mamá Lochi once. The grandmother turned to face her granddaughter. Emilia could never be sure if she was going to scold her for asking stupid questions or if she was going to indulge her with a twinkle of her eyes. Days could pass before she responded. When the answer would come, Emilia had already forgotten the question. She had to think hard to understand why, without warning, Mamá Lochi would suddenly say something like:

"The center is in the inside of each of us."

Submerged in those memories, Emilia walked away from the barracks and when she looked up, she was close to the room that they were using as a kitchen—she stopped, a stone's throw away. A stream of light spilled out from the crack under the door and another flooded down from the building's one tiny window, high up the wall. A dense cold rushed in, like something was chasing after it. Rowdy laughs crashed into each other inside those walls. An unexpected sound, metal clanging, startled her—around her, shadows were moving about. A shiver passed over her.

Ándale, chamaca. There's vermin nearby.

The voice slid down her back. First, a pang of fear. Then, she looked side to side, and didn't see a trace of anyone. It had to be Mamá Lochi's very own, gruff voice. That calmed her—better to hear her ghost than her silence. The mumbling voices and laughter burst forth again from the keyholes of the dingy room. Emilia dropped her pants, squatted, and peed in a hurry. The hiss of the warm, relieving stream flowed between her sneakers but didn't touch them. As she pulled up her pants she looked around and was overcome by an anxiety to return to the chicken coop as soon as possible.

And she would have, but her anxiety was beat out by the nibbling of her damn curiosity, that thing that got her into trouble, that convinced her to stick her nose where she shouldn't. Afraid that her beat-up sneakers would crunch the arid ground beneath them, she stealthily approached the building. Güera's scandalized laughter boomed out, her inhospitable cackle more like a groan brought by a stomachache. Emilia crept around the room and couldn't find a hole or nook to spy from. Tiny streams of light filtered through the cinder block walls, but she couldn't distinguish anything inside when she pressed her eye up to them. She managed to hear a few disconnected words, a piece of furniture being dragged across the floor. She looked up to the tiny window high up on the wall. Piling up junk metal and some crates she found strewn about, she managed to build a tall-enough base. Her agility and light weight helped her get up to the right height. Clinging to the edge of the concrete, Emilia Ventura looked inside.

In the middle of the dingy room, there was a stove where they were warming up food. Beyond that, a shabby table with a bottle, three cups, and an ashtray sitting on it. The two men and the woman sitting around the table were playing cards, drinking, smoking, and laughing loudly. A few crumpled bills sat beneath a cup on the table.

"Fucking Güera, you're killin' me. . . ."

"What, you can't handle all this heat?"

"All this fuckin' bullshit . . ."

A guffaw sliced through the air. Emilia noticed a cot behind the table, but the woman's body blocked it from view. It looked like it was moving. She managed to make out a military-green bag, some bills scattered over the mattress, and more piled in stacks as though someone had attempted to impose an impossible order on them. There was a gun and some bottles strewn about. Suddenly, she saw it: A gray cat leaped onto a flattened cushion and that sudden movement made her start, making the support under her feet sway until she fell into a pile of junk and crates.

"Who the fuck . . ." she heard Vaquero say on the other side of the wall. There was a scraping of chairs and voices.

Emilia jumped up and didn't have time to check herself from the fall—she snuck off as best she could to a point where the brief light couldn't reach, her heart now a bird desperate to escape from inside her. Through all of it, she managed not to make a sound or shout out, though it wasn't easy as she crouched and stumbled through the dark. Finally she wriggled into a hiding spot between an abandoned car and a pile of rusting scrap metal. She folded herself up as best she could.

Staying very still, she tried to work out which way she needed to make a break for it.

"It was probably one of those desert rats," she heard Donojo say in that harsh and composed voice of his.

"I haven't seen any . . . well, other than fuckin' Vaquero," Güera responded.

"Get me another drink, fuckin' Güera. C'mon, cutie."

Ay, Calandria, what have you gotten yourself into.

The voice came from over her shoulder, but she didn't dare to turn around. Suddenly, one of those silences. *It's like something's coming, from over there*, Emilia thought, all balled up in her spot behind the broken-down car. She sensed a tension, an alert unraveling its stiffness into the air, into the silence. And then, whispers—inside the room, they had lowered their voices. Emilia closed her eyes to focus on their murmurs, and, when she opened them again, she found herself surrounded by tiny fireflies. They came and went before her eyes, glowing, buzzing out their messages. She closed her eyes and covered her ears. Her head, squeezed between her knees, was filling with an unexpected and total pain.

"Not again . . ." And it seemed to her that her voice came from far away.

That feeling that she hadn't felt for so long was back: that warmth flowing through her, forcing her into stillness. She opened her eyes and uncovered her ears. It wasn't long before the images paraded past. There they were: Donojo driving a car. Yelling. Next to him, Vaquero, a bottle in his hand. Yelling. They were fighting. Vaquero was hitting Donojo. The car was accelerating: trembles, leaps, deep potholes, somersaults. Quickly, the image became distorted or shaken—it spun and spun and there were shouts and cries. An instant before the images dissipated, she had the unsettling impression that she was there, too. When the images disappeared, Emilia Ventura grabbed her head. The intense pain made it impossible to move. Falling over to the side, her contact with the old car's metal returned her to her body. Her pain unyielding, she guessed the direction and distance that separated her from the chicken coop where Goyo was sleeping. Why was she waiting to run? She looked around to make sure there was nobody near. The voices and laughter sounded from the room again, and she could smell the rust and rotting garbage. She emerged from her hiding spot with the weight of the night on her head. And once she was out, she looked up to the sky.

"So you're the little fuckin' rat that's creeping around and spying on us."

Something tugged on Emilia's hair and brought back the headache at full force. She tried to break free, but she was trapped. That body, reeking of alcohol, marijuana, and stale sweat had stretched out its tough claws. It was the one with the mustache, the hat: Vaquero. He appeared out of nowhere, like a pest dropped from the sky, evil, prickly, and venomous. He snatched her up by the neck, grasping her so tightly she lost her breath, and dragged her away. Right there, in that soulless place filled with dust and trash, he jerked her around, her head bobbing like a rag doll's. Emilia tried to yell, but the calandria took over her voice.

"Shut up! You sound like a fuckin' hysterical chicken," Vaquero hissed as he pressed his hand over her mouth. "And where the fuck do you think you're going, you little bitch? I'm gonna teach you a lesson. Throw you to the snakes to scare the thief outta you. Isn't that right? You were gonna steal from us?"

With a yank, the man pulled her head onto his cock and rubbed her face against it.

"Look at this giant snake. You're gonna eat it. It's what you get for being a thief. Shut the fuck up and open your trap, you fucked-up dumbass chicken!" And he smacked her face to the side, splitting her lip as she thrashed in his grip. "This is the only way to make you bitches understand anything!"

Emilia Ventura felt her blood boiling. The crazed, disturbed calandria banged against the walls of her chest, looking for a way out.

Vaquero shoved her again, forcing her head into him, when a scratchy voice spoke out from a few steps away.

"What the fuck are you doing, bastard?"

A fist yanked Vaquero by the shirt, twisted, and then shoved him to the ground.

"You're going too far, shithead! I already told you this one is off-limits! Asshole!"

Emilia's calandria chirped wildly, its sound jumping out her open mouth. And it didn't stop, not even when she picked herself up and ran, stumbling and tripping, like a soul being chased by the devil. The entrance to the barracks was filling with people.

Shoving his way through, Gregorio managed to reach his sister.

"What's wrong, Calandria? What happened to you? Where were you?" The alarm in his voice mixed into the surrounding din. Emilia's breath came out in pants of fear, and that exasperating trill wouldn't stop coming out her mouth, swollen from the slap.

The sound provoked a sense of strangeness in everyone who heard it. "No wonder he calls her Calandria," someone said, followed by two or three bewildered laughs.

Emilia gasped like a dying fish. She tried to say a word, but soon gave up—it was useless. Not until she settled down.

"Calm down already!" Goyo grabbed her by the shoulders and shook her twice. Then he hugged her tight. That was the only way his sister could get back her voice.

"So what happened to you?" the teenager tried again. "Just look at your mouth. . . ."

"Over there," Emilia stuttered, finally, still short of breath. "The one with the hat. . . ."

They shone their flashlights out at the emptiness.

Donojo came out of the shadows. Vaquero followed him, straightening his rumpled hat, looking down and rubbing his swelling cheek.

"Better watch your sister! She was trying to steal from us," Donojo insisted, looking at Gregorio with his dark capulín eye.

Goyo looked at Emilia, and she looked right back at him: They understood each other perfectly. The murmurs stopped.

"That's not true. My sister doesn't steal." At his side, he felt Emilia trembling.

"Are you calling me a liar?" the man said in a harsh voice. Gregorio felt Emilia at his back, inching closer to Demetria in search of protection.

"I asked you a question. Fucking answer!" Donojo took a step forward and brought his twisted face up to Gregorio's.

"My sister's not a thief and neither am I." He noticed a slight tremor in his own voice.

"So what was she doing sneaking around places she shouldn't be? Watch your fucking sister if you don't want me to fuck you both up, got it?"

Emilia felt her blood reach its boiling point. It was a hot spring overflowing from her veins. A hot spring that took away her fear and her understanding. Without a thought to warn her otherwise, impulse took over and she threw herself onto Vaquero, kicking.

Surprised, Vaquero gave her a hard punch straight to the face, knocking her far. The sharp pain and the blood, quickly streaming down her face, clouded her view.

"You little fucking . . . ! You're lucky I didn't put a bullet in—" He hadn't finished saying it before the brother was on him, fists flying. The man reacted with a quick punch that knocked him over, before Donojo could intervene.

"Stop it! Motherfucker." Donojo planted himself between them and looked fiercely at Vaquero and then at the two kids. "Get the hell inside and stop starting shit if you don't want to end up completely fucked!"

Demetria stepped toward the siblings to help.

"Órale, get up. He's right, you should come inside."

"If you act like fucking dumbasses, nobody's gonna take care of you. Got it?" Donojo warned them, and he walked away, kicking rocks and trees.

Güera, who had just emerged from the shadows, went up to the siblings.

"I don't want to hear about bullshit like this again. Stop picking fucking fights," she said, and directed herself to the group. "Did everyone hear me? That son of a bitch"—she pointed at Vaquero's back, disappearing into the darkness—"doesn't have a heart. A fucking coyote devoured it, okay? Am I making myself clear?"

Nobody dared respond.

"Just look what they did to you," she said to Emilia, grabbing her by the chin. "You were such a cutie. . . . No one will want you like this." And before she turned around to head back to the kitchen, she said to Demetria, "Go on, fix the kids up. I'll bring you something to help." And she returned to the shadows.

Demetria and another woman worked on cleaning their injuries. Goyo was more messed up than Emilia. The fist to the face had sent one of his teeth flying, his lip was split, and his face was swollen.

An insistent exhaustion reached deep into Emilia's soul. She looked down at her shirt, covered in blood, and touched her nose carefully, as though it belonged to somebody else. She was out of pain to feel. An enraged wail was trapped inside her, and it wanted to creep up to her eyes.

"You gotta stop gettin' into trouble," warned Santiago, a man with white hair, a dense mustache, and a sharp gaze. "You're dealin' with enough being so young—and alone, too. These sons of bitches don't have heartstrings to tug on. Stop lookin' for fights. Stick together. And even better if you do it quietly, in the shadows, under the radar."

Goyo and Emilia couldn't get any words out.

"It wasn't on purpose. The girl just went to the bathroom— you know how these people are." Demetria didn't even look up. She was concentrated on washing and bandaging wounds.

"Really, Caco—I promise I won't go anywhere again without telling you first," Emilia whispered to her brother as she watched him, grimacing every time Demetria dabbed at the wound on his mouth.

"You should change your shirt, Calandria, you look like a gutted goat." He pushed the backpack toward her with his foot.

"I'm sorry, Goyito, I really didn't . . ."

"That's enough, niña," Demetria cut her off. "These things happen, and sometimes it's even worse than this. Thank God they didn't do anything to you—" She stopped and lifted her eyes, looking fixedly at Emilia. "They didn't do anything to you, did they, chamaca?"

Emilia felt many eyes fall onto her body like stones. Checking her over. Looking for clues. It gave her a scare, the kind that doesn't come with a warning—the calandria nearly broke free, but she contained it and shook her head no until she was dizzy.

The flickering light from the greasy lightbulb turned off again. A tense, cold, soulless silence clung to the room like a bad omen.

Emilia curled up next to Gregorio. Demetria spread herself out a short distance from them and in just a little bit they heard her measured breathing.

"Caco, I for sure heard Mamá Lochi's voice. And then I *saw* something. . . ." She felt her brother tense alongside her: He knew that his sister's visions were never wrong.

"What did you see, Calandria?"

"Well, I don't really know what it was. Those assholes . . . they were in a car . . . they were fightin' and then they crashed and then I don't know."

"Good. Let those sons of bitches kill themselves."

"But, Caco . . . it's just that I think that I . . . I was right there."

Gregorio Ventura sat up. "What do you mean?"

"Well, I don't know . . . I just felt it . . . I couldn't see much. I pretty much just heard everything."

"Calandria, promise me that you won't go anywhere without me."

A silence. And that look, shared between them, deep, the kind of look between two people who know each other from far away and from up close.

"I promise you, Caco. Really."

"Seriously, Calandria. No matter how much Mamá Lochi is protecting us, if we fuck up, we'll be meetin' our maker."

"Yes, Caco. I promise you. Go to sleep now."

Goyo returned to his spot curled up against his sister. A stubborn sense of unease wedged itself between them.

They heard the truck start up and drive away down the road. Emilia breathed out deeply. If only Mamá Lochi was still nearby. If only she could bring back even just one breath of the perfume of her skin. If only she would talk to her again. Her Mamá Lochi. Her refuge. Her warmth.

Calandria, sweet little Calandrita, she'd say to her. *Don't get down on me now, a woman has to be strong—¡ándale!* But no matter how hard she squeezed her eyes shut and focused, no matter how much she murmured her name to call her near, no matter how much she breathed in with that stubborn desire that sometimes took over her, all that reached her nose was that rancid smell of old chicken shit.

That evening of the thunderstorm was the first of many that Mamá Lochi let me go with her to her cave, which is what she always called it. That's where she hid the secrets of her life, some of which she would gradually tell me. In my child's heart, after following her on her adventures through the mountain, I understood her inexplicable wanderings. And even though she didn't respond to my questions or give reasons for her actions, her powerful gaze, overflowing with mystery, told me that her invitation for me to get to know that place had its own destiny, purpose, desire. That sooner rather than later, the answers would come, revealing a truth that had everything to do with me.

Several months passed before Mamá Lochi took me back to her cave. First, I had those fevers that changed my way of seeing everyone around me. Incredibly high temperatures that lasted a week, during which my abuela looked after me day and night.

"Let's see what they have to say. I think there's something pickin' at your soul." That's what she said: *they*. And *they* were the ones who whispered news into her ear.

Who knows what got into me, or what it was that I'd eaten, that brought me those fevers. Sometimes, when we went out on walks alone, Caco and I stuffed ourselves with whatever we found out in the fields: so many herbs, so many fungi, so many fruits. We'd get caught up in some wild hallucinations, and soon enough we learned to distinguish which ones to eat and which ones not to. But sometimes we screwed up and ended up flat on our backs, overcome by fevers and vomiting that felt never-ending. During these burning hours I went straight from dreams to hallucinations, without a stop in reality. I remember seeing a man pass through the adobe bricks in the kitchen like a wisp of smoke and become solid again. Even though my eyes were shut, I immediately sensed his presence every time and opened them to see him. He would sit by the fire to smoke a cane pipe and turn to look at me like he knew me. His white clothes glowed on his body and he had wide-open owl eyes. Sometimes he would laugh wildly and speak in a language I didn't understand. I was never afraid. He spoke gently, with a sweet familiarity that calmed me. Little by little I started to understand him, though later I couldn't remember what he'd said to me. Sometimes I waited for a word or a gesture but he would just stay sitting there, smoking the pipe between his lips, touching the scarf tied around his neck with the tips of his index and ring fingers. Every so often, he'd scratch his head and ululate just like an owl.

It took Mamá Lochi no time at all to realize what was happening—nothing that had to do with the other world got past her. She sensed it the very first time I saw him. But she couldn't see him, which was weird because she saw apparitions all the time.

"Who knows what you swallowed, chamaca. You're seein' spirits, aren't you? Well, what do you see, Calandria?" Between shivers and shakes I had tried to describe him to her and tell her where he was sitting. But what came out of my insides was half words, half chirps from a scared chicken.

"Seems to me like it's Don Jacinto, sendin' us his spirit to heal you. But don't you try to go with him anywhere, in case it's Death herself in a disguise."

But that spirit never wanted to take me anywhere. He just spoke to me in his language or sang like an owl—then he'd turn into smoke to slip between the adobes and disappear.

During those feverish days, my head weak, creatures I'd never seen before also came in through the door hinges and cracks in the adobe. Giant insects and a whole bunch of figures and objects I couldn't describe. A tangle of images like shots in the middle of a battle. Like a channel had opened inside me. A channel that I wouldn't ever be able to close and that turned the adobes into rubber, made the walls go saggy, sunk the floor down and cracked the roof open.

The night I started convulsing, Mamá Lochi got scared for real. She swore that an evil spirit had entered me. Later she told me that my eyes got glassy and then went white, that my body bounced from the shaking and that she had to plug her ears with cotton balls to dull the sound of a deteriorating calandria's clucks. She called her closest comadre so that the two of them could work together to help me. For days she rubbed me with herb pastes and alcohol and cleansed the air with her incenses. The fever went down. I started to wake up, saying I was really hungry and wanted to get out of bed. At that point, that man's spirit was gone and

I even forgot what he looked like.

Once I started running around like before, Mamá Lochi kept observing me very quietly. She intuited or knew that something was changing in me. She wouldn't take her restless eyes off of me. She kept asking me if I saw apparitions, if I felt different. It wasn't until the day that I *saw* my papá that I knew something had changed in me. Several months, maybe even a year had passed since I'd had the fevers. It was midday. My father was in a hurry to go to Temixtlán to run an errand. I was absorbed in my mug of atole, blowing on it so it would cool off, when my vision was filled by little white lights jumping right in front of my nose. I thought I was getting dizzy—I grabbed my head and shook it and, when I raised my eyes, I saw an enormous white butterfly enter the kitchen. I thought it was weird because it wasn't the season for white butterflies, and I was scared she had come to chew my eyes out. Before I got too scared, she settled onto my father's head and then the lights trembled around me—that's when I realized they weren't lights but rather tiny insects that buzzed and shone so brightly they spooked me. I lowered my head to my chest, closed my eyes and covered my ears.

"What's up with you, Calandria?" my abuela's voice asked from far, far away. I felt her shaking me by the shoulders. And then I stood up.

"Some bugs got in, mamita," I lifted my head, but I didn't have the nerve to open my eyes. All of a sudden I felt the clear sensation of a warm air flowing through my head. Warm and drowsing. Then I opened my eyes and uncovered my ears—my father, the kitchen, and the atole were no longer in front of me. The lights turned into images that ran into one another as if they were on a screen: I saw my papá hugging a really thin woman with long dark hair. He rubbed her back gently and called her Lucre. There was an intermittent point of light flashing on the woman's stomach, like a heartbeat. Then I saw her in a dress stained with blood—she was crying and my father hugged her, stroked her hair.

"Calandrita, what's wrong with you? You look like you just saw a ghost. Ándale, your atole is getting cold!" Mamá Lochi's voice dissolved the image, and I returned to the kitchen to find my abuela in front of me, scrutinizing me with eyes wide in fear, and my father with his mug halfway from the table to his mouth. The white butterfly and the glowing insects had disappeared.

"What's goin' on, then, niña?" My abuela lifted my face by my chin and looked deep into me. "What are you seein'?"

How does she know, I remember thinking.

"I saw Lucre: that's what you call her, right, Papá?" tumbled out of my mouth, as though my lips were moving on their own. My eyes, too, since they fixed right on him.

He choked on his atole, and Mamá Lochi stood up to pound him on the back. His eyes went as big as tortillas.

"What did you say, Emilia?" he yelled, like I'd said something obscene. He avoided my abuela's eyes, which she didn't take off him.

"Yes, Lucre. That's what you call her," I said with a little thread of a voice, wary. My head hurt and I pressed into it with one hand, but I needed to tell them what I'd seen. "She has long black hair, Papá." And then, in a very low voice, I let it out: "The baby died, Papá, the one she had inside her. Not even the sun could brighten her up right now."

I remember that right as I said it, I regretted it. I felt like the words had been dictated to me. My father's lip trembled, and then he bit it to pretend otherwise.

"What are you teaching this chamaca, mamita, that she's saying stupid things like this? The atole must have done something to you, dumb little brat," he said, swallowing down a sob, a cry, an I-don't-know-what. Even though he seemed angry, I knew that something in that story was really hurting him. He stood up with smoke coming out of his ears and threw the mug, still full of atole, into the bucket of dirty dishes as if I had offended him. He grabbed his hat and his bag and left, slamming the door closed like the devil himself was chasing after him.

"As if we didn't know . . ." murmured Mamá Lochi as she rinsed the dishes and dried her hands. Then, looking at me intently, she sat next to me, put her fingertips on my temples, and moved them in circles.

"Your head hurts, doesn't it? What got into you, hm, chamaca? I think you've had visitors."

"It's just that I *saw* it, mamita."

"What do you mean you *saw* it? Where did you see it?"

I thought about it. I didn't know how to respond.

"I *saw* it. How do I explain it. . . . There were a bunch of insects and they buzzed real loud, mamita. My eyes and ears hurt. Then everything disappeared and I saw it. . . ." I finally said, not sure if I had invented it, dreamed it, or what. But still, I didn't want my abuela to think I was a liar. "Mamita, I swear on all the saints that I saw it and that I didn't do it on purpose. They must've been the kind that you say bring messages."

"Well, that's just what it must've been, Calandria," she said, and I felt how she pierced me with the force behind her pupils. "It must've been."

I looked for the white butterfly, but it had disappeared. The warm air escaped from inside me with a shiver. Mamá Lochi put one hand on my forehead and the other on my belly.

"No, well, you don't have a fever," she said, and went back to looking at me intently, the way she did. "This happen to you before, Calandria?"

I shook my head and felt strange. And I went back to looking around.

"It was that big troublemaker, the white one that flew in. Right, Calandria?"

"You saw it, mamita?"

She nodded. "They're really something, I already told you. They don't mess around. And if they choose you, well, you're screwed: She's going to keep shakin' you and showin' you things you'd never imagine. If it happens again, tell me."

"I think it's happened to me before," I clarified, both to her and to myself. Suddenly I'd realized that these things had been happening to me for a while, but I hadn't clearly distinguished what they were about. This was the very first time it happened so intensely.

"It was like I was right there, seein' everything, like it was on the TV."

"I knew you weren't just a discombobulated calandria. There had to be some other rarity in you."

Soon we would learn that the so-called Lucrecia was a woman in Santiatepec that my father visited often.

"That damn kid just doesn't learn," I heard my abuela repeat a lot in those days. But she didn't step up to say anything to my papá, who had been quick-tempered ever since he was a boy. Quick-tempered and a womanizer. When my Mamita Estela got sick, rumors ran through the town that he was off with some woman called Rosina. Mamá Lochi always said that woman put a spell on him to stay with her, and she must have done something evil to my Mamita Estela to get her out of her way. But she didn't manage to stay with my father. I don't know if Mamá Lochi had something to do with that.

"Don't get involved in my life, Mamá. Aren't I grown up now?" he'd say to my abuela whenever she brought herself to suggest anything to him. Mamá Lochi would shoot him one of her tough glares and not say anything more. I knew that she prayed to her saints about him, and that every so often she passed her incenses over his clothing to cleanse him of his bad habits with women.

The *seeing* thing, which is what Mamá Lochi and I called it when it started happening to me from then on, didn't happen very often and wasn't something I could control. The only thing that announced it was coming were the bright spots that sprinkled down around me, then the hum, and then an insect or a full swarm of them filling my vision. Next came the pull inside me, that warm air flowing through me quickly. Over time, I discovered that sometimes they were things that happened in the past, sometimes in the future, and that not even the person whose heart I could *see* knew about it. It was unpredictable. Mamá Lochi insisted that I needed to learn how to control it, to use it, but I think we needed more time for her to help me. On my own, with everything that happened after, I didn't try very hard. Plus, I don't think

I ever liked all that about knowing everyone else's secrets —it felt like a weight that I didn't want to carry was placed on my shoulders.

I could *see* lots of things about life, mine or that of others, but the only person I never *saw* was Mamá Lochi. No matter how hard I tried, no matter how much I attempted to enter into her secrets, I never managed.

"Don't even try it, chamaca," she'd say, a step ahead of me, as she flipped the tortillas on the stove. All I was doing, sitting near the warmth, was looking at her. "It'll be a long, long while before you can control when and who it's about, and only if you work real hard. But by the time that happens, I'll have jumped over the old stone wall to the sky already." And after she threw me a twinkling glance, her laughter cleaved through the air like bells.

In the dark before dawn, the sound of a motor woke them. It was the stake bed truck, returning to the camp. The bruises on Emilia's nose and mouth hurt. Despite the ointments Demetria had smeared over them, the swelling wouldn't go down. The barracks' lights came on. A new group had arrived, and they went about settling into the room's unoccupied corners.

"You look like a beat-up turkey," Goyo told her when he saw her.

"And you look like a bruised pig."

And they were overcome by an endless laughter, the kind that comes when everything hurts and the only consolation is to laugh until you can't anymore. Gregorio's face was swollen, too, and he was missing a tooth.

"It looks like you both got run over by a train," said Demetria.

Vaquero and Donojo passed out water and food to the newcomers and went around to charge the second fee. They would have to cough up the rest of the money before the crossing.

"Get the cash out of your other shoe," Goyo ordered his sister. "With that, plus what I've got, we'll have enough."

Vaquero planted himself in front of them and received the money. He gave them one of those looks: "And where'd you find this bill, huh, crooked foot?"

"What's it matter to you, mister," Goyo responded. "We're payin' you, aren't we? And don't call me crooked foot. I have a name."

"Don't get smart, fucking crooked foot, I'll whoop your ass, motherfucker. I'm asking because I don't like dealing with thieves."

Goyo's thoughts advised him: *Better to stay quiet.* The moment to respond would come. Vaquero wasn't happy, either: "And, anyway, just so it's clear, you two still owe us. Chato told us he covered for you. Don't go thinkin' it's gonna be free."

"Owe you what? We already paid!" Gregorio lurched forward, but Demetria yanked him back.

"Calm down, can't you see he's trying to—"

"Fuckin' crooked foot, you're a damn idiot." The man in the hat pocketed the money and walked off to charge the others.

"That bastard wants to screw us over," Goyo muttered, wiggling back into their spot. A bird's trill sounded—multiple people lifted their faces to the sky, as though they could see through the ceiling. When the shrill sound repeated, Vaquero stood, frozen, and then exited the chicken coop in a hurry to scream curses into the air.

"Fucking piece-of-shit bad-luck bird," he returned saying.

"Fuck, Vaquero, stop it! Let it go," Güera yelled as she

came into the room. "Can't you see it's just a fuckin' bird? Are you really so fuckin' scared of it?"

"That thing brings me nothing but bad luck whenever it pops up," he complained, adjusting his hat, not bothering to hide his trepidation.

"I hope that fucking bird eats him alive," Emilia whispered, mostly to herself.

Goyo looked at her intently. It was obvious to him that she was upset. She was surprised by his searching voice, by the tense tell-me-the-truth of it. "What did that asshole do to you?"

She didn't want to tell him. Why would she. It embarrassed her, and she was scared that he'd get mad at her for disobeying their agreement. She didn't know if it was just his tone or if that thing that sometimes happened with them was happening—when it was like they could read each other's minds or know what was in each other's heart.

"Tell me, Calandria. Don't lie to me. What did that piece-of-shit asshole do to you?"

"Nothing."

"I'm gonna kill that son of a bitch."

"Calm down, Caco. He didn't do anything to me, really—he didn't get the chance to."

Goyo gave her his hand, and she squeezed it hard.

They took the opportunity to refill their water bottles. They were ready to get out of there—the putrid smell of chicken shit burned their nostrils.

A while later it was announced that it was time to grab their stuff and head out. Vaquero led them to the back of the truck, and they shuffled in like a bunch of turkeys. Güera was at the steering wheel. She was wearing a hat and dark sunglasses as if it was the middle of the day.

The lights from the hall fell farther and farther away. The truck plunged into the desert on a rocky dirt road, full of deep potholes and uncertain shadows.

"Stay on your toes now, chamacos. This is like a game of roulette. If you're not quick, you get the bullet," Demetria warned them, still not tired of giving them advice. "There's no time to think. Everything happens in a flash. There's a lot of us. They're probably gonna separate us into groups." As soon as she heard those words, Emilia stuck to her brother's shirt like a hungry tick. Just the idea of being without him made her tremble.

After a while there were no longer any traces of electric light. The round and enormous night rose above them, like it was looking down at them with an exhausted resignation.

A tangle of tiny lights shone up high. Below, a hungry darkness. Little by little they got used to the bumps and shakes. Surrounding them were the shadows of enormous yuccas and saguaros. They appeared on one side and then on the other, close up and far away. It occurred to Emilia that they were guardians of the entrance to another world— spirits tired of watching others pass by, never getting to go anywhere on their own.

The truck stopped and the motor turned off. Donojo and Vaquero got out of the truck and left Güera at the wheel.

"C'mon, the first ten, on this side: get out!" the man in the hat shouted as he opened the cargo hold. Then he climbed to the side to let the people pass and indicate who should go with who.

The first ones started to clamber out of the truck. Goyo and Emilia were the last of that batch. When the boy jumped out of the stake bed, Vaquero grabbed the girl's hand and tugged so that she had to let go of her brother, and he held her back.

"She stays! She'll go with Donojo's group. You'll find each other on the other side," he ordered, and then started motioning for the rest of the group to hurry on out.

Emilia threw herself forward to break free, but Vaquero pushed her to the back of the truck with a shove.

"Goyo!" she screamed, and launched herself forward again to try to get out.

Gregorio, who had stepped away from the truck, tried to push through the crowd. Vaquero rushed to shut Emilia in.

"My sister comes with me!" he repeated, his shout now turning into a plea, like his soul was jumping out of his throat.

"Let her out!" Demetria interjected, stepping forward so that the people inside the truck would hear her. "What are you thinking, separating them? Besides, these kids are with me! Órale, Emilia, get out of there! Jump!"

"Let her out!" The outburst of voices continued, one after another, mixing with the dark night.

"I'm in charge here, motherfuckers!" Vaquero shouted. "If I say she doesn't go, she doesn't go! Got it, crooked foot?"

A slam from the front of the truck and Güera's harsh voice stopped the discussion short.

"What the hell's happening? These fuckin' brats again?"

"I don't want them to go together. I already told you, Güerita. Plus, they didn't even pay in full," Vaquero declared as he looked at his dirty fingernails.

"What do you mean they didn't pay in full?" Güera observed them over her sunglasses.

"Well, with a kid her age and the other with that crooked

foot, they should pay more, right? We have to take care of them."

"Nobody has to take care of us!" Goyo shouted with rage.

Güera looked them up and down. A dense silence spilled through the air.

"Don't be fucking stupid, Vaquero. It doesn't matter! Do you ever think? Think, asshole!" And turning to Emilia, Güera charged forward with a firm shout: "Get down from there, brat! Fucking hurry, before I regret this!" And before anyone could take a breath, Emilia was standing next to her brother.

"You keep pissing me off, fuck," the woman burst out, turning around. "I really don't care how, let's just go! Wastin' our fucking time, sons of . . ."

Donojo took a step forward and lit a cigarette. Then his dry capulín eye searched for Vaquero's gaze, he signaled something to him, and he climbed into the truck bed.

Emilia and her brother squeezed against each other and started to walk. The night was dark and their sense of unease had no end in sight.

"I have a bad feeling about this. There's something up with that Vaquero," they heard Demetria say, at their side. "Watch out for yourselves, chamacos. Stay close to each other—don't get separated."

The truck's back lights shrunk in the distance.

"Just in case, stick with me. And with that señor"—she pointed to one of the men in the group, who was always near her—"he's watching out for me."

So the two of them started to walk with Demetria.

"Fuck, Calandria. If you separate from me, you'll see. Promise me you're not gonna go anywhere without telling me."

"I promise you, Caco."

Vaquero turned on his flashlight and planted himself at the front of the group.

"These are the rules: I carry the light, nobody else. We go in a line. Follow the person in front of you. You have to be quiet in case a Vulture or Dog comes by. If a Vulture comes by, we split up and run and everyone has to get down on the ground and hide. And if a Dog comes near, same thing. If you find a snake, don't make any quick movements or you're fucked. Got it?"

A dispirited yes. And soon after they began the walk in their silence.

"Vulture or Dog?" Goyo whispered to Demetria.

"Border patrols who can hunt us as soon as we cross the line."

"And the snakes?"

"Those are the real kind," she laughed. "The kind that slither on the ground. Watch out if you hear a rattle or if you think you spot one anywhere near us. Stay real quiet and don't even move. They can jump up to two meters, the sons of bitches."

Demetria's shape bobbed in the darkness, walking a few steps ahead. *Wild animals everywhere*, thought Emilia. And she imagined what Mamá Lochi would say. That wild animals were less wild than people. That they'd never do anything to her if she didn't attack them.

Gregorio was busy passing his tongue over the hole where his tooth was missing. His mouth hurt. Dragging along his crooked foot, with his exaggerated little steps, he tried to keep pace with the group.

Emilia wanted to shake away her tangle of misgivings. She thought about her Papá Milo. She missed him. She thought about how happy they'd all be when they showed up and surprised him. When they could see each other for real, and not just in thoughts or in dreams, which is what she was used to lately.

The line advanced, Vaquero at the start lighting up the path with an intermittent flash. The group following him was made up of seven men and three women, if you counted the light-footed chamaca. Only four came from the same area, from the same landscape of jagged mountains, from the deep gullies filled by old jocote trees stubbornly clinging to the rock. They carried inside them the same river, the same sky, and the same air as Gregorio and Emilia Ventura. The same world that fell away as they advanced through the middle of that broken nothingness.

Months passed before Mamá Lochi took me to her cave again. I never got tired of asking and asking her to—I'd say it in a low voice, so nobody else would hear. She'd throw me one of those harsh looks, brimming with words. With her wide, serious eyes, she finally warned me that if I kept bothering her, she wouldn't even take me to a shack next door. My tongue burned, itching to tell her that I wanted to keep visiting her special place and learning her secrets, which I could sense by then were many. But I knew it was better to keep my mouth shut. I didn't want her to get mad and not let me go with her ever again.

In a town like ours—save for holidays when it was filled by festival wagons; dart and marble game carts full of stuffed animals and ceramic knick-knacks for the winners; stands selling pastries, candies, quesadillas, and chicken tamales; and people selling kitchen utensils and furniture—there wasn't much to distract yourself with. There was the television, that's true. The one that our abuela's comadre, Tomasa, had. We didn't have two pesos to rub together, much less enough for a television. Some afternoons, Goyo and I would knock on her door. She would let us in and turn on the TV without even saying a word. And we'd stay there a while watching cartoons. But I was always the weird one because, pretty much as soon as I learned how to read, I started to prefer the books and comics that my godfather and Tomasa's husband, José Clemente, brought me from the capital. I treasured them like they were made of gold dust, reading and rereading until I knew them by memory. That was the one connection I had with my godfather, who I only talked to when I was telling him what the comic book he'd given me was about. Mamá Lochi also asked me to read them to her, because she never went to school and didn't know her letters—she could just barely half-scrawl her name, with difficulty. Sometimes she asked me to recite the stories like I was just talking with her, which was how she preferred to hear them. I knew that it gave me a power over her. I would stand beside her and tell whole stories in one go, until I ran out of breath. But, to tell the truth, there was nothing better than when Mamá Lochi told me her stories about apparitions, elves, spirits, and magic spilled anywhere you could imagine. Her tongue almost always let loose during those trips up the mountain. Our long walks dusted off her memory and at any point in our route, even on the most strenuous and winding climbs, she'd give herself over to storytelling. Like she was telling a long story, broken into chapters, that she could pick back up wherever she wanted.

". . . and we were drinking an atole when we heard the sounds right outside. The squeaking of a sandal, no mistaking it. They were short, quick little steps. And then my comadre says, 'Now you tell me, who could that be? All the chamacos are asleep already.' Because it was midnight, but Tomasa had asked me over to give her something for the kidney problems she was having. . . . We both felt like it wasn't something from this world. And when we went to look—"

And just like that, just how she started, suddenly she went quiet and there was no human power or prayer that could make her finish the story.

"C'mon, mamita. Tell me what happened. Whose steps were they?"

When she was in a good mood she'd say to me, "Don't be so impatient, Emilia. Everything has its moment. And today, this is as far as the story goes."

And she plunged into that silence that was so hers, so dense with feeling. It settled down and swaddled me as I walked beside her.

". . . when my comadre opens the door to see who's there, well, she gets so spooked she jumps back and yelps. And so I run to her side and look out. There was a strange man at the door. He had a real huge face and looked up at us with wide owl eyes. He was dressed in glowing white with a bow tie, and his shoes were even polished. I jumped in to ask him: 'Can I help you?' And like I expected, not a peep in response. He just stood there, looking at us. I already knew he wasn't from this world, but I played dumb to not scare him off. I didn't want him to snap on us out of fear. Plus, I didn't want my comadrita, who always really suffered whenever apparitions came around, to get the air spooked out of her."

Again, the silence. And me, as always, swallowing down my antsiness so she would keep telling the story. Because I knew real well by then that it was better not to ask her for anything. She'd finish telling me on her own, whenever she decided was most convenient. Sure, she could take weeks to tell a single story. I had to keep stitching together the parts in my memory, and sometimes it took me a while to understand which story she was adding to. Because she didn't tell one at a time, she told a bunch. And always piece by piece like a puzzle.

We'd walk around without saying anything pretty often. Just as often, she would sing while we kept busy. Cutting pieces of ocote bark, gathering seed pods from the colorín trees, or collecting their red seeds sprinkled all over the dust, sparkling. She sang with that deep intonation, like a calandria, which she also had inside her. Except she knew how to hide it better than I did—she used it only to bring joy to her soul.

When I learned my letters, Mamá Lochi picked up right away that those drawings on paper, which is what she called writing, could reveal unknown worlds. Sometimes, after one of our long adventures, we'd sit together next to the comal where she flipped her tortillas and she'd ask me to read her parts of whatever book I had tucked away under the cot where I slept. I liked sitting next to her and reading or reciting a story for her while she rolled the ball of masa in her hands, smashed it between her palms, opened them to peel off a perfectly round tortilla, tossed it on the heat, then flipped it at the exact right moment. They came out warm and perfect. She said that she didn't feel anything with her fingertips anymore. There was a little dish of salt above the stone where she kneaded the dough and, even if I was in the middle of telling the story, she'd interrupt it to say to me, "Ándale, Calandrita: Make yourself a taquito with salt. Nothing better when you're hungry." And I'd come over the stove and open my hands waiting for her to give me a hot tortilla so I could sprinkle it with salt, roll it up, and take a little bite. "Okay, keep going now, chamaca. You got me hooked with your story."

Little by little, reading and telling stories that I pulled out of my sleeve gave me a power over Mamá Lochi. A power that none of her children, not even my father who was her favorite, ever had. I could reveal things to her that she found interesting, and that gave me the right to ask her about things that she didn't tell anybody, except for the other curanderos who came to learn her healing secrets and recipes. But it wasn't that easy. I had to be careful and find the exact right moment to toss in my questions.

Sometimes she would tell me about my Mamita Estela— about her sad eyes, her singsong voice. About when she started calling me Calandria. Back when I was all tiny and snot-nosed, when I was still drinking from my mamita's chichi, I'd start whistling when I was happy, when I was sad. It was a while before I'd burst out with the wild trill that jumped from my guts when I was scared. Even back then, Mamá Lochi said, she suspected that I had something special inside me. Suspected it. But it wasn't enough to just have suspicions. The calandria's trill was, for her, something very intimate, something straight from her own core. The fact that I had a pretty little whistle wasn't enough proof to say that I'd really inherited something of her magic.

When we went back to visit the cave, I had already turned eight. The rainy season had just passed, and it took us more than an hour to arrive at the trickiest peak of a tall mountain.

After that we had to walk for more than a half hour on a trail between crevices formed by overhanging rock faces. And at the end of the path, between two crags, there it was. The landscape had changed completely. That's just what happened from one month to the next in those mountains. As if the trees, the earth, and the plants shifted. I wouldn't have remembered the way there on my own. Especially because, on that rainy day that she took me for the first time, both the fear I felt from the thunder and the falling water that barely let me see past my nose made it impossible for me to record the terrain we were stepping through into my memory. But what I do remember is what we talked about on the way up and what she told me once we were in the cave. That I can't forget.

We were halfway up the path on that second trip when she decided to continue the story of the man in white:

"Well, there he was, all dressed up, with polished shoes and everything. His eyes, you should have seen them, they shone like he was trying to communicate something just through them. Like he was trying to send a message just by staring. 'Tell me, sir, how can I help you?' I told him. I kind of wanted to hear his voice. To see if he was really from another world. You know they say apparitions don't have a voice. And so then my poor comadre starts to pray and pray, inside the house, with a crucifix in her hands. She was getting real spooked, like she gets sometimes. Not for nothin'. Even me, and I know about these things, I felt something was really off with that guy. 'Well, tell me, sir, really, how can we help you?' I repeated. What if he was bringing us a curse. And he, still staring straight at me, without even blinking a little bit, what does he do but start pointing to the mountain, specifically

WHEN YOU GET TO THE OTHER SIDE

to the maize that was next to the land. And so I turn to look over that way. I managed to make out some glimmers of light. Barely. The fire was just starting, right there, right in the middle of the cornfield. I lifted my head and then shouted to Tomasa: 'Comadrita, the corn! It's burning!' And I look back to thank the man, but, well, nothing. The rascal had disappeared. Not even a trace of him. But there was no time to think or get more scared about it. Everything turned to lugging buckets of water to put out the fire. If it wasn't for that guy who appeared at the door to warn us, we wouldn't have harvested anything that season. Even the house would've burned down."

The rain kept falling as we reached the heights. I looked over my shoulder as I moved forward. I didn't want the guy with polished shoes to be following us.

The entrance to the cave was half hidden. At first glance, it didn't seem like the opening would lead anywhere, unless you took a few steps to the side. It smelled like mold, and a pair of bats flew out when we took our first step in.

Once the firewood caught, Mamá Lochi lit the reed pipe that she often smoked from.

"Tell me something from the story you're reading, Emilia," she said, and picked up a stick to push a piece of firewood that was falling off to the side. "Or make one up. Or just go ahead and sing me a little song, the kind you make up when you're whistlin'."

And I went along telling her whatever I could remember from the latest thing I'd read. They were short fables, which I mixed with my own inventions for long passages, trying to surprise her, searching her face to weigh what she might be thinking. But she didn't give away any emotions, never taking her eyes off the fire, smoking her pipe, and poking at the wood every now and then. Even though it seemed she listened to me attentively, I worried that my story was boring her, and when I ran out of air, with her scratchy voice full of smoke, she said:

"That book you were carrying around really says all that? I don't understand how they can fit so much into such a little thing." And she threw me a look, like she was searching for the truth or the lie in me.

"Really, mamita. It says all of that, and even more." And we stayed for a while, quietly watching a log let loose embers.

After taking a few deep inhales, she stirred the firewood and continued:

"Well, now it's my turn to talk and yours to listen. You're going to learn how I ended up in this cave for the very first time, more than fifty years ago now." She breathed in deeply, maybe to encourage herself. She looked at the wood burning in silence for a good while, before letting her words break out. And she didn't stop until the birds announced the arrival of the evening.

It was still night when they arrived at the fence. Emilia and Gregorio stopped before the tall, thick metal sheeting and looked up, then to one side, then to the other. Their gaze was lost in the absurd endlessness of that obstacle that split the landscape in two. They hadn't imagined it like that. They'd imagined a line, drawn clearly across some stretch of land. With all that talk about how when you cross the line, this; before you cross the line, that; after you cross the line, the other. No matter how many photos they might have seen, no matter how many stories they might have heard, in their minds there was a line. A line that divided the world, and that you had to cross to arrive at another. Gregorio wanted to say a word or two, or however many came out. To name what was waiting for them beyond that point. He sensed the step before them was big. But nothing came to mind. *Who the fuck knows what's waiting for us* was all that came to him, and he decided it was better to stay quiet. Emilia thought of Mamá Lochi. What if she didn't want to follow them. To leave her homeland, her spirits and her walks there in her mountains.

Maybe she had just guided them to that spot. "Mamá Lochi," the girl whispered, "don't stay back. Come with us. C'mon, mamita. Don't be mean."

Vaquero hurried them forward—what were they doing standing there like dumbasses, staring up at the wall like they were at the movies. He led them along the edge of the fence, crouching and silent, until they came to a slope in the earth. The descent led to a tunnel just recently covered by rocks and organic debris that, with their many hands, they uncovered quickly. The air was cold and the night black. The travelers began to drag themselves, one by one, through the low tunnel and come out on the other side, like beings birthed by the earth, covered in dust, pebbles, and dry brush.

Vaquero ordered them to walk with quick and light steps as soon as they came out the hole on the other side, to scurry as quietly as possible to a spot he pointed out in the distance. The border patrol would be making their rounds. They needed to stay alert.

Of the two siblings, Gregorio crossed first. At the opening on the other side, he waited for Emilia, his chest on the ground. A police truck passed by slowly, lighting up the edges of their path. Goyo warned those behind him to stop. They stayed in wait, breathing tensely. The truck went away and then Goyo gave them the green light with a gesture that they could hardly make out in the darkness.

Emilia came out spitting dirt from her mouth and followed her brother's crooked step. They ran in the direction they'd been told. The shapes of the travelers rose and disappeared in the distance. They tripped over plants and invisible rocks in the dark, never daring to look back. When they reached the meeting point, a little more than a half-kilometer from the crossing, they gasped for air. They waited for Vaquero—he had crossed last and soon arrived, walking casually like nothing was going on. He ordered them forward another stretch, so they'd end up far from the border line.

They walked beneath the pink-and-yellow shades of the sunrise that was stretching over the edges of the world. With the arrival of the light, Emilia was surprised to look around and see the figures that surrounded them: cacti, thorns, shrubs. She thought of Mamá Lochi, of her last breath, of her fierce tenderness. She thought of her mountains, of her river, of her father walking with a hat on his head and a machete in his hand, an empty sack for wood hung over his shoulder.

A dust storm swelling with inconvenient emotion spun around inside her.

"What's wrong, Calandria?" Goyo could sense something in her. He looked at her sideways.

"Nothin'," she responded, still contemplating the golden sunrise.

The spines on the cacti snared them, sticking in their feet and pants.

A bird cut through the sky, flying low with an ominous caw.

"Fucking bird." Vaquero stopped to take off his hat, scratched his head, and made the sign of the cross over his chest.

"C'mon, hurry up!" he said, before picking up his pace.

From one side to the other, the saguaros stood in their quietude. After walking a long stretch with steady steps, the travelers started showing signs of exhaustion.

"Ten minutes," Vaquero ordered. "Drink water, rest. We gotta take advantage of the time before the sun gets too strong. It'll be right over us soon."

They spread out and looked for places to settle down and stretch their bodies. They drank and ate. Goyo and Emilia went to Demetria's side.

"Supposedly a truck is waitin' for us. I don't see one anywhere." The woman's voice dragged with exhaustion.

"Don't worry, doña. We've already crossed. You'll see, everything's going to be okay." Gregorio felt optimistic. They were already on the other side, whatever came next couldn't be that difficult.

The landscape opened up like a fan decorated with wandering figures—the saguaros, giant yuccas, and playful clouds sketched in as they met the light. Morning birds cut through the sky, singing to the dawn. And the deep nocturnal cold crept back as though embarrassed by the sun's arrival. To the north, far away, the mountains rose up like giants, unaware of what was happening at their feet.

When the travelers started marching forward again, their tiredness lingered. But they walked until the ruthless heat of midday forced them to stop.

Bunched together under a group of trees with thin shadows, some took off their shoes, jackets, and backpacks. They drank, took a sad bite of food, and did everything they could to stay out of the harsh sun. Gregorio took the bean-and-rice taco out of its plastic. It was starting to stink. They devoured it. Emilia pushed through the nausea its taste brought her. Like food scraps for pigs.

"This bastard is taking us the long way. And where's the fucking truck that was supposed to come get us?" Demetria burst out suddenly in a tense whisper, like an unwished-for thought had escaped her mouth.

"What do you mean, doña?" Goyo's misplaced optimism was deflating.

"Shh! Don't talk so loud. Even the rocks listen here. At this point the truck should be here or at least at the base of the mountains. It's like he's taking us the long way. I'm not gettin' a good feeling about this."

The brother and sister exchanged a broken glance, and Gregorio tried to recover his sense of good fortune: "Don't worry, doña, you'll see. We're going to get there safe, really, I know it."

At Vaquero's signal they started walking again. Their feet hurt more after taking a break. Vaquero went slowly. He'd pull a bottle out of his pocket and take a gulp. Then he'd spit, clean his lips with the back of his hand, put the cap back on, and stow the bottle away.

They stopped before sundown. There were those same mountains. The same saguaros. The same burning rocks. The sky with its streaks of white clouds turned orange, and an eagle flew over them.

"It's like we haven't moved at all," Emilia dared to say.

"Yeah. It seems like that. I think the doña is right," her brother confirmed, drying the sweat that slid down his face with his shirt and, at the same time, shaking off the remains of his optimism.

They sat down hungrily to eat, but took their time to draw out the taste of the small mouthful of tuna that Demetria shared with them.

"So how much longer, Vaquero? It feels like we've been goin' for a long time," ventured one of the men sitting farther away.

Vaquero was standing, making circles in the dirt with the

sole of his boot. He barely lifted his gaze, his eyes blocked from view by the brim of his hat. A stiff silence tied up the air. The heat came in brutal waves.

"I'm talking to you, Vaquero. Seriously. We want to know how much longer."

Before lifting his head, the man in the hat let some hostile seconds pass. Finally he raised his eyes, pulled the bottle out of his pocket, took the lid off, and drained it all the way.

"We're asking you. We just want to know."

Vaquero burped. Then he turned to the man who had spoken and approached him slowly, never taking his unwelcoming and unhelpful glare off him.

"Motherfucker. Don't you want me to take you on the safe route or what."

"No, it's not that, no, Vaquero. That's not what I mean. It's just that we want to know if we're almost where we're supposed to go."

"Can't you see, are you fuckin' blind, or what?" The travelers looked in the direction that Vaquero was pointing. At a distance, if you looked hard and squinted, there was a gleam of light.

"What's that?" another spoke up.

"That's where we're meeting the car. We have to get there when it's dark, so they can't detect us." And, finishing his statement, he lay down with his backpack under his head, put his hat over his face, and started to snore.

The sun brushed up on the edges of the earth as they gave in to the discomfort of a rest upon rocks and exhaustion, waiting for the full arrival of night.

Emilia and her brother had just a little bit of water left—their dry mouths burned. Goyo reached deep into his backpack and pulled out a piece of tamal and a tortilla that they'd hidden among their clothes. They seemed like they were made of rubber.

"Calandria."

"What's up, Caco."

"If we end up losing each other for any reason, whatever it is, promise me that no matter what we'll meet up in the mountains."

"But how will we know where?"

"Well, just go to the mountains. There, where you can see them split. And we'll leave each other signals, you know, like we do when we walk up our mountain. That way we'll find each other for sure. You promise me?"

Emilia, her head between her knees, continued making marks in the dirt with the sharp rock in her hand. She thought of their games, running through the mountains of Amatlán. Goyo had a secret radar that helped him find her. He climbed up trees and over piles of rocks, clever as a cacomixtle. He could fit anywhere, silently, lightly, to find whatever he was looking for or get where he needed to be.

"You promise me, or what?"

"Yes, Caco. I promise you. But I don't want us to split up ever."

"We're not going to split up. It's just in case."

"But, Goyo . . ."

"What's up, Calandria."

"What if the border patrol gets us? And what if they send us back? What will we do?"

Gregorio glanced over at Emilia. He didn't want her to sense his nervousness.

"No, Calandrita, that can't happen to us. You'll see, we'll

be okay."

She squeezed herself up against her brother and let her exhaustion take over. Curled up with each other, they couldn't resist falling into an uncomfortable sleep, littered with anxious, fearful dreams.

It happened to her during the rains of September, when the puddles fill up and rise to the edges of the tall rocks, along the sides of the gully where the river runs. Mamá Lochi was just a girl then. Together with her siblings and some other kids from town, she'd gone down to the river to splash around. Her mom, Goyita, who'd be my great-grandmother, had warned the little chamacos not to take long, that the storm was coming even if right now the sun was shining.

"We were just kids," Mamá Lochi remembered. "When playfulness and joy come together in the soul of a chamaca, worry and danger get pushed aside and there's no fear that would show its big ugly face."

The hours passed as they dove from the tip of a tall rock and stood under the waterfalls that splashed over the riverbank's edge. The sky turned black, and, before they knew it, big drops were falling on the water's reflective surface, sending ripples across it. The first boom of thunder caught them in their underwear. Before Mamá Lochi, the smallest of all the siblings, could pull her dress over her head, the rest were already running uphill to get out of the gully and find safety under some roof cover so the lightning couldn't get them. Mamá Lochi said she didn't feel afraid. She knew the way back. And even though they'd taught her to be afraid of lightning, she felt strangely protected. But the raindrops turned into a downpour and a dense fog came down so quickly that, when she looked up, she was walking along a dark path and couldn't see farther than the tips of her toes. The lightning lit up the way every now and then, filling it with specters, with glimmers that took strange shapes. My abuela, at seven years old, told herself that all she needed to do was to keep climbing up to get out of the gully. Plus, she'd already started to wander through the mountains a while back, leaving behind not only the riverbed but also the way back to her house. Guided by the eyes of her feet, she skirted around the edges of the cliffs that were growing deeper and deeper. She sensed a fit of fear coming and decided to call out to her brothers and sisters who were surely looking for her. She shouted, but her voice scattered in the fog, lost in the furious sounds of the thunder and the dense rainfall.

Suddenly, she walked into an old jocote tree with a wide trunk. She felt like the tree was stopping her, like it blocked her path, and she hugged it tightly. She thought of her father, who didn't allow himself to be hugged, but whose hands were tough like the tree's bark. She found a branch and started to climb. She thought that from high up she'd be able to see the way home, which the low fog had impeded her from making out. She climbed up swiftly and was getting settled, balancing on her haunches on a branch, when she felt a hard blow against her shoulder. A deafening boom of thunder, a fiery cold running through her veins, through every pore of her flesh, and pain that centered on her arm and radiated out through her bones and skin. It threw Mamá Lochi to the ground, leaving her facedown on the earth.

Who knows how long she stayed like that—under the harsh rain, unknowing and unfeeling from the jolt that had just run through her. When she woke up, she felt the pain again, clear and open—and also a profound strangeness. She was dizzy, confused. The buzz in her ears was incessant. Her body burned and she smelled something singed. She couldn't move her left arm very well, and when she turned to look at it, she saw a sketch now marked into her skin, from her shoulder to her hand: pink, perfect lines, like they'd been traced with a paintbrush. She said she contemplated the little leaves of that impeccable fern and felt afraid that her Mamá Goyita would get angry at her for drawing on her skin.

Her hands, arms, and face burned. She tried to sit up straight—a struggle since waves of dizziness kept passing over her. Though the first few steps took work, bit by bit she felt a great strength in her feet. She started to walk—dazed, with that buzzing in her ears decreasing slightly—leaving behind a vivid smell of burnt kindling with every step. And because it was still raining, she continued walking without knowing which way to go.

At that point in the story, Mamá Lochi settled into a dense silence. I knew that I shouldn't interrupt her thoughts, that I should accept that she didn't want to keep telling the story or that she would continue whenever she wanted. She raised her gaze, which had stayed fixed on the fire, and hooked her black and bright eyes onto mine. After getting up and looking for another log, throwing it into the fire and waiting for it to catch, she returned to the story, like someone returning to a difficult chore.

That day of the downpour she kept walking as if her feet had their own will and an invisible force told them where to go. Everything looked different to her—it was like the mountain had transformed. What she saw with her eyes made her forget the pain throughout her body. The plants' leaves shone with intensity. She could sense the flesh of the tree trunks and the sap running through them. Their cracks, traced by the lightning or a lumberjack's ax, were open wounds, bleeding, oozing a silent pain that grabbed her by the insides. Rocks pulsed beneath her feet, full of secrets she could hear them whispering. The wet earth exhaled in deep breaths, told its stories. She could see animals and insects walking in the distance. They exchanged looks and she saw them stop by her side, like they recognized her. They murmured to her, in their animal voices, and she trembled when she understood them. She had to draw up her courage to follow the golden threads that came and went around her and connected her with every being on the mountain. Every sound transmitted its story. Mamá Lochi told me that it was like her ears, her skin, and her eyes had shed a veil and were able to see the universe how it really is. And, even though she was too little to explain it, she soon knew that something deep inside her had transformed completely.

She walked until the night took over, never crossing paths with anybody from this world, never looking for her way back. Returning home was a distant concern, lost in some corner of her thoughts, which were more occupied with seeing what the flashes in the dark were offering her as welcome gifts. Every now and then she was overcome by the fear of meeting up with one of those spirits that wanders the mountain, the malicious ones that Mamá Goyita said steal the souls of badly behaved children. But, despite the blackness that embraced her, she erased fear from her mind—the trees, shadows, and spirits wandering this mountain revealed themselves to her as forces nobody needed to fear. She climbed down the rockiest part of the mountain until she was overcome by an exhaustion that made it impossible to take another step. Curling up into a little ball between two shrubs and against a boulder, she waited for a coyote to come eat her.

The first lights of daybreak were beating out the shadows when she felt eyes on her, looking her up and down. At first she couldn't see clearly if it was a coyote or some other animal. Then she realized it was a person that was observing her so attentively. Mamá Lochi tried to get up, but she ached all the way up to the hairs on her head, which had been burned by the lightning that struck her. Now she did feel afraid, thinking the spirit might be an evil one, looking for lives to haul off to another world. She wished with all her heart for it to be Mamá Goyita, even if she'd come to scold her and beat her for her disobedience, for getting lost. Even that would seem sweet to her compared with a spirit taking her away from this world forever.

When the figure in front of her came into focus, she saw that it wasn't Mamá Goyita or anyone she'd ever seen before, but there was something familiar in the woman's face, in her demeanor, in her way of looking. Two black eyes ran over her, like she had turned into an animal that the old woman couldn't quite recognize. A long braid flecked with white and silver fell down her back. She had thin, tough legs and carried a burlap sack over her shoulder. Suddenly, she stretched out her arm to help my seven-year-old abuela up onto her feet.

And Mamá Lochi made a great effort to stand up, but the pain clinging to her skin didn't let her. Her legs buckled. The old woman tried to steady her and my little abuela let herself fall—this time to the bottom of a dark hole that opened up beneath her feet, which she didn't emerge from until several hours later.

When she finished this part, Mamá Lochi maintained such a powerful silence that I thought we were about to leave the cave and head home. She'd continue with the story on some other occasion, as she tended to do, and I consoled myself by listening to the murmur of the trees. The branches and trunks of the oldest ones crackled, covering my skin with goose bumps. With the wind blowing, they sounded like a rushing river in a storm. The air swirled about the branches, the dry leaves and mature fruits moving with it as though they might fly away of their own accord. The birds in the sky let loose their chirps, and Mamá Lochi trilled along, like she was responding to them. I whistled to encourage them to sing. Even the shadows made sounds, mumbling among themselves.

When I didn't let fear stop me, I'd try to open my heart and see the invisible. I would look for spirits in the brush, at the bottoms of ravines, or in the clouds that ran over the world. I could only do it when I didn't let them see that I was afraid. A darkness would cross a clearing and when I'd turn to look at it, it would have already disappeared. Or suddenly I'd find my eyes glazed over and trained on a figure that looked like an animal, but before I could fully recognize it, it'd vanish between the clumps of brush or flit across a grassland. I'd feel the spirits come closer. They would touch my shoulder or breathe on my neck, on my face.

At night, after one of those walks or visits to the cave, full of spirits and invisible beings, I tended to sleep restlessly. I'd wake up screaming, immersed in darkness, sweating and terrified because I felt very clearly that a weight had fallen on me and it didn't allow me to move or open my eyes—a weight that kept smushing me down no matter how much I fought against it. That's when my abuela, woken by my yelling, would say to me, "That night hag's sitting right on you, Calandrita. We'll send her far away soon. Breathe calmly, because they like fear and the more you fear, the more she'll stick to you." And she would rub wild jasmine petals on my neck and hands, make me drink lime-blossom tea, and speak to me softly in her language so I would fall back to sleep.

That evening in the cave, as I heard her murmuring silence, her way of looking at the flames and pushing around the firewood, I suspected that she might pick back up with her story. I curled up on the blanket. Sleep, difficult to resist, was taking over me, but Mamá Lochi turned to look at me right as I started making my sack into a pillow.

"Don't you want to hear what happened next?"

"Yes, mamita. It's just that I thought you were done telling for today. You know how sometimes you do that. . . ."

"What are you talkin' about? That's the whole reason I brought you here." She poked at a burnt log that had escaped from the fire. "What I'm going to tell you now, Emilia, is for you to save in your heart." She tossed a handful of herbs into the bowl where she was preparing tea. "What I'm going to tell you is what I'm going to leave you of me, of my mystery, my legacy. It's only going to help you when you're far away. When you learn how to draw words on paper real, real well. And you're only going to remember it when you feel totally lost in the middle of nowhere."

"But there's nowhere I'm goin', mamita," I said, convinced.

She returned her gaze to the embers. "That's right, chamaca: You're going to no where, in so many words. Destiny put grasshoppers in your feet. Wings on your back. You're going to carry with you the story of your family, my history, the history of this very mountain that is your home. The history of your ancestors, even though you don't know it. And one day, when you miss me and you feel like you're going to forget me, you're going to sit down to sketch it all out on pieces of paper, so that other people know it. So that not even you can forget it. It's going to come right out, you'll see. You won't have to call for it." And before my questions could rain down on her, she returned to the day she was struck by lightning, right when she was awoken by a cold sensation.

When she opened her eyes, she was spooked by the face of the old lady with the long braid. She was leaning over her, holding a damp cloth to her left arm. Mamá Lochi looked around. They were in a cave, and she heard the rain falling. She felt the warmth of the air and the light of a bonfire a few steps away. The crackling of the trunks as the flames embraced them calmed her, as though it was proof that she was alive. She turned back to look at the old woman. What if she was a spirit who'd come directly from the beyond? Maybe she had died and this was heaven, and that woman was the Virgin herself. Though it did seem weird to her that the Virgin would appear as an old lady. Maybe she was a saint, one of those that are really good while living and go straight to paradise the moment they die.

Mamá Lochi tried not to move around too much, as if the stillness could ensure that nothing bad could happen. The woman dampened a rag in a bowl full of water that smelled of herbs like chamomile, fennel, and mint, then wrung it out and put it right back on my little abuela's arm, forehead, and other parts of her body. Her skin stung from head to toe. She wanted to tear it all off to free herself of the burning.

The old woman did her work in silence. She only looked at her with her shining eyes, and my little abuela looked back up at her, searching the face for something that would clarify things. She might be a dead spirit, an ancestor that came down from the other world to help her. She also had that mosquito bite of a birthmark under her left eye, characteristic of some of the women in the family. That's why she looked so familiar. Maybe it was her great-grandmother Rigo, or her great-great grandmother Carmen. Her Mamá Goyita talked about them often, about the bunches and bunches of years they lived, about the things they knew, about their powers, how they didn't put up with anything from anybody. But it wasn't until the old lady with the long braid took a knife to split open a leaf of aloe, rubbing the sticky innards over her skin, that Mamá Lochi noticed the fern that covered the woman's left arm. The lines weren't as pink as the ones she had on her own small arm, and the sketched branches were smaller than hers. Mamá Lochi remembered raising her hand to touch it. The woman, as though she was waiting for that gesture, didn't seem upset. She let her do it and brought the tips of her own wrinkled fingers, soft to the touch, to the drawing that the lightning had tattooed on my little abuela.

They stayed like that for a while, measuring each other up. The old woman recognizing what she already knew. Mamá Lochi faintly starting to make out what, in some corner of her soul, was pushing forward to reveal itself.

He and Emilia float above the earth: They are held up by ropes attached to their backs. The ropes are losing their rigidity—if they don't manage to grab hold of another rope, swinging out of reach, the open hole at their feet will suck them in and swallow them up. Emilia opens her mouth to shout to her brother. He can't hear her voice, but he sees her throat trembling and watches her fall away and cannot reach her. A force coming from the black hole pulls her down and Goyo wriggles his feet to take flight and grab her, but she keeps falling away, plunging down and disappearing into the hole. . . .

"Emilia!" Gregorio jerked awake at the sound of his own shout, his agitated breath, the wail trapped in his chest. "Emilia! Calandria!"

His sister wasn't at his side. Alarmed voices surrounded him.

"Run! Run! Vulture! Vulture!"

The shadows came and went, scattering, spreading out over the land in search of somewhere to hide. In the distance, a helicopter sent out waves of incredibly powerful light, illuminating the surrounding darkness in segments.

The commotion of the scattering bodies was fading away, but Goyo still hadn't found his sister. The rumble of the helicopter was coming back toward him. He heard a voice falling from above, threatening to shoot. Distorted, it sounded like a malicious god speaking from the heavens.

"Emilia!"

He looked around him with no luck. The group was now an anthill disseminating in the distance, while the Vulture continued flying over them. His sister's backpack was abandoned in the exact place they'd laid down to sleep.

"Fuckin' hell, Emilia. I told you to tell me if you were going anywhere." The anxiety grabbed at a place deep inside him. It chewed at his insides, settling in with its usual ease.

He could make out some running figures, illuminated in the middle of a useless race. From a distance, he saw them throw themselves on the dirt, hands on the backs of their heads. A beam of light coming down from the sky briefly flashed at a car parked in the distance. In a blink, Goyo managed to make out the silhouette of a man herding people toward it—a gut feeling pushed him to start running that way. He ran as best he could with his crooked step, tripping over rocks, plants, and bumps in the earth invisible at those hours. Despite his efforts, before he came within reach, the car started and was swallowed by the night.

He ended up alone in the middle of that heartless emptiness—with just his anxiety and a dust storm of disconnected thoughts, all built from total desperation.

The helicopter flew overhead, continuing its hunt. Goyo saw it approaching, with the haste of a hunter—they'd seen him. He squatted down against a thicket of creosote bushes, ducked his head, shoved his arms between his legs, and stayed still, adjusting his breathing so he could sink down into that part of his spirit that he knew well. The light passed over him without detecting his presence.

"Ay, Calandria, don't let them get you. I'm coming for you, don't worry," he murmured, and felt a tightening deep in the very center of his chest. What if it was her that they'd taken away . . . who they'd tossed into the car. What if they got her. Maybe it was the Dogs. He shook off those gutting thoughts that weren't helpful at all. The helicopter flew over him again. Mamá Lochi hadn't shown him his tricks in vain. They didn't call him Caco, like the sneaky, ring-tailed cacomixtle, for nothing—with his elastic and flexible body, his ability to turn invisible wherever he went. But Emilia. He hoped to find her huddled in some hiding spot just like him, with her head between her bent knees, her thoughts and heart far from the earth, breathing serenely and erasing the borders between her skin and the world. Their abuela called it becoming air. But Emilia never got it right, her body wouldn't do it—she could do other things, but not that.

"Push everything all down inside. You'll get mistaken for the invisible and nobody'll be able to find you, no matter how much they want to," their abuela would repeat when she showed them how to do it. For Gregorio, with his bubblegum joints and his ability to go unnoticed to the point of complete erasure, it wasn't difficult at all to learn how. Mamá Lochi told him again and again that he had a special gift and he took advantage of it, using it more frequently than his own abuela would have liked.

"Just don't stay on the other side forever, chamaco.

You have to know when to come back," she'd say when he, called to do some undesirable chore, would disappear and spend hours hidden while the others tried to find him in the corners of the house or out in the backyard.

The huge beam of light passed over him several more times. Finally it stopped, along with the shouts, the fleeing voices, the sirens. He strained his ear—maybe he'd catch Calandria's trill. But there was nothing. Then the brief flash of lightning—*the gringos use those super powerful lights to send aliens signals*, he thought as he floated in his invisibility. Where could his sister have gone. Rebellious Calandria. And he thought back: Before she curled up to sleep next to him, she'd taken off her sneakers to relieve the pain in her feet, to take care of her blisters. She had fallen asleep first. Goyo tried to encourage himself. Once the Vultures were gone, surely they'd find each other.

"Ay, Emilia, I hope you're not bein' stupid."

A hazy intuition progressed toward certainty. His sister was in that car he'd seen take off: They'd gotten her. But how could he be sure? The bright light from the Vulture had made it difficult to make out what was happening far away. The certainty embedded itself deep inside him, like a hungry tick.

From within his invisibility, Gregorio Ventura heard distant gunshots and was tempted to get up, but he got the feeling that it would be better to stay still. Releasing himself into the measured rhythm of his breath, he sunk back into his invisibility, dove deep under his gathered-up skin, and floated in that empty space that was his discouraging refuge, far from the world. When he returned at last and opened his eyes, he noticed the density of the silence. The darkness wrapped around him had no soul.

He felt like he heard his sister calling him. He raised his head from between his legs and looked around. He had no idea how much time had passed. Around him, a tense calm. He heard his heart beating, the uproar of his hungry innards, and, coming from some other world, her voice calling him. He shook himself out of his self-absorption, stood up, and walked in circles.

"Emilia!" The letters trembled as they tumbled out of his mouth—her name emerged laden with bad omens. "Fuckin' hell . . ."

He pulled a bottle of water, some soggy tortillas, a few sets of rolled and mildewy clothing, a knife, a couple bills, and some loose change from the bottom of an abandoned backpack. He added everything to the bigger backpack. He called for his sister again, walking the area in overlapping circles until he was sure he was completely alone.

"Now I'm really fucked."

He felt his own voice, as soon as it joined the dark and cold night, become lost. A reminder of how alone he'd ended up. He started walking to the mountains, the ones with the gash between them. He hadn't forgotten the promise they'd made each other: No matter what happened, that was where they'd go if they got separated or lost sight of each other. He imagined her aboard a patrol car, being taken back to the border, to the other side. He imagined her in Vaquero's hands and that's where he stopped imagining, because inside him a cruel river's shadowy waters flooded over, threatening to drown him if he let himself lose heart.

"Hopefully you're with Demetria," Goyo wished, and, without stopping his forward steps, he asked himself if it would be better to let himself get caught so he could find her.

A distant sound jarred him out of this wandering within himself. Frozen, alone in the middle of the desert's open shadows, he listened. It sounded like a roar. He imagined a wild animal creeping up on him.

Just what I needed.

He shook away the thought. The sound was more like a machine, maybe a siren. *The Vultures are coming back,* he told himself with sudden distress, *they're coming for me.* He quietly looked for a spot to hide. And the noise returned. It came from far away and stayed far away. It didn't take him long to identify it as a car's horn, maybe, or an alarm echoing who knows where. He looked around. A pair of bright points flickered in the direction of the mountains. Maybe it was a building. Or someone with a flashlight. Hard to know what. He observed the light carefully to see if it moved and soon determined that it was staying still. It was far enough that he would have to travel a ways to reach it. He took the knife out of his backpack and stuck it in his jacket pocket, holding it tight with one hand, and started to walk in the direction of the glimmer in the middle of that emptiness.

The cold pierced his skin and he picked up his pace to warm up a bit. He figured there must be a couple more hours until sunrise. What if the distant light was something that could help him get out of there, or that could give him news about his sister? What if it was hope? He livened up and that's how he walked until the dawn. Inside his shoes his blisters and scrapes chewed at him like angry bugs. He went in and out of basins, with labored breath, rushing to arrive who knows where, until the sun started to color in the night. And then he saw it. Far away, really far away: A car that shone with daybreak. He looked at it like it was a strange animal stranded in the middle of that nowhere. Calmly, weighing the possible outcomes of the meeting. There didn't seem to be any movement around it, but how could he know for sure at that long distance. A vague premonition lit him up inside. He sped up his uneven steps, feeling the burning of the frozen night that was just slipping away, its remains still drifting through the air.

The lightning didn't only scar Mamá Lochi's skin—it also left a mark deep inside her. When she managed to pick up her story again, about her meeting with the old woman with the spot under her eye, her high-pitched voice had to work to make itself heard. We were in the cave and Mamá Lochi wouldn't take her eyes off the fire. It was clear how difficult it was for her to return to those memories, which she'd never told anyone before. I couldn't have known because I was very small, but to tell the truth, I sensed it—by telling me all that, my abuela was turning me into her clay pot, her pewter pan, so that I would hold them for her.

After being rescued by the old woman, Mamá Lochi remembered spending hours sleeping inside the cave. Between dreams she saw the old lady exit and enter the cave with her burlap sack over her shoulder, reviving the fire every now and then and singing in a tongue that my abuela recognized from hearing her own abuelos speak it. From time to time, the woman sat at the opening to the cave, facing out, sending smoke over her head as she smoked a pipe whose tobacco smelled like banana leaves. She didn't stop taking care of her. Giving her sips from an intensely sweet tea, pieces of piloncillo, and boiled eggs. Rubbing aloe and tepezcohuite on her burns. Helping her get up to relieve herself in a bin, which she then took out of the cave and returned clean to its spot.

Mamá Lochi remembered watching the daylight fall away and become the dark of night several times through the cave's opening before she felt strong enough to go look out on her own. When she did, the old woman was out of sight and my little abuela walked outside and looked around. They were on the tallest peak of a mountain. It was early. She recognized the landscape. The same trees she'd always seen. The same smell of the earth. The same sounds. Birds chirping, the wind rumbling like a river over the foliage. But the feeling that that world had transformed was still with her. She perceived every miniscule movement, sound, aroma, silence, or nearby space with complete clarity.

Turning her gaze to the right, to the edge of the cliff, my little abuela found the old woman squatting to look down at something. She was still as a rock, facing the gully. A few seconds passed and she intoned a song, a light murmur that could be confused for the sounds of the mountain. From time to time, the old woman raised her face up to the air, then lowered it to the container at her feet. It was a deep gourd, and she leaned over it like something inside was trapping her gaze. My little abuela thought it could be a newborn creature of some sort, though she didn't manage to see it because the woman leaned so far over the container that she almost put her whole face inside. Mamá Lochi felt like she was being coaxed forward by a spirit, greedy to know what was in the gourd. She approached slowly and suddenly, when she was a few steps away, the old woman turned. Her eyes were alight like flames, like they weren't from this world. The woman made a gesture to send her back to the cave while, with the other hand, she covered up the container. Inside the gourd something was moving, but the force with which the old woman demanded she go away made her double back over her steps. The woman followed her with her gaze, and when she disappeared from view she turned around and went back to her songs.

Finding out what the woman had inside the gourd hooked into Mamá Lochi's mind like a bee's stinger. She waited for her to return to the cave to stoke the fire that stayed lit day and night. She waited for her to rub her body with the tepezcohuite and aloe, to run her fingertips over the fern tattooed on her arm, to give her infusions to drink and food to eat. She waited and waited, alert as an owl, until the moment came that she saw her cross her sack over her chest and exit the cave. My little abuela had spent enough time there to understand her rhythms, and when she saw her leave, she got up and went to the cave's entrance. It was close to midday. The rocks radiated a scorching humidity. The shadows were just barely sketching in, and, despite the cool air inside, drops of sweat pearled up on her forehead. They must have been from nerves, I remember she said. She already sensed that her disobedience was going to bring her an evil difficult to expel, she explained, looking at me intently, like she wanted me to really understand her so I wouldn't even think of disobeying her like that.

From the entrance to the cave, my little abuela looked around. The idea of the woman's flaming eyes catching her in her disobedience scared her. She felt the simple calm of midday. A clear calm. She felt the eyes of the birds flying over the mountain, in circles, monitoring her movements. She felt the alert silence of the insects between the rocks, behind a leaf, above her head.

Mamá Lochi headed for the gourd, which lay on the edge of the gorge. As she approached, she felt like the gap, in its devouring immensity, was opening wider before her. An emptiness that seemed to want to swallow her up.

A flat rock covered the gourd, which, she could see now, was embedded into the earth. A light wind started to blow when she took the rock in her hands to lift and set it to the side. The water contained within the gourd rippled, giving her a welcome. There wasn't an animal or anything extraordinary inside, Mamá Lochi remembered thinking. Just water. A gourd with rainwater, nothing more. Squatting in front of the container, my little abuela contemplated her reflection. Whispers, distant voices that seemed brought by the wind's hands, reached her ears. A fresh, calming breeze came from far away to take away her fear.

Take a look, Eloísa.

At first she didn't understand where the voice was coming from. Turning around, she only saw trees, rocks, the dark and cool cave where there was nobody.

Ándale, niña. Get down and look, she'll be back soon.

Mamá Lochi leaned over the surface of the water a little more. The voice was coming from inside the gourd. At the bottom she saw the sky with white clouds and a bird flying across it. She leaned in more and recognized her own face. There were her black and prominent eyes, which shone like sparklers as they looked at themselves. The mosquito bite of a birthmark right under her left eye. Her hair, thinned out by the scorch of the lighting, hanging alongside her ears, and her mouth, closed like she was afraid, not sure of what to say. But what could the old woman have seen inside the gourd, Mamá Lochi asked herself, that seemed to have sparked her up like a firework, to the point that her eyes even lit aflame. And the voice continued.

Look, niña; don't stop looking. C'mon now, keep goin', keep looking. If you don't keep looking, you'll have nothing to see.

Mamá Lochi said that what happened next happened in a second. A second that lasted a lifetime. My abuela's little girl face started to unravel in the water and the lines of her features took new shapes, and as they did, distinct figures started to run inside the gourd. She said that inside there, she saw images from her life pass by. I imagine it was like a movie, even though she never went to see one. She was there, inside it—with her Mamá Goyita, her father, her abuelos, playing by the river with her brothers and sisters, in the town's central plaza with all the other kids, at church, running through the dirt roads. And she saw herself on the mountain, walking through the rain, and the lightning bolt that struck her and ignited the branches of light inside her. She saw the old woman who carried her up the mountain, who cared for her, who healed her. She saw herself in front of the gourd. And that's when the images accelerated: She saw her life pass by after she was found unconscious at the bottom of a ravine. A life that ran like a stormy river inside the gourd. She saw herself as a girl, as a young woman, she saw herself talking to an iguana, a snake, a centipede. She saw the day her father died, struck by a bullet, and other days: when my abuelo Güero stole her away, when Mamá

Goyita died, the day she gave birth to her chamacos, the day her first son died and then another, until her favorite was born, Emilio. She also saw Jacinto Estrella appearing to her in dreams, in corners, telling her on every occasion not to be stubborn, that she needed to accept the gift she'd been given. She saw her questions, her dreams, her suffering and her joys. She saw the moment that the curandero Jacinto Estrella passed his healing instruments on to her, in a cloud of smoke and with a bird flying over his head. She saw herself walking up the mountain, older now, with her tough legs, her long white braid, her burlap sack, talking with plants, with the spirits, with the wind. She saw my birth, my Mamita Estela's death, and she saw me walking through an arid and desolate expanse, dying of thirst alongside my brother, Goyo. And it wasn't until she saw, in the depths of the gourd, the face of the old woman who had been healing her up to that day, that my abuela fell back on her behind out of sheer fear, and, turning around and seeing nobody around her, she fully understood, with a shock that left her speechless, who that woman was who had been taking care of her all that time. Mamá Lochi said that she felt her feet being pulled by the depths of the earth, that all of a sudden she saw herself falling into a dark hole. When she opened her eyes, she was looking into the terrified faces of her Mamá Goyita, her Papá Emilio (which was her father's name, too), and her four siblings. On the other end of the palm bed mat were the eyes of Don Jacinto, wide as an owl's.

"After that, Emilia, my ignorance abandoned me," my abuela said to the seven-year-old me who listened to her story with a mouth wide open. "Since then, my dreams haven't let me have peace, with their truths. And I can't stop feelin' the pains of the world."

I wanted to talk, to ask her to explain, because I didn't understand it clearly—or couldn't. But as soon as she arrived at that part of her story, Mamá Lochi shut her mouth and threw dirt over the fire to extinguish it. That could only mean that it was time to return to town. That her story would stop there, at least for that day. I was itching to ask her, but it was better to stay quiet so she wouldn't regret telling me her secrets.

It wasn't easy for Emilia Ventura to peel open her eyelids. Everything twisted and spun as she tried. Her head, her stomach: useless volcanoes of nausea and pain. Where was she. What had she gotten into. She felt the scratchy touch of the cloth wrapped around her. The smell of pigs. The world jostled her around—she felt an uncontainable urge to vomit and the shaking didn't help. A graceless suffocation. A desire to shout. Deep inside something advised her: better to stay quiet. Where was she. She listened to the sounds. Scattered impressions and confusion pressing against her intestines and understanding. She wanted to clear up her memory. It wasn't easy. And those voices. The groans. She recognized the stench of Vaquero's laughter. She recognized Donojo's voice, his snarl. And the groans—a duet of wails that couldn't hold themselves in, with Vaquero already lunging toward the sound:

"Shut up! Motherfucking bitches!" And there was the sound of a fist making contact.

Emilia felt the trembling that came from within her.

"We're gonna get good money for the meat we've got back here!" Vaquero and his alcohol-soaked yell froze the girl's heart. "I just wish I could've stayed back just to see the looks on their faces when the Vulture got 'em."

"Fuck, Vaquero. Güera was right about how a coyote ate your fuckin' heart."

Emilia tried to move around inside the sack to find a way out, but she was tied up tight.

"The girl is already spoken for: She goes straight to the boss. How d'you like that? That Chato has a good eye. He sure knows how he wants them. Got a nice big payday comin' to us. We'll see what they say at the junkyard about the other two."

"Hey, maybe the boss will want one of them, too . . . even though they're way too old for him." Donojo sounded tired.

"You know he likes tender meat, he likes to crack them open and eat good." Vaquero's laughter sounded like hiccups. "Then he sets them up all nice. He doesn't leave them without a job. Even when it comes to that, our boss is a fucking good guy. . . . Isn't that right, Donojito?"

"Well, to each his own. Doin' all that with kids doesn't seem right to me. Really I'm just here 'cause I don't have anywhere else to work." A sadness snuck into Donojo's serious voice. He drove on, attentive to the broken road ahead—its sandy bumps, dips, rocks along the way.

"Don't play the saint, fucker. You're tellin' me you don't like fresh meat, huh, Donojo?" Vaquero took the bottle from between his legs and held it out to him. "C'mon, have some," he cackled, before gulping down the rest of the bottle.

Emilia felt her calandria stirring. *Please stay quiet, don't let it start now*, she prayed. A whip of fear lashed against her chest.

The nearby groans made her realize that, other than the two men, there were at least two more women in that car, and she wondered to herself if Goyo was there, too.

A sudden silence made her harbor an omen, approaching with gigantic steps.

"Listen, man, what if we had a little a taste now? You know, without ruining the merchandise. . . . These bitches are makin' me horny. C'mon, what d'you think? Fucking Güera wouldn't let me borrow them. And honestly I really wanna get into the girl. . . . I kinda got a cravin' for her. . . ."

"No, asshole. No tastes. Don't fucking start. And she's a kid, you piece of shit! You don't even have a drop of compassion for the girl? Fucking asshole."

"Don't be a little bitch, fucking Donojo! What the fuck are you talking about, fuckin' compassion. What does it matter if she's a girl? Girls are for fucking too! Or no? That's why you lost that eye: 'Cause you're a fuckin' idiot. And anyway who's going to find out? Don't tell me you're goin' to snitch? Look, it'll be quick—she can just suck me off and nobody will know."

"I already said no. And right now I'm in charge. As long as I'm at the wheel, don't fucking try it, asshole." Donojo's voice was dry. Firm.

"And what are you gonna do when the boss wants to fuck her, idiot? You gonna tell him the same shit you're saying to me? Gonna give him a sermon with all that bullshit about how she's a little girl and fuck-all? He'll give you two bullet holes for that, dumbass!"

"That's different. The boss is the boss. Over there he's in charge and we do whatever he says. And he's not such a bad guy. He'll take care of her in his way. And anyway, while we're here I'm in charge, asshole, because they trusted me, not you. So shut your mouth unless you want me to shut it for you."

A coarse silence. A tension: the kind that comes before a plunging collapse, a cliff's edge.

The last thing Emilia could remember before that moment was when she curled up against her brother to sleep. And then she'd felt her stomach cramp. "Fuckin' pig food," she'd said to herself, dodging rocks and brush, looking for a private place to relieve herself. She didn't have time to tell Goyo she'd be back soon. When she headed back to where Gregorio was, someone grabbed her from behind and covered her mouth with a humid rag that smelled horrible and that's where the memory went out. After that just a black hole, like a snake nest.

"Ah, fuckin' Donojo," Vaquero complained. "Really. You don't make any sense. What about . . . So if the boss tells you to fuck the girl, you'd fuck her."

"The boss isn't going to tell me something like that, asshole. He respects me. He knows that I don't like little girls and he doesn't carry the fuck on about it like you."

Vaquero tried to get one last swig out of the empty bottle and there was a brief silence.

"So I'll fuck one of the others. These ones aren't girls anymore." And reaching his hand into the backseat, Vaquero stuck his fingers between the legs of one of the gagged women.

"I told you no, fucker," Donojo elbowed him hard to get him to stop. "You better calm the fuck down if you don't want me to take out one of your fuckin' eyes so we look the same."

The jeep stumbled forward, jumping over dips, holes, and rocks on the road. Through the holes in the sack, Emilia tried to see: no light snuck in, not even a furtive, rebellious ray. She tried to rip open the threads so she could breathe better and look around. It was difficult because she was so tightly wrapped up that she couldn't move. With effort, she stretched her feet away from her stomach and managed to tear the cloth a little. Then there was the clanging of bottles and Vaquero's strident voice insisting that they stop and take the women.

A wave of cold sweat ran over her. Her body shook from the top of her head to the soles of her feet. She squeezed her eyelids closed.

"Mamá Lochi," she whispered. As if she could hear her. She couldn't even get herself to imagine her face. She thought of her brother. Where was he, how was he. Ay, Caco. She repeated it to herself, and just thinking of him choked her up with tears. And suddenly, the bird. Its warning trill filled her ears.

"Fucking bad-luck bird!" shouted Vaquero, with an even harsher bark than ever. "I bet those sons-of-bitches Indians I fucked with sent it after me. Get out of here! Hit the fucking brakes, Donojo! I'm getting the gun. I'm going to kill that fucking piece-of-shit bird!"

The jeep accelerated.

"Shut up, jackass. What the fuck are you talkin' about, Indians. It's just a fuckin' bird. We're in a hurry."

"I said stop, motherfucker! I'm going to get it before it gets me! Fucking stop, I'm telling you to stop!"

They kept arguing. Accelerations, shaking. Their voices rising and the bird that wouldn't stop its shrieking.

"Don't be an asshole, fucking Donojo!" Vaquero howled. "You owe me and it's time to pay. . . . I've had it up to here with you, fucker."

A hard swerve, a jolt, and a bang on the door brought forth the screams of the women, of Emilia and her uncontrollable calandria. The jeep accelerated as the screaming continued, and the girl smashed up against the walls of the trunk, her "ay, ay," inaudible to the rest.

"Shut the fuck up, asshole! Stop fucking around! I'll kick you out right here so the bird can peck out your fucking eyes!"

"Let's see you do it, fucking cyclops! I dare you, son of a—"

A hard bang from one side, a crash, and the car's leap into a deep crater, which opened the back door. Emilia felt the void, then the fall that ended in hard contact with the rocky earth. Her torso came out of the sack, tattered by the crash—she was a newborn that didn't know how to face the world. The car tumbled over in the distance, a crash of somersaults and bounces. And when it finally stopped, a long honk. Really long. With no end in sight.

Beat up, tangled in the torn sack, and scared down to her bones, Emilia stayed still, stuck in a mess of dry plants. She wanted to move, but all she could manage was to take off the smelly rag that gagged her. The horn kept blaring, bursting her eardrums. In the racket she heard voices, a wail. Maybe her name or someone calling out. But she was far away and wrapped up in her own bewilderment. In pain all the way down to her bones.

I need to move, she told herself. Just thinking it made her feel as though her legs were nailed down, the roughness of the dry branches piercing her flesh. And a dizziness, a flip of her soul that pushed her into a deep faint.

When the world came back, she didn't recognize where she was, though it didn't take her long to shake away the amnesia. With effort she escaped the sack and brush she was buried in. The horn had gone silent and there wasn't even a fly around her.

She was still disoriented. It wasn't long until sunrise and she looked around: nothing but desert. A few meters away, in a narrow basin, she saw the overturned jeep and was overcome by a new wave of terror: What if those assholes got out of the car and grabbed her again. She set off in search of a hiding spot. She didn't feel any pain because she also didn't feel her body in her desperation. Blood ran down her face. She wiped it away with her hand like it was sweat.

"Gotta be kiddin' me," she said to herself when she saw the sticky darkness on her palm. "Death herself's really comin' for me now."

And anyway maybe it was better to just die already. The thought calmed her.

"Well, what's the point. I should just go be with my abuela."

And she huddled up beside some shrubs. Hidden there, curled into a ball, she spent a while trembling, hardly daring to breathe—no way to even try counting the time, no sounds to listen to. Nothing moving. And looking down at her feet she realized that she was missing a sneaker.

"My sneaker," she mumbled, and raised her eyes.

The sky: total immensity. The light of daybreak was just starting to suggest itself. And inside her, that hesitant cry that clawed its way up from deep within.

Emilia, órale, don't you get down on me. None of this about jumpin' that stone wall to the sky now, you have to go look for your father.

She got up with a start. She whirled around to look this way and that. But nothing. She would have liked to hug her. To feel the warmth of her skin. To sink into her scent of wild jasmine, of lumber, of rain, until the ache disappeared. A cry crashed into her, but it was so dry that not even the memory of a tear came out.

C'mon now, don't cry. You'll wake up the dead.

"Ay, mamita. But you're dead," she whispered. "Why don't you take me with you. It's just that it really sucks to be alone here. And I can't lie to you—I'm really afraid."

Just saying it made her swallow back her invisible tears. Thinking it over, she didn't want her abuela to think she was a wimp.

"Mamita, where are you? I want to see you."

The shadow of the bird came back to slice through the air and made her lift her gaze. She looked at the jeep. Total stillness and silence. And Goyo, who knows where he ended up. And the crying women. One must have been Demetria. And there was another. And her sneaker. She needed to find it, whatever it took. And that damn thirst. She looked around: Nothing was moving. With little steps she drew closer to the jeep. Like a lizard, like a little bug that doesn't want to be seen or stepped on. When she was up against the car, which was flipped on its head, she looked in through the shattered windows. A whimper: just one whimper that seemed to come from another world. She needed to hurry—they weren't dead and they would want to grab her and put her back in the sack. And her sneaker? She needed to get her sneaker back.

She couldn't make anything out and walked around the car to the back door she'd flown out of. It wasn't difficult to get in, crawling on her knees on the ceiling that was now the floor. There were objects scattered in the backseat on the body of a woman. She was dead, and Emilia recognized her as one of the women in the group of migrants. And the other one, where was she. She was sure there had been two.

In a hurry, she tossed the things she found out of the car: a jacket, a backpack, a handful of rope, a bottle full of water. But as far as her sneaker, there wasn't even a shred of a shoelace. She leaned into the front seat: The men's bodies were a jumble of clothes and tangled limbs. A groan interrupted her thoughts and made her jump away. She shoved the things into the backpack and tossed it over the shoulder before taking off running to hide behind a bunch of shrubs. From there, not daring to go anywhere else, she kept spying. One of the men opened a door and crawled out. Emilia couldn't make out who he was. She stayed quiet, waiting for the right moment to start running. But where to? She looked out into the distance.

Get goin', chamaca. Move. Do you want them to get you again?

The voice rose from her own feet.

She was right. What was she waiting for. She opened the bottle and took a gulp—water. Sweet water. She looked out into the distance again. The mountains were starting to define themselves with the glow of the dawn. But Goyo. Where could he be. She studied a point in the distance to guide herself by: the break between two mountains. That, and nothing else, would be her destination. That's what she and her brother had agreed on. She looked for little pebbles and twigs to use to show him the path. In case he reached them. He would understand.

Emilia Ventura hitched the backpack over her shoulder. It didn't weigh much, and she didn't pay attention to what it had inside this second time either. She walked toward the mountains to get away from there as soon as possible, scanning the ground in case, out of sheer dumb luck, she might find her other sneaker and wouldn't have to limp anymore. In a few steps, she found the other woman, thrown over some boulders, and drew close to listen to her breathe— but not even a faint breath rose from her chest.

"She's real dead," she said to herself.

Discouragement started making a nest deep inside her, and she began walking, her feet and body already starting to ache.

They said that Jacinto Estrella hadn't aged since his arrival to Amatlán, that he was the most powerful healer in the region, that he'd brought dead people back to life, that he didn't only speak to animals, as all curanderos tend to do, but that he also spoke with insects, with trees, with plants, and even with the grass and herbs—above all, they insisted that he came from another planet. More than one person swore, on the Virgin herself, that they'd seen him arrive to town on a spaceship that landed in the middle of a cornfield, wearing a golden spacesuit and a glowing helmet, shaking off the ash from the fire that ignited during the landing. That the gold suit turned into a white shirt and pants, that he put a white bandana and a wide-brimmed hat on his head, and that, after taking off his stainless steel boots, he stepped into some rope sandals, the ones he always wore.

Jacinto Estrella rolled around with laughter when he heard those stories. He would exclaim, with the full power of his lungs in his gruff and decisive voice: "They're really damn stupid. Why does nobody ever believe that good could come from right here?"

Mamá Lochi remembered his dark face. His immense nose, flat and wide like a tamal, and those sleepless owl eyes of his—which stared unblinkingly at her seven-year-old self the same day that they found her unconscious on the edge of a riverbank, with her hair singed and those marks etched into her skin. They ran to bring her back into the house, laid her down on a palm mat, and tried in vain to wake her. When Mamá Goyita sent for him, cracking her knuckles, she was sure that her chamaca wouldn't survive. As soon as the curandero entered the room, my little abuela woke up and fixed her eyes directly onto him. She saw blue-and-yellow sparks jumping around the man, just like fireworks. Eyes and mouths that, at times, made signs or spoke in her ear. Mamá Lochi heard the same distinct tongue that she heard the old woman on the mountain speak, and that I myself, years later, would hear when she spoke with her spirits. But at her seven years of age and sitting there before Don Jacinto, who would not take his sharp pupils off her, Mamá Lochi already understood the meaning of that language that her abuelos had spoken. Even though they hadn't taught it to her—because nobody in town used it anymore—it ran through her veins.

That day, when Jacinto Estrella checked over her, passing his hardy fingers over the ferns etched into her skin, my little abuela felt like electricity was running through her body. And even still, maybe out of politeness and a little bit of fear, she let him smell her head, look extensively at the soles of her feet, study her mouth, return to look at the leaf-like scars over and over and, finally, bring his giant pupils up to hers, so close and with such a desire to look inside her that Mamá Lochi felt like her blood was boiling, rekindling that tremble that she'd felt before.

"This chamaca was struck by lightning," Jacinto Estrella said in his raw voice. "It must have been just now—her body still smells like the embers."

"Ay, blessed María," Mamá Goyita crossed herself. She was a big believer and spent her life praying to the Virgin and all the saints.

"It wasn't just now," came out of my little abuela's mouth. "It's been days."

"Don't be silly, chamaca," Mamá Goyita scolded her, still doing the sign of the cross. "It's only been two hours since the downpour started. God wanted you to survive. Thanks be to Him."

Mamá Lochi looked at her the way someone would look at a stranger who shares a private secret that nobody knows, and she felt a light tremor run through her body. Don Jacinto's eyes latched onto her, attentively—they waited for her to reveal the truth of her experience. Nothing. She wasn't going to tell them what she'd experienced just like that. They were going to think that she was crazy like her great-grandfather Ildefonso.

"Well, it seems like, to her, she spent more time on the mountain than that," the witch doctor said at last.

Mamá Lochi retreated into her silence.

"Give her some lime-blossom tea so she can rest. This girl will heal on her own," Don Jacinto said before leaving. And shooting a meaningful look at Mamá Goyita, he added: "Your daughter has a special gift, doña. Let her sleep as much as she wants. The dreams will put her back together. She has the gift, and they sent it to her from up above." And he pointed with his index finger up at the ceiling. "Just don't let her out in the rain—lightning likes to go after heads like hers. Bring her to me when she looks better to you," he said before looking one last time at Mamá Lochi, whose hairs stood up straight when she heard his request, like a hurried spirit had jarred and shaken her.

As soon as Don Jacinto disappeared through the door, Mamá Lochi announced to her mother, in her little girl voice but with that character that she always had, even when she was small: "I'm never going to go with that guy." And she pulled the blanket up over her head, fell asleep, and didn't wake up until two days later.

Mamá Goyita told her that she took care of her in her sleep all that time, never leaving her side, and that, as she slept, she heard her babble in the language of the ancestors. Twice she got up like she was possessed, walked around the room several times, and her mother couldn't wake her. Sleepwalking, she drank two spoonfuls of chicken broth and then lay back down, covered by the blanket all the way up to her head.

Mamá Goyita promised herself that she'd take her to Jacinto Estrella as soon as she woke up. But when Mamá Lochi opened her eyes, she repeated that she didn't want to, didn't want to, no matter how much her mother shook her and pulled at her to force her to go.

"I already told you I'm not goin' with him. I don't like how he looks at me. And plus, who knows what he does with kids and animals," she pronounced, with that strength of character that was so like her.

"That's just talk, chamaca. You're going to make him mad and then nobody will be able to cure you of his evil eye."

"Let him be mad, then. I don't want anything to do

with him."

And faced with this stubbornness, my great-grandmother Goyita finally gave in.

Don Jacinto came in search of her a month later, and the next, and the next. Every time he reminded Mamá Goyita of her promise to take her to him so he could initiate her in the wisdoms, and she assured him she would, trembling for the fear of making him angry, that it wouldn't be long until she made good on her promise. But Mamá Lochi refused with such vehemence that my great-grandmother ended up throwing in the towel.

"She doesn't want to go with you, Don Jacinto," she dared to tell him one of those days. "She says that she doesn't want to learn how to make cures. That she just wants to learn how to cook. And I don't have the heart to force her."

Jacinto Estrella looked harshly at Mamá Lochi, who didn't lower her eyes, standing there beside her mother.

"It's on her," he said at last and he left to where he came from.

"That time that I told him no, lookin' into his eyes, I felt worse than when the lightning struck me, Calandria," Mamá Lochi stressed as she told me the story one afternoon, while she mended the cloth she used to wrap up the instruments for her cures.

"That Jacinto, he had burning hooks instead of eyes. A heart woven from tough fibers. Who knows what that man was made of. One thing I'm sure of, Emilia: He knew how hard I was workin' to close myself off—to what my eyes, ears, and skin couldn't stop perceivin' from the moment that lightning bolt passed through my flesh and soul."

Don Jacinto warned Mamá Goyita that if her daughter

didn't give herself over to her gift, destiny was going to be furious with her. That the lightning was the least of it. It would keep looking for her until the spirits themselves retracted their protection and, then, matters would become ugly, as ugly as a dead man's face: Those same spirits, pissed off now, might end up killing her. For being stubborn, for refusing to accept what destiny ordered of her.

From then on, as soon as she saw one raindrop fall or the sky light up in the distance, Mamá Goyita would send her daughter to the stone hut where she stored grain—she didn't want her to be chased by the little snakes of light that now followed her wherever she went. There, Mamá Lochi spent the storms counting seeds, which looked like points of light to her because she could visualize the life they carried inside. And she separated them by groups: according to the amount of life that she estimated each one had, and according to the intensity of the light in their interiors. When she touched them, she could clearly sense the tingle of lively palpitations, the magic hidden inside their skins. A few times, when Mamá Goyita remembered to go get her daughter out of the silo once the storm had passed, the girl refused to leave because she wanted to keep playing there.

"But why didn't you want to be a curandera, mamita?" I asked her the afternoon that she told me the story. She kept her eyes glued on the piece of cloth she was piercing with a needle and thread. Only her voice rose: a voice that came from deep inside her.

"I think it was pure stubbornness, Emilia. Just wantin' to go against Don Jacinto and show him who was more powerful. Pride and stubbornness have always been my biggest sins, though life's taught me how not to keep carrying those burdens. Plus, there were lots of stories going around about Don Jacinto. About what he did to badly behaved kids. They said he threw them into a pot of boiling water to melt them down and then drink them like atole. They also said he did nasty things to girls, or that the spaceship he'd arrived on came back every now and then and took away disemboweled kids to another planet. All just talk. Just that fear people have of what they don't know. Including me—see, I had an image engraved in my mind from this time when I was just a little chamaca and we were spyin' on him. We were being nosy, Rosa the neighbor and I, peekin' through the gaps in the adobe bricks of his house, lookin' for gossip. We saw him take the feathers off a live hen, open up her guts without breaking her neck first, all while singin' to her. The hen only let out two clucks, like she'd been hypnotized. Then he ate her guts one by one, and he was totally covered in blood. We were watching him when we heard a voice behind us: 'That's what I'll do to you two if you keep spying.'

"You have no idea how much that scared us! It was him. We got frozen by the fear. We were watchin' him right there in front of us and—who knows how—at the same time, he was behind us. You can imagine how we took off, lookin' like starving vultures, each of us runnin' to wherever God sent our feet, not wantin' to know anything more about that son-of-the-devil witch doctor."

Her long laugh, as if the fear from back then had turned into pure comedy, flooded the room.

"But why are you laughin', Mamá Lochi. That's not something to laugh about," I responded, scared out of my mind just from imagining that man eating raw chicken guts.

My abuela stopped laughing, but she didn't drop

her smile.

"Well, what's wrong with eatin' chicken guts? Are you tellin' me, chamaca, that you've never eaten them?"

"Yeah," I confessed, because I really liked their little hearts fried with chile, "but I don't eat them raw, mamita."

I had seen my abuela eat the guts of an animal as she prepared a cure. And not just chicken, also pig and even snake. So it was better not to say anything more.

"At first I didn't like how I heard everything the animals and plants had to say. How I could read people's thoughts, how I could see calamities comin' in my dreams. But you can get used to anything, Calandrita. And now look at me: I've learned to live with it."

The sun appeared on the horizon when Gregorio Ventura made out the jeep in the distance. *Just a stone's throw away*, he thought. But no. It still took more than an hour to get there, his feet throbbing like agitated hearts inside his shoes. His crooked right foot, stubbornly turning inward, bothered him more than the other.

"This place is fuckin' deceptive as fuck," he heard himself say, like he was speaking to his shadow.

Once he was close, he took careful steps, half crouching, his movements slow. He didn't want to be surprised. He couldn't be sure of—or, even less, trust—whatever was waiting for him there. The car was flipped over in a dry basin. He thought he recognized the jeep from back at the chicken coop, and hope invaded his distress. Calandria could be right there. The car looked like an animal with its feet in the air, dead or badly injured. A tattered uneasiness gnawed at his insides. What if she was inside the jeep. She might be injured real bad. Or dead.

He ran. Before he got to the vehicle, a few meters from it,

he was surprised by a body, facedown, stretched out on the ground. When he turned it over, he could tell the man was alive. He hesitated when he recognized Vaquero.

"Son of a bitch," he muttered, and the image of a squirming bug came to his mind. He felt the ruthless lashes of the sun, now starting their travels over the world. That face, swollen from the crash, shook in a coughing attack that made him spit up blood.

"You're getting what you deserve now, fucking asshole piece of shit," Gregorio whispered, squatting down beside the man. He looked into his murky eyes, barely open and filled with supplication.

"Help me . . ." the man rasped, and, between tremors, he closed his eyes. Goyo felt an irrepressible urge to kick him. That bastard was for sure the reason the Vultures had come, the reason his sister had disappeared, and even the reason the fucking unforgiving sun slammed full-force against the back of his head.

"Give me water . . ." The voice, hoarse and like it was coming from another world, irritated him even more.

"Where's my sister?"

Vaquero half opened his capulín eyes. Goyo felt another lash of that desire to kick him until his skin fell off. To crack his bones until they turned into tiny splinters that would stab him from the inside.

"Where is Emilia, you son of a bitch? I know you know, bastard." He grabbed him by the neck of his jacket, covered in bloodstains.

"No . . ." The man made a useless attempt to sit up; the teenager sent him back into the dirt with a furious shove. A groan of pain burst out of Vaquero. But he composed himself, cleaning his mouth with the sleeve of his jacket. And, concentrating on making himself heard like his life was hanging in the balance, he whispered with those vocal chords destroyed by tobacco, "In the car."

Goyo threw off his backpack and ran to the jeep. Overcome by the fear that he'd find his sister dead, or nearly dead, he looked in the windows with a ball of anxiety gnawing at his insides.

"Emilia! Emilia! Where are you?"

She might be crushed under the car—her brains turned to mush, the calandria squished and totally dead.

"Calandria! Where are you?"

First he saw that there was a body in the front seat. He stopped when he recognized Donojo, his one pupil still, frozen in surprise by the nothingness that got him without warning. Gregio understood everything at once: The Vultures had to have seen them. They had lit up the jeep with their spotlight and hadn't done anything to stop them. Vaquero and Donojo were on the hunters' team.

"Sons of fucking bitches. That's what you get, fucking asshole bastard." And he pounded his fist on the car window. But Donojo—nothing. He was bunched up over himself, his neck twisted like a sacrificed turkey. His face covered in cuts and scratches. His tongue out.

"I hope you're burning in hell, you son of a fucking bitch," the boy said before doing the sign of the cross over his chest. Just to be safe. He didn't want that departed spirit to decide to follow him around.

When he looked into the back of the car, he saw the inert body of a woman. He could hardly make out her battered face. Her eyes, wide open with shock, looked at him from across an uncrossable distance. He did what he could to drag her out of the car and closed her eyelids. Where could she be. And he turned on his heels, looking out into the distance.

"Where are you, Calandrita?"

He returned to the jeep and in the back found broken bottles and trash. Beside a tire he found Vaquero's metal flask, dented and half full. Hoping for some courage, he took a gulp.

The burning heat ran through him. Suddenly, he felt emboldened: He'd kill Vaquero, that son of a bitch, if he didn't tell him where Emilia was.

When he returned to where the man was, he saw that Vaquero had tried to drag himself away. A useless and unseeing worm under the sun's radiance. Gregorio stood at his side: "Where's my sister, you son of a fucking bitch?" And he kicked him, hard. The man didn't even have enough strength to groan.

Goyo raised his face, his spirit faded, his head empty. He looked out at who knows what when a flash of light in the distance, a few meters away, made him turn his attention to a spot and walk that way.

"You've been around here, little sis," he said as he picked up the orphan sneaker. "Emilia!" He heard his voice dilute into that soulless expanse.

She'd gone. Or they'd taken her. And if they'd taken her . . . The thought was a twist of fear. He looked around until he was sure she wasn't there. What he found was another inert body, a woman thrown over the boulders, her head split by the impact. He remembered her, she was in the barracks and he had hardly heard her speak.

"Well, I'll never hear her speak now." And he crossed

himself again.

He returned to Vaquero. "What did you do to my sister, you bastard. You'll die right here if you don't tell me."

The man looked at him from across an arid darkness. "In the car . . ."

"She's not there, you son of a fucking bitch!" And he let his foot fly into the stomach of the man on the ground, feeling a wild jolt of joy when he heard the responding shout of pain.

"If you don't tell me right fucking now where Emilia is, I'll break you apart." Not even he could recognize the crackling of that rage that howled from within him. He lifted the man by the neck of his jacket. And he saw Vaquero's desire to kill him in his eyes. If he could.

"You tell me right now where my sister is or I'll kill you right here, I don't give a fuck, you bastard."

"I don't know . . ."

Gregorio burned with rage. Fury. The kind of fury that is thoughtless, acidic, poisonous, crazed.

"I'll kill you right here if you don't tell me what you did to her!"

He could have killed him right there. It wouldn't have mattered what kind of cry that miserable good-for-nothing let out. Even though God would punish him by sending him to the worst hell. He would have done it right there, if not for that sharp intuition, a sense of alert, that made him lift his head: in the distance, a barely visible dot. Coming closer. And the sound of a motor, still imperceptible to an ordinary ear, but not his.

Gregorio Ventura took off running, crouched over, like a dog chasing after the devil. He slid into a basin about a hundred meters from the jeep and, pressing himself against an embankment, huddled into himself, sticking his arms between his legs, making himself into a ball, and went quiet, waiting for his breath to calm down. His eyes closed and his ears opened to pick up what was happening in the distance. An open-top truck braked beside where Vaquero lay. Three men with machine guns and army uniforms got out and surrounded the fallen body. One of them looked into the flipped car, opened its doors, took out Donojo's body and let it fall carelessly—he dug through his pockets, through the glove compartment, through the jeep.

A military boot planted itself upon the body of the woman dead on the rocks. The tip of the shoe lifted her shirt. And stayed like that for a while. Looking at the unmoving flesh.

Vaquero considered the newcomers with a dry fear.

A deep voice spoke broken Spanish: "Time for pay, Vaquero." The fallen man felt a boot's movement beside him. His broken bones chewed at him from the inside. The blond hair of the man standing over him shone beneath a green military hat. Two big white hands with well cared for nails reached into a jacket to take a cigarette from a pocket. Another gringo, red-headed and freckly, flicked the lighter.

The third man came up to them from the car. He was holding a woman's underwear, which he showed them like a trophy.

Everyone laughed.

The one with the cigarette made a quick gesture to the man on the ground. The other two flipped him over. They went through his pockets, between his legs, shoes.

"Nothing at all." The conclusion came in English.

And they finished off the search with a stomp to

Vaquero's gut.

"Honey, you have a debt to pay. . . ."

"In the car . . . your share's in the car . . ." Vaquero groaned in a thin voice. Two of the men went back to the jeep, rummaged through it, and returned empty-handed.

"No money. You're dead, Mexican."

In no hurry, and with a degree of indifference, the redhead took a small gun out of his pocket and pointed it at the dying man.

Vaquero coughed. He didn't take his eyes off the gun pointed right at him.

"Okay," the boss said. And he turned around so he wouldn't have to see the shot that sliced through the hat and burst the head of the man on the ground.

A puddle of blood poured over his face.

"Fuck you," the redhead said, and then he spat on the dead man.

Coming to him from a far off beyond, the sounds of what happened a few steps away reached Gregorio, on the other side of the ditch: the gunshot, the laughter. He lifted his head just a little bit and got a quick look without losing his connection to his invisibility, with that state of being where the limits between his skin and the air fade away. The Dogs passed by his side a couple times. They stood on the top of the jeep, peeled over the whole area with binoculars, emptied his backpack, cut into the tires, and took apart the motor, all without noting the boy's presence. He was lucky they hadn't seen him before, when they were driving up. Finally, they got back in their truck, slammed the doors hard, started the engine, and left.

When Goyo took his sweaty chin out from between his

legs and returned from the other side, he felt like his brain was boiling. A heartless sun fell directly onto him with so much power that he could hear the panting of the savage heat. Not a breath of the Dogs remained. A crimson stream surrounded Vaquero.

"That's what you get, asshole."

The jeep was a butchered animal. The dead thrown in every direction. A deep disheartenment overtook him, a degradation of the already degraded, from seeing so much disembowelment.

"But who are those bad guys that kill the bad guys," he asked Vaquero's still corpse, as if he could get a response from him.

The fear that they might return revived his nerves. He thought of Emilia. She'd better not run into those guys. But what if they were the ones that took her. He put the things strewn on the ground back into his backpack, rescued the forgotten flask from the branches of a bush, and took a gulp. When he turned to look at the mountains, he saw the long sack. Made of rope. Torn. And he sniffed it. Underneath the scent of a horse stable he breathed in the aroma of orange blossom, his sister's smell. He looked for her inside, like he couldn't believe it. She had been there. He turned it over, looked at its bottom: holes and rips with faint bloodstains. As though she'd disappeared through those rips in the fabric. Where was the thread that would pull her out of there?

"Now I know you're alive still, Calandria. And I'm going to find you, if it's the last thing I do in this fucking bullshit life."

He tossed the backpack on his back, took a new gulp from the flask, and started walking toward the mountains.

He hadn't even been walking for ten minutes when he discovered a clue: a sneaker. Some drops of blood. And some rocks and sticks that made him raise his eyes to see what they pointed to, in that language that only he and she could decode.

"Just like we do on our mountain, Calandrita. Me followin' your clues, you leavin' me hints wherever you can. You'll see, with my cacomixtle nose and owl eyes I'll reach you real, real soon."

And he lit a fire under his crooked step, keeping his eyes on the emptiness ahead, hoping to trick himself, at least with his mind, into forgetting that unbearable thirst and that son-of-a-bitch heat that was torturing him already.

Mamá Lochi said that after the day the lightning struck her, nothing was the same. Her world was switched out for another that was hard to recognize. My abuela had a rebellious disposition, and didn't want to accept all the new things that were raining down on her through her senses like an August storm. She couldn't stand when Don Jacinto Estrella reminded her of what she wanted to deny. She couldn't stand to feel the heat of those spirits graze against her back, her arms, when those gossipy shadows came and whispered what was coming into her ear. Mamá Lochi didn't want to know any of it. She made impossible efforts to drag those senses out of her soul, to make them disappear into her memory. But it wasn't easy to ignore them. They imposed on her thoughts, filling her with fear. She spent nights awake, watching the shadows speak with each other. She looked for a way to exorcise them, to push them aside so they would leave her in peace—without telling her Mamá Goyita or her Papá Emilio so they wouldn't get scared. She would sing at the top of her lungs, chirp like a turkey and make everyone who heard her laugh. She preferred their teasing over that confusion of being in constant contact with that other, restless world. The minute the spirits appeared to her, she sent hens flying with her loud, off-key voice, and wouldn't stop until they settled and gave her some time in peace. The whole family ended up thinking that the lightning had not only disoriented her but had also left her a lunatic. They listened fearfully to the fiendish screams that she breathlessly gave herself to every night, and were shocked to see her shoo away shadows invisible to them. Mamá Goyita tried multiple times to get her to go see Jacinto Estrella. But my abuela didn't want to know anything for several years. Though in her dreams he wouldn't stop coming to her. He would appear himself or send others that, she soon understood, were his messengers.

The old woman who saved her after the lightning, whose face she now recognized as her own in the future, also persisted in her dreams. Telling her not to be stubborn, to take up the tools, to stop taking so long. She insisted on showing her the path to the cave hidden in the depths of the mountain. Every time she appeared to her, the next morning, my little abuela was tempted to go looking for that cave the old woman wouldn't shut up about. She hated to be called a wimp, but even worse, stubborn. Mamá Lochi and I have that in common. One time she told her mother about it, but she just looked at her with clear concern and warned her she'd better not go wandering off alone on the mountain.

"Another lightning strike like that and you'll kick the bucket right there."

All it took was someone telling her she had to—or couldn't—do something, for her to become obsessed with doing the opposite. But she did have respect for lightning.

She didn't hesitate to go into the grain silo when the rainfall picked up. Little by little, she started cobbling together the memory of what happened on that afternoon she was struck. More than the burning heat, what she was most afraid of was that if another bolt struck her, the voices she heard and visions she had wouldn't stop torturing her—not even when she screamed over them.

After one of those dreams with the old woman, she finally decided to look for the cave. She was twelve years old and her fear of the lightning, though she never forgot it, had subsided. She waited until the dry season came, when not even one wayward cloud was in the sky. Without telling anyone about her intentions, she threw a box of matches, a candle, a calabash filled with water, and an orange into a sack. She thought it would take a while and didn't want to go unprepared. She left the house early in the day, telling her Mamá Goyita that she was going out to get some herbs, and she went deep into the mountain. Right away the voices started speaking to her. She sensed the power of the tree's hearts, trickling out through their branches and leaves, concentrated in their trunks, dropping incandescence on her path. She ended up letting go of her resentments and let herself be taken in by the restless contact of the insects, the plants, the animals, the earth itself. Out of view from other human beings, it was easier to relax.

She let her feet lead her and walked up the mountain for an hour. Her steps took her away from the path marked by human footprints. She climbed the rocks until she went through an opening covered by grass and boulders. In a blink of the eye, she found herself standing before the cave. The thrush's song made her lift her gaze. It sat on a nearby rock, silently, with its chest yellow and its crest raised, its attentive little eyes fixed on her. Mamá Lochi understood that it was there to welcome her, and she entered the cavern to find that there were no signs of it having ever been occupied before.

It was like a dream or an apparition, she said she remembered thinking, because she didn't understand that which is impossible to understand with reason.

She spent a couple hours in the shelter: She observed the cracks in the stone, the creases in the rock wall. She contemplated the swaying of the crowns of the trees that grew from below, there where the gully began.

Mamá Lochi picked up the habit of hiking to her hideout more and more frequently. She started leaving her things there: a blanket, a sack, a candle, her box of matches tucked well into a dip between outcroppings of rock so that it wouldn't get wet. And her special gourd. She found it on her way up, on one of those long hikes. She carved inscriptions into the hard external skin and completely cleaned it out inside. She buried it on the edge of the gully, in front of the cave, looking out over a landscape of full and leafy trees and a row of the mountains in the distance. Sometimes she saw images in the water that accumulated at the bottom of its curvature, but she preferred not to look inside more than necessary. Instead she chose to use it only to collect rainwater, leaving it out in her absence so she could drink from it when she was thirsty. She would spread out the blanket inside the cave and lay back to look out, letting herself be taken by the waving of the branches in the distance, the trills of the birds, until she was numbed by the portents that empowered themselves through her, and she ended up falling into a deep and restorative sleep. The dreams she had in that cave were clear, like she was really inside them, seeing it all. They could be announcements about events that, sooner or later, would come to be. She dreamed of big balls of fire coming out of a mountain, and then she'd learn from the radio about the devastating eruption of a distant volcano. She saw the earth split, swallowing up trees, houses, people, a couple days before the radio announced that a big earthquake had destroyed a neighboring country. Soon the dreams became less distant with their announcements, and they started to warn her about catastrophic occurrences very close by. She dreamed of an earthquake that knocked over the church tower, but no matter how much she proclaimed it, her mother paid her no mind. She dreamed of a hailstorm that demolished roofs, ruined the harvest, and killed any animal it caught off guard—an entire night with hail as big as rocks that didn't take a breath and leveled out everything. The next day, the landscape of snowy mountains and the ice that carpeted the streets and gardens with white made the town unrecognizable to everyone in it. It took them days to recover from the disaster, and the town smelled like cadavers for weeks. Then she dreamed of the thieves who broke into and stole from twelve houses. Mamá Lochi warned her mother about what she saw in her dreams, but Mamá Goyita, now that she saw that the things she told her really did happen, begged her to stop dreaming, sure that she had such a powerful mind that she herself provoked these misfortunes. But no matter how much she tried, my abuela couldn't put the brakes on it.

The afternoon that Mamá Lochi dreamed her father was full of holes and there were branches growing through his body, a ferocious downpour broke out while she was in the cave. With time, she and her mother had both forgotten their worry about keeping her safe from lightning. It was the height of the rainy season and, even though she'd climbed the mountain early in the day with confidence that it wouldn't rain until the evening, the storm caught her unprepared. She was dozing at the mouth of her cave when she saw her father's body in her mind, sliced by balls of fire that ran through him and ignited his intestines. Before the image itself could, a crack of thunder made her leap off the blanket. From her refuge, Mamá Lochi was startled to see that in the distance a tree was lighting aflame. The deluge accelerated soon after, and a series of lightning strikes made her huddle into the depths of her shelter, covering her ears and lacing her fingers around a candle with a flickering flame. She prayed to the saints that the lightning wouldn't reach her, and begged for her dream not to turn into reality. Though she guessed, rightly, that her begging would be useless—her father's torn-apart body in her dreams couldn't mean anything good.

The downpour stopped after a few hours. When Mamá Lochi arrived at her house at last, slipping down the muddy riverbanks and scared of the whipping that her mother would give her for being out so long, she found that rather than everyone worrying about her, there wasn't a soul in the house.

"There was an emergency and they took your dad to the hospital in Santiatepec. Some guys in ski masks shot at him."

My abuela explained how she felt an endless hole open up under her feet, which swallowed her for hours even though only a few seconds had passed when Doña Matilde, the neighbor, spoke to her again and she returned to the world.

"Look at you, all covered in mud. Come in, hurry up now, dry off and have a wash. I'll make you a warm atole."

Mamá Lochi said it was like a million wasps were stinging at her brain and insides. She was to blame. She'd dreamed it. If she dreamed it, it happened.

As soon as she saw her mother's face, my abuela knew. Then a car arrived with the bullet hole–riddled body of Don Emilio Ventura, and the wake was in the evening. Mamá Goyita, just looking at her daughter through her tears, recognized her guilt.

"Don't tell me that you dreamed this too. Because if you did, you need to get out of this house, right now. All these disasters, my God!" my great-grandmother cried out.

Mamá Lochi stood there, lonelier than a cactus, moving her head from side to side like a broken machine. She wasn't there, or anywhere, anymore. It was like the cold sweat that ran over her body had erased her completely. Like a phantom, she wandered around the edges of the house, silently, hoping nobody would notice her presence, repenting for murdering her father, asking the heavens to forgive her. She told me how it hurt her to feel invisible, to the point that she really believed that nobody could see her—nobody spoke a word to her, not at the mass or at the burial. Though at times she felt eyes on her, burning with hatred, reminding her of her guilt. She was twelve years old and Don Jacinto was the only one to look at her differently, guessing her thoughts, the only one to speak to her when they gathered at the house to mourn.

"Look at you, niña, look what you've become. You haven't come to see me. It's about time," he said.

Mamá Lochi said that even though she felt grateful for the compassion that Don Jacinto showed her, without even thinking, that word burst forth from her:

"Never! Never! Never!" my abuela yelled at him, pushed by her old belief that it was he who had cursed her that day the lightning struck her. She was convinced that he had provoked those torturous perceptions in her, just to force her to go to him so he could eat her, stirred into an atole, or take out her guts, or send her in a spaceship to another planet.

My abuela went more than five nights without sleeping, terrified by the very idea of dreaming up another misfortune. Her eyes sunk into shadow, watching the spirits pass that didn't try to hide themselves. She didn't eat or drink water. She had high fevers and walked like a sleepwalker through the house and through the town, thin and with dark shadows under her eyes, saying that she had killed her father. Then she started to speak in that language that sounded like: xiquiyehua inxochiltl xiquiyehua ipanoyotl . . . and she was so lost that she didn't put up any resistance when her mother took her to Don Jacinto to be treated.

"Leave her here with me until tomorrow," the man said, biting his reed pipe. "I'll fix her up."

My abuela said that, when she opened her eyes, she thought Death had come for her. She was in a place she didn't know. The walls were crowded with masks, gourds, and images of saints, all flickering in the light of lit candles, like nothing she'd ever seen before. She was covered by a blanket and there were feathers from a speckled hen and animal bones around her. Despite the fear she felt, a deep tranquility invaded her. Something deep inside her was appeased.

A soft song made her sit up. When she saw Don Jacinto seated a few steps away, swaying as he intoned that song, she was impulsed by a deep fear, leaped up, and started to scream like a pig in a slaughterhouse. Then, as though she'd seen the devil himself, she took off running through town in the middle of the night.

She said she ran and climbed the mountain in the dark until she arrived at her cave. There she waited for the dawn, trembling from the cold, watching what the shadows around her did, though soon she realized that there were none and that she didn't hear the voices huffing endlessly. She couldn't see through the animals and insects to their hearts anymore, like they were transparent, nor the bleeding sap running through the trunks of the trees. She felt like a being from another world without it. Like they'd removed something from her body. Only two days passed before they came back to her—plus even more, as if they'd only gone out to bring back more guests with them.

Entrenched in that turbulence, my abuela, at twelve years old, had already made her decision: She would never go back home. She needed to distance herself from her loved ones, so she wouldn't end up killing them all.

Emilia walked a good stretch to distance herself from the jeep, and its dead, until midday distorted the shapes of the world. She stopped to take a breath alongside a clump of creosote bushes, raised her head, tired of bearing its own weight, and contemplated the twisted waves of the heat. She passed her fingertips over her face and traced the shapes of the scrapes and cuts that covered it. The blood stuck to her skin was a map of unknown roads. She took the two socks off her right foot and then the sneaker from the left. She'd tried to create a stand-in for a shoe with the socks, but it didn't work how she'd hoped. Her popped blisters were just dirty, old chicken skin, and she entertained herself by scratching at them until she reached the living flesh. So many bruises. The memory of her abuela saying that her feet looked like they belonged to a ceramic doll, like the ones they sell in markets, as she massaged them with camphor and rosemary to calm her growing pains or relieve the exhaustion of days on the mountain, came in as a burst of comfort.

"If you could see my burned-up pig hooves right now,

Mamá Lochi, you'd burst out laughing."

Her own voice sounded unfamiliar as she stood there, barely hearing, in the middle of the wasteland. Like it belonged to someone else, someone she'd never met before.

She walked for several hours with just one sneaker. She'd count one hundred steps and then switch the shoe to the other foot. That kept her distracted. It turned out to be as uncomfortable as limping along. She also tried to walk in socks only. Then another attempt, completely barefoot—but she still ended up with really messed up soles. The thorns and pebbles didn't make way for her step. She returned to the method of swapping the socks and the sneaker after walking a certain distance. Her eyelids were shutting on her, but it was more important to keep going. When she finally stopped, she closed her eyes and saw herself: so skinny, so dehydrated, and so alone in the middle of all that nothingness.

"Skinny but tough," she heard that voice that was hers but another's say.

When she walked with Mamá Lochi on the mountain, there was no *I can't keep going Mamá Lochi*, no matter how much her feet burned.

"Ándale, Calandria, don't be a crybaby," Mamá Lochi would say to her whenever she whined. "So your callouses will get strong, and you can climb up to the peaks."

Emilia learned quickly that whining carried no weight with her. Being called a wimp was worse than getting hit with a belt. That's why she put up with the blisters, bruises, achy muscles or bones, until they really didn't hurt her anymore. Sometimes they'd spend five, six hours walking through the mountains, until night returned them to the house. The next day, and the one after, the exact same. Especially when her abuela couldn't find the herb or animal she needed for her salves. Or when she ate her mushrooms—then there really was no end in sight.

Emilia half-closed her eyes. The sounds around her became clearer, as did a voice. It seemed that the wind brought it from who knows where.

Emilia, where are you. First he was a diffuse shadow wandering around her.

"I don't know. I'm going to the mountains," she said. "It's cold. It's almost dawn."

Emilia. Tell me where you are. Take strong steps. Leave something along the way.

"I can see you kinda blurry. I'm leavin' you things along the way."

Take strong steps, Emilia.

"Caco, I'm going to the mountains."

Something tells me you're close. That I'm gonna find you real soon, Calandrita.

"Caco, I'm hungry and thirsty."

Hold on, Calandria. And watch out: Something's circling you.

Goyo dissolved and she opened her eyes, startled and afraid. Her calandria flapped hard inside her. She looked up and then around, a tiny grasshopper in the middle of the universe. Seated on the hard and dry earth she saw how the sun twisted the shapes of the world, and a distracted happiness came to her like sweet candy because she'd contacted her brother in her dreams. Something was circling her, Goyo had said. Well, what could it be. She stood up and turned around in circles. Surrounding her, just the soulless desert.

She touched her fingers to scrapes, bruises, cuts.

Over and over she tested her face with the tips of her fingers. She had leftover dry blood from her forehead to her cheeks and she removed it with the small bit of saliva she had left. Her injuries didn't hurt so much—it was that battered mess that was settling inside her that ached the most.

She remembered that she had water and took a drink. She wet her fingertips and washed her face. Then she spread the sticky insides of a cactus over the scratches on her face. The cactus looked like one that Mamá Lochi had used often. She sucked out the bitter pulp: She was hungry. She rubbed it on her burst blisters, and she wrapped her feet with two pieces of cloth that she tore off the lining of her jacket.

A bird covered her with its shadow. She raised her eyes to follow its flight until she saw it come down on a shining and distant mesquite tree. If she hurried, she could reach it before the heat beat down its hardest. She placed some rocks and branches down to signal to Goyo where to go if he came this way, toward the mesquite. She set off walking in her handmade shoes and didn't look back even once. Mamá Lochi always warned her: Never turn around to see the path you left behind when you have a long way to walk, if what you want to do is to get far away from something bad. Once Emilia had asked her what would happen if someone turned around on accident, and all she did was raise her shoulders. "Who knows, but it can't be anything good if the shadows say not to."

Emilia walked a while and stopped to look at the distant mountains. What was *behind* that endless desert? She'd traveled inside a jeep, gagged, blindfolded, stuck in a sack, without knowing her endpoint or her origin. She'd flown through the air during the crash, without understanding where she was coming from. She'd spent hours walking, now without knowing whether what was in front of her now was what was behind her before. If she looked over her shoulder, she couldn't be certain that she was looking backward, so she risked it—she turned in a circle, like she had done before remembering her abuela's warning. The heat drew ripples into the air. There was a sorrowful and sluggish murmur squashing the world down with its breath. The mesquite tree and its shade were close and lit a fire under her step. Bearing the pain of her worn-away skin, she picked up her pace to get there.

The earnest glints of light, slipping through the tree's small leaves, received her kindly. It was like getting to the house of a neighbor who had been waiting for her for some time. She tossed off the bag she'd been carrying, took a breath, and leaned back on the tree to take off the one sneaker and the rags on her feet. Her flesh throbbed under her skin. Thirst squeezed at her mouth and hunger bit her insides. The blisters on her feet screamed at her. She took the bottle of water out and looked inside the backpack. At the bottom there was an enormous black plastic bag that filled almost all of the interior. To the side, a box of cigarettes, a lighter, a pen, and a bag full of weed. She tossed all that to the side and scratched hurriedly at the black plastic bag, hoping there was food inside. It was green bills. A ton of dollars. Disappointment gave way to the idea that she could use them to buy food and water. She looked at them closely, she smelled them: hundred-dollar, fifty-dollar bills. She looked around. What good were they? There was nowhere to buy even a cup of water, much less an egg taco. She tossed them into the bag and rummaged through the weed—what if there was a dry tortilla. But nothing. And she tossed it to the side. She lifted her face, the warm density of the air grew deeper. An immense loneliness spilled all over. Everything felt so distant: eating, finding her brother, her father. And she wanted to cry. What did it matter if they called her wimp, crybaby. She undid herself in tears. When she finally ran out, she returned to the backpack, with a renewed hope that, besides the money, weed, and cigarettes, there might be something to eat inside there. She stuck her hand all the way to the bottom, under the plastic bag, and found the hard and cold metal. From the bottom, between the folds of the cloth, she pulled out a gun. Other than in the movies, or when her father used a buckshot rifle to hunt doves, she'd never seen a real one before, and she leaned her face away from it like the thing was alive and could shoot on its own. She turned it over in both hands. It was loaded. She considered it from all angles as she thought that it would've been better to have found a bag of cookies, some bean tacos, or some potato quesadillas. At least one of those rancid pig-scrap tacos that they'd eaten in the barracks. Her mouth even watered as she remembered it. But there wasn't so much as the shadow of an animal's skin here. What the hell was a gun going to do to help her. She grabbed a handful of the weed and put it in her mouth. Even though it wasn't food, maybe she could trick her intestines. She chewed it slowly. Like she'd seen her abuela do so many times to prepare her ointments for rheumatism. She always said that just chewing it made her hunger go away. Though she always spit it into a bowl of hot water. Emilia swallowed it and then even took another handful—it was dry, bitter, scratchy. The gun beside it seemed to look at her. What was she going to do with that thing? And like that, looking at it, she saw a crowd of insects approaching, fluttering about before her eyes, emitting that unreal shine that she knew well. Then the air plowing through her veins, opening the pores of her skin. And there it was, infallible, the image filling her vision: the gun thrown out onto the wasteland, between thorny bushes and the moon growing in the sky. A dirty hand with polished nails picking it up, bringing it up to eye-level to look at it. Then, surrounded by scrap metal and dust, another hand, shooting, *pow, pow, pow*, and blood running down the body of one, two, three men. She saw herself: running between old scrap metal, broken-down cars, popped tires, scattered all over. And a group of kids running like they were being chased by the devil himself. It left her with goose bumps.

Emilia wanted to see more, but the familiar and intense headache came suddenly and the images dissolved quickly. She grabbed her temples with both hands, protecting herself from the light, not moving so that the tearing she felt in her brain would settle down. Finally it began to subside and, upon lifting her gaze, she looked at the gun. She grabbed it with the tips of her fingers, skinny and dirty with black fingernails.

"Before they stick me in another bag, those bastards are going to taste lead," she heard her voice as she turned the gun over and over in her hands, and it brought her a fit of laughter, until she ran out of air.

"Taste lead—" And she started to laugh again. "What would that taste like."

She stood up with the firearm pointed into the distance and she turned in a circle. She was ready to kill whoever stood before her. She noticed the tingle that rose from her feet, filling her body with joyful energy.

"Let's see, c'mon now. Come for me, let's see if you make it here, you sons of bitches." And again that laughter until she got a stomachache.

Between bursts of laughter, the memory of a movie she'd seen at Tomasa's house came to her: A detective, who was being followed by some mafiosos who wanted to take her out, took a gun out of her bag and shot at their legs, leaving them knock-kneed with their mouths wide open, twisting like worms on the asphalt.

"That's exactly what I'll do to whoever tries to steal me."

And she felt relief, even happiness, because she felt safe.

She leaned against the trunk of the mesquite: She felt the life of the tree run through the trunk at her back. And that tingle that made her sleepy. Not even a shadow moved around her. Between the tree's tiny leaves, the rays of midday poked through—projecting unmoving figures onto the earth, wrapped in mystery.

"Where are you, Goyo," she heard herself say, and her voice fell into an empty well.

The tiny joy from having heard him in her dreams had melted away completely by now. She would probably die before she found him, and she sighed with disappointment.

She considered the mountains, still so far away. How could it be that she'd spent so long walking, and those mountains hadn't ended up any closer. Maybe she was just imagining them.

Mamá Lochi's decision to run away didn't last long. First she wandered around the mountain until she remembered the cave and got herself there. She didn't want to let the lightning get her on the bald mountain. She collected water in the gourd, stored up wood to make a fire, and went about eating herbs and mushrooms when her hunger intensified. She had stopped hearing the voices of insects and animals. For a time, she thought that she'd gone back to who she was before the lightning and felt relieved to not hear any more words or sounds from the other world that didn't belong to humans. But that enjoyment didn't last long because her hunger led her to eat the rainy-season mushrooms, the kind that they call little birdies and the others that they call landslides, and her senses went wild again. Though there were some differences: When she ate them, strange animals appeared to her, and far from being shadows that spoke to her, now they appeared as figures with monstrous features. Who knows what depths of the soul my abuela was in back then. When she tried to tell me about it, it wasn't easy for her to find a word, or even a gesture, to put a name to her experience.

She didn't know how much time she spent inside her cave. What she did know was that one evening, the kind of storm that makes you think the world is ending came. Torrents of water fell over the entrance to her shelter, pouring down into the gully and forming mud rivers all around her. It seemed like it would never stop, and, wrapped in darkness, she thought she deserved to die. Why not let herself be taken by a lightning bolt? It'd be better if it just killed her already. That way she wouldn't have to suffer those damned dreams that brought so much misfortune. And so that's what she did. She left her refuge in the middle of the storm and hiked up to a peak full of trees, where she could touch the sky. And there she turned herself in, her arms wide open, her face to the clouds, imploring that once and for all a lightning strike powerful enough to send her six feet under would strike her in the head, charring her with a whip of flame. And there she stood for some time. Begging, yelling, crying until her legs gave in and she fell to her knees, exhausted. Finally, she told me, she returned to her shelter, dragging her feet.

After several hours of rain her hunger grew, and she took the fungi and the roots she'd collected and made a broth that tasted like the earth. The visions came. She saw, in the streams of rain that fell over the opening to the cave, huge boats filled with people. She saw a tree give birth to a rainbow. She saw flocks of bats with the faces of people enter the cave, until finally she herself turned into a bullet approaching her father's chest. It was a slow and painful journey. First she broke his skin with a harsh sound and then she ran through the flesh inside him, while in her own body she felt a burning that scorched her skin. My abuela said that she felt wounded by her own screams—it was like when they came out of her mouth, they pierced through her flesh. When her mind returned her to her body, the pain now settled, she looked into the holes planted all over her skin. Within them she saw her father, alone, walking through the sierra on his way to work the cornfield. Her father with her mother, eating a bean stew in silence. She saw herself with him, when they went to the cemetery to leave flowers for her abuela. Her pupils ran over the fissures in her skin and she cried over every pore, until she fell asleep.

"Be calm now, chamaca. You didn't have anything to do with this. I died because I was a dumbass. Because I was stickin' my nose where it didn't belong."

Her Papá Emilio, whose name was the same as my papá's, was in the middle of an empty space, like he was floating. His voice was echoing, he was naked and he covered his privates with both hands.

"Go back home already, your mamá can't stop cryin' because she thinks that you kicked the bucket, too."

Mamá Lochi saw the holes in her father's body. Golden branches sprouted out of them, full of small and deep green leaves. With the blank background, the green turned into a happy phosphorescence and it felt like, suddenly, that eased away her sadness.

"I promise you that I'll go back. Please, really, forgive me for going and killing you," my abuela told him between sobs.

"Don't be silly, chamaca. My own dumbassery killed me, I already told you that," he managed to shout out before disappearing.

When she opened her eyes, she realized it was sunrise.

She smelled the humid, fresh, lively earth. But still, it was really damn cold, and she wrapped herself up tighter in the blanket to watch the drops slide over the rocks. She was still wearing her damp clothes. Before she got busy at hiding away her stuff, gathering it in a corner and taking off back to her house with her soul lightened, she drank the rainwater and felt like her thoughts cleared up.

Mamá Goyita received her with a hug. The whole family surrounded her to kiss her and touch her, thanking the heavens for returning her alive and kicking. They'd gone looking for her in the mountains, in the day and at night with torches, until they'd given her up for dead. After that last thunderstorm, they were sure she was lying, burnt, at the bottom of a ravine, buried in the mud, and they wouldn't find her bones until the dry season. Mamá Lochi devoured the tamales, elotes, and tacos they put before her—and spent the rest of the afternoon vomiting up all that stuff, which her body couldn't handle after a week of just broth made from manure mushrooms. The next day she went straight to the graveyard and left a bunch of flowers on her father's tomb. She promised him that she'd take care of the house, her siblings, and her mother, so he wouldn't worry.

I think it was from then on that Mamá Lochi started to visit the graveyard often. It didn't need to be the Day of the Dead for her to make her rounds. Many years later she'd also take us, every two weeks, to clean the tombs, place fresh flowers, and sing to the departed. After one of our visits to the graveyard, a little before my father crossed to the other side, I asked her if she'd seen the dead come for the things that we left them in the cemetery. Especially on the days for the dead, when everyone puts so much food, drink, and all sorts of other things on the tombs, when they visit us from the beyond. When I asked her that question, I meant the dead we knew, our dead, because I had no doubt that she saw others, strangers who came to visit her—she threw me a harsh look, like my question annoyed her.

"Of course I've seen them, Emilia. Not as much as the others, but I see them when they have something to tell me. And on the days for the blessed dead, I see more than one at once. Don't you see this is their only opportunity, the whole year, to return and enjoy whatever they liked the most? To see the ones they loved the most when blood ran through their veins?"

"Don't be mad, mamita, but do you really see them, like they're really real, like when they were alive?" I insisted and I noticed a tremble in my voice, I think from the fear that she would get angry that I was asking these things.

"No, Calandria, of course not. They look different. Like they're made of smoke. Like they're pale, discolored."

"And do you think that I'll see them someday, mamita?" I piped up.

She kept arranging the altar that we were setting up, and without taking her eyes off the votive candle lit right next to the photo of our abuelo Güero, she told me, "Well, we'll see about that, Emilia. We'll see." She stood up and stayed silent, intently considering the flickering flame.

"A spirit is circling us, Calandria. It must be my Güero . . . let's see if we can hear him."

And she started to sing in that language she spoke: "Xiqui yehua in xóchiltl, xiqui yehua ipan noyótl." Who knows what she could have told him that day.

How could he follow the clues his sister left, with that overambitious heat that wouldn't stop rising? Gregorio's head sunk between his shoulders and his steps, which were strong at the beginning despite his limp, slowed as he pressed forward. His thoughts became scattered by the gulps he took from Vaquero's flask, which he ended up emptying. After walking for a while, he stopped under the red-hot sun. He squatted down and waited a few minutes to regain his energy. A bit of air blew over the sandstone that covered the ground and it outlined the shapes of a hand, of a leg, of a skull. The desert's bones, he said to himself shakily, fearing that the excess of heat, alcohol, and exhaustion were making him see things. Those unknown dead, buried by erosion, appeared every now and then like a warning.

"How shitty. To die and not even make it to your grave. That's fucked up."

Here and there he found a pair of pants, a shirt, a shoe. Pieces of a life, abandoned along the way.

A white hare crossed his path a few meters ahead and

stole away his attention, distracting him from his exhaustion and that feeling of death that those bones presaged. For Goyo, who was a good hunter, all it took to trap a prey was a rock, a slingshot, a stick, even his bare hands. He'd learned from his father, spending whole nights with him out under the open sky, chasing down opossums, cacomixtles, and rabbits, or looking for the birds with succulent meat that nested up high. There was a time when wild ducks flew over the area, just before they'd sold the buckshot rifle. When that happened they spent all of August coming down from the mountains with two or three prey in hand, which they cooked in a spicy mole sauce that was so good they licked their fingers clean. It made Goyo's mouth water to remember it. Afterward, during a time of crisis when they didn't have money or hunt or harvest, and Emilio Ventura had gotten rid of the rifle—they spent a season eating roots, herbs, and fungus, living off loans, though even the people who lent didn't have anything to lend.

A hare. The little saliva he had left reminded him of his hunger. He imagined the animal impaled by a stick, its meat roasting, its skin browning over the embers. He imagined the crunchy, greasy skin and took a dry gulp. And it was like the animal guessed his intentions: It jumped away, extending its svelte feet to go faster. *Nobody could keep up with that*, thought Gregorio, measuring up his own lack of strength. Even still, energized by that discovery and the possibility it brought with it, he set off in the same direction that the animal had gone, keeping it in his sight.

He remembered more: When his father sold the rifle, they still climbed up the mountain to hunt, unarmed. They had to put food on the table. Their hunger kept growing and the lack of food had no end in sight. "Even if it's with our fingernails, we're going to catch something," Emilio Ventura would announce. "We won't come down the mountain until we've got meat in our bags."

And they did as he said: They would hike up to the peaks, delve down the paths, and could end up spending two or three days wandering through those hills, sleeping beneath the jocote or morning glory trees, lying in wait for the sounds of rodents, of birds. The traps they set in the trees or right above ground level only worked with patience. Goyo was an expert in throwing himself onto prey after pursuing it for a while, and, when he had it in his hands, he didn't hesitate to snap its neck with just one twist.

"You really are like a little cacomixtle . . . or a mountain lion," his father would say, surprised with his son's fluid ability.

They hunted volcano rabbits. And some small birds with little, but juicy, meat. And snakes, too. They tricked Emilia into eating them. They told her it was chicken; she'd devour it in her hunger, but then once she was satisfied, she'd furrow her brow and suspect: "I have a feeling this isn't chicken . . . right, Mamá Lochi?" And she looked at her abuela, because there was nobody who could trick her.

The white mass, in the distance, moved steadily forward through the evenly spaced waves of sun. When he stopped to look around, Gregorio realized he had strayed from the point he'd meant to follow: a distant mesquite tree, on the way to the mountains, which Emilia had pointed out with her little towers of rocks and sticks.

"Fuckin' animal distracted me."

His dry tongue stuck to the roof of his mouth when he

opened it. The last few gulps of alcohol had dried him out and scrambled his head. He was nauseous, thirsty, and hungry all at once. It tortured him that he hadn't been able to take care of his sister; he shook off the idea of having lost her, of never seeing her again, and he felt an uneasy void tugging at his will to live, gravelike. He kneeled down for a while with his gaze fixed on the cracked earth and started to cry, but no tears arrived to refresh him. Finally he lifted his face and looked to the mountains. It wasn't long until evening fell. Night was coming, with its cold, and just imagining Emilia alone, or in the hands of some son of a bitch, twisted his insides and made his desire to disappear beat down on him. What was the point of all that walking. What was the point of crossing the line. What was the point of going on. What was the point. What. Let the night, when it erased the world, erase him, too. The dust floated like it was breaking apart the air, and the mountains stayed in place. Still. Silent. They knew everything: the entire world at their feet, dominated by their peaks. *Fucking asshole mountains*, he thought.

Then he remembered: Emilia had left her clues. And as long as she left her clues, she was fighting. And as long as that happened, he'd continue following her.

Tic, tac, tac. The animal again. Goyo asked himself who was following who. *Tic, tac, tac.* What was it doing to make that sound. He asked himself if it was doing it with its mouth, with its feet, or if he was imagining it. Maybe the sun had cooked his brains, and he was hearing things. But the *tic, tac, tac* interrupted his sorrow and he saw it again, only a few meters away. There it was, the hare, raising up its white shine, its super long ears, looking at him like it was calling him. It looked brilliant from that distance, like a glowing phantasm that carries an urgent message.

"What's your problem, you fucking animal," he yelled, and his throat stung. He thought of Chucho, a man back home who'd lost his wits and spoke to himself or with animals. He remembered how he chased hares up the mountain without losing his breath. That thought brought his strength back and he stood, puffing out his chest.

"You'll see. All I need is to grab you and just like that I'll sink my teeth right into you." As soon as he said it, his insides twisted with hunger.

He remembered that in his backpack there was a knife. A lighter. He'd approach it slowly, calmly—there was no hurry. With one jump, he'd land on top of it and snap its neck right there. He'd skin it and save its soft skin as a souvenir. He'd save a foot for Emilia, for good luck. Another for himself. He wouldn't leave even a bone. He was going to eat it whole. Skin, meat, guts.

"You're not getting away from me, you fuckin' rabbit."

He stood up slowly, with the knife hidden in the back pocket of his pants, and he walked toward the quadruped, moving stealthily and pausing frequently, to not scare away his prey, to focus his dormant violence, usually unnoticeable in him. The hare wasn't disturbed. It chewed on a bush, throwing furtive glances at the young man, who watched his every move like it was a matter of life and death. When he was just a few meters off, the animal lifted its head and leaped away a few times, not stopping until it was a sufficient distance from its hunter. It stopped again and took up chewing on a new bush. Goyo kept going in the same direction—he wasn't going to give up just like that, even though his hunger, thirst, and the oppressive sun drowned him with a turbid energy.

Without realizing, he found himself a few steps from a man splayed out in the middle of his path. His confusion lasted an instant, wondering if the vision was real or not. How could he know, if he wasn't sure of his own skin, his own thoughts. The fear that there might be more people shook him out of it: He looked around quickly. Nobody. Or at least nobody in view. That's when he noticed the vultures flying overhead.

"Fuckin' death-gobbler birds," he thought. And, with some hesitation, he approached the man, thrown out over the earth, whose lifeless eyes seemed to follow the circles that the birds of prey made just a few meters from his own head.

That night hag's sitting right on you.

The bird's chirp woke her abruptly. She watched the leaves of the mesquite shine above her head, like restless butterflies beneath the afternoon light. That awful heat had died down, leaving behind a freshness as the light retreated. She tried to move but couldn't. Instead, she felt like the tree was considering her.

That night hag's sitting right on you.

Mamá Lochi's voice was coming from right inside her guts. Then the high-pitched bird's twittering—a tense and engulfing shriek that made her open her eyes and return to the world.

Emilia remembered: Sometimes, back home, she only came to from that state with a scream that broke the tough ropes that tied her to the other world. Pulling in the air like a newborn. Now, a smelly sweat fell over her forehead. Her mouth was sticky with a harsh thirst that rode along the back of every moment in this desert.

Once she came out of the mess her soul was in, and when

she finally managed to open her eyes and feel awake, she wished she could have seen the mountains of Amatlán, the sky framed by the foliage of the blooming jocote trees, the sweet song of the wise and gossipy robin that spied on the world of men from atop stone walls. And yet, except for a slight break in the light and the heat, foretelling the death of the afternoon, the landscape was the same as before her sorrowful sleep. Dry desert, impeccable in its distant aridity, filled by that loneliness that just depleted her willpower. A new twittering from the bird, standing atop the crown of the mesquite, made her lift her face. She recognized its song as the same as from the previous nights, that same clucking that flew over the jeep when she was kidnapped. If Mamá Lochi had shown her anything in their walks through the mountains in Amatlán, it was to distinguish the songs of birds. She always said that she was a whiny calandria because she was her granddaughter. That in her heart, a bird vibrated—she could tell because in her own there also lived a bird that was never calm.

The white feathers, fluffed out, grew over the bird's crest. The sharp beak, the twinkling and cunning eyes that observed her. White feathers with blue shades over its back, lined up in a way that made them seem like leaves flowing in the wind. Emilia and the bird observed each other. It came to tell her something and she waited to hear its voice. But, other than the slight movement of its eyes, nothing stirred until it shook its wings and took off into the air, dragging along its scandalized twittering. She stood up and followed it with her gaze until she watched it disappear, way in the distance, into the rocks of the mountains.

"You want me to follow you," she said. "Well, that's

where I'm headed." She hurried to stick the gun in her pants pocket, then took a hundred-dollar bill and a pen out of the bag. On the bill, she wrote to her brother: *To the split in the mountains.* She looked for good-sized rocks, stacked them in a tower next to the mesquite, and stuck the bill between two boulders. She tied the dusty rags around her feet and slung the bag over her shoulder, determined to follow the path traced out by that nosy bird.

The fading afternoon light exposed the bones embedded in the dust. *How many bones must the damn desert have swallowed up. How many lost spirits must be wandering under this sky,* the girl thought. And she walked for much of the night, facing the mountains that rose up in the darkness filled with stars, like stewards of the universe. The bastard cold started biting at her skin like a lumberjack's ax. She stepped up her pace, refusing to register the pain in her feet. But her exhaustion—that made itself be noticed.

"I need to get there before dawn," she heard her trembling voice say from somewhere in her guts. "In case you catch up with me, Caco. So we can find each other."

She built a pair of rock towers and sticks to show him the way.

Ándale, Emilia, don't get down on me now, you still have a way to go.

Her abuela's voice grew in clarity as her body drained of energy. Soon enough she forgot about the bird. Arrive at the foot of the mountains—that's all she had in her mind. Her bag was heavy, and she ended up throwing it off as she walked on. She could barely carry on with her own weight. When she fell to the ground, totally worn out, she'd gone hours dragging herself forward without even knowing where she was going. She chewed on the dust that stuck to the roof of her mouth. To her soul. She'd reached her limit and saw a tiny cliff dropping into the abyss before her. She looked up at the mountains: Now they looked pretty close. And so far.

"I'm going to die right here," she murmured in a drained voice, and her thoughts got tangled in themselves.

Daybreak was far away, but some distant gleam of light arrived suddenly and she could make out the shadows of the vultures sliding down the mountain's creases, its banks, its slopes of boulder and harsh vegetation. The world's color snaked down the ridges, too, and fell away over her body. Soon the vultures were only a few steps from her, already smelling her death. All that Emilia Ventura had left was fear, and even that was fading by the minute. All she had left was a glide into a space without sensation, a place flashing brilliantly with memories. She heard the twittering of the bird crossing the air and escaped into its sound, flying high above her to who knows where. Then she imagined herself reaching the tall cliffsides and going into their high climbs and deep dips to protect herself from the scavengers that wanted to devour her.

She thought of Goyo.

He must be a goner by now.

It was probably his spirit speaking to her in her dreams from the beyond. And she noticed how the desiccation broke her thoughts to pieces. She sunk into a time of tranquility that was taking her to the other side. She saw herself again, thrown on the earth, made of the dirt and pebbles that stuck to her skin.

I better be real dead when those fuckin' vultures stick their beaks in me.

The voice in her head unraveled like the afternoon. Now and then, she half-opened an eyelid to look toward the mountains, and the dim view shimmered in waves until her reality was erased. Like a spark, she flew into a memory: One day, collecting herbs on the mountain, she'd found a dead bull in the middle of the path. Sad and enormous. Surrounded by dogs and vultures having a feast of the still-fresh intestines and flesh. An enormous and abandoned bull, so alone in his death that she wanted to give him a hug to console him.

Thrown on the ground, with the gun at her side, she guessed she wouldn't take long to extinguish, and she was just able to reach a thought: *I'm going to get at least one of those fucking death gobblers.* The night, its stars heavy with omens, was still crowning over the earth when she grabbed the gun, begging the ground to stop moving so much beneath her so she wouldn't miss her shot.

Kill them all, Calandrita.

The voice inside her turned into a long thread moving through the air like a kite. Soon that thread of letters disappeared in the breath of her thoughts, interspersed with voices.

Don't leave a single one of them alive, Emilia. If you do, they'll gobble you alive. Don't you let go, chamaca, you know that a woman has to be strong. . . .

The vultures were coming toward her, only just a few steps away when she squeezed the trigger. The shot echoed. She heard the rustling of their squawks, their flapping wings, and, holding on to them, she started falling into a desolate pit with no bottom in sight.

From the other side, Emilia Ventura wasn't able to hear the rumble of a car's motor nor see the lights that shone onto her body.

"Here!"

She didn't make out the moving human figures or the men's voices or the radio at full volume. The beam of light fell onto her and she didn't even notice. Embedded in an engulfing silence that came from within her, Emilia Ventura fought for her life like the flame of a candle assailed by a gust of wind.

Emilia, ¡ándale! Hold on . . . don't you die now, it's not your time yet.

Mamá Lochi was walking in front of her on the butterfly-filled mountain, soaked with rain. That harsh rain that fell in bucketfuls in the summer evenings. Emilia was happy, with her face raised to the sky and her mouth open, and she let the generous drops of life fill her body—they slipped over the corners of her lips and satisfied her thirst. There it was, the green mountain, immense, covered with trees and herbs and overflowing with humidity. She smelled the fennel, the mint, the freshness of wet earth. She descended through the mountain's ravines, surrounded by white butterflies, to another season where the jocote trees' autumn-yellow leaves, small and brilliant, floated through the air before descending on the golden carpets woven through the uneven earth. That soft raining, of water, of leaves, of humidities sprouting between the moss and ferns on the rocks, calmed her with its caresses and took her away from the torment and the deserted, ice-cold night, where her body lay.

From that world, the one she was slipping into, she didn't hear the words of the men that surrounded her, nor did she notice when they lifted her up shakily to take her to the car where more people waited. She also didn't see when the truck went into the heart of the mountains, far from that patch of land where, in her agonizing dreams, she believed she had returned to her hometown.

Mamá Lochi talked to me about her visions of the world when we walked alone on the mountain. She liked to talk about time, about changes. We'd stop to rest on a boulder that served as a lookout from the highest part of the mountain. She tended to splay out, silently watching the clouds pass and the birds fly over us. She would be quiet for a long time and then she would start to whistle, like a little bird. She could spend up to an hour like that, and suddenly she would say, for example, that the shapes the clouds were taking were like the reflection of the world of men, that one could believe that something was a certain way and all it took was a blow of the wind for it to disappear and turn into something else.

"That's how the world is, Calandrita. You need to learn that well. You shouldn't cling to anything. Nothing can be eternal as long as you're alive: It's better to let things happen and move with them when they move." I would stay quiet. I was turning her words over in my head, not understanding very clearly what they meant.

She was in one of those moods when she talked to me

about her Mamá Goyita. About how when she was a girl she would go up the mountain with her, about how she showed her the secrets of herbs before Death took her away. She had a stand in the Cerro Gordo market, and all the curanderos in the area were her clients. I asked her one day why she, Mamá Lochi's mother, wasn't a curandera herself, and she answered me very seriously, like I'd said something completely outrageous:

"Well, it's not as easy as just saying, 'Roll me up another taquito.' To be a curandera, you have to be born with the gift. And it didn't matter how much she knew about herbs—she didn't have it."

When Goyita got sick and died, Mamá Lochi was fifteen. My great-grandmother was really hurt by the death of her husband, and two years after his murder, she started to lose so much weight that in a few months she looked like a skeleton. Back then, Mamá Lochi kept waking up in the middle of the night, frightened by the same dream: a big mass eating Mamá Goyita from the inside. The mass slid through her intestines and gnawed at her with a tiny mouth filled with sharp teeth, until it destroyed her insides. Mamá Lochi said she would wake up sobbing, screaming, and the whole family would surround her to ask her what was going on with her. She looked at her people, not trusting her very own eyes, as though putting her gaze upon them could hurt them.

"You're havin' real bad dreams, aren't you, chamaca?" she said Mamá Goyita had asked her. But my abuela denied it. She didn't even want to think about it. Better to avoid letting her memory go back to those images.

I should get out of here, she thought. *I'm gonna kill them all.*

She would go to her mountain, to her refuge, and she'd spend days away from home. Or she'd wander through the town—there was nobody left who didn't think she was crazy. A bad spirit was possessing her, they gossiped. Those were lonely times, she didn't have anyone to talk to about what she was experiencing. When she returned, her mother would get pissed at her, she'd beat her with a cane made from ocote to get her to stay put.

It was around then that she noticed a chamaco they called Güero, because of his light eyes. He was the son of an out-of-towner and a woman from town, and he was lost in love for my abuela. He followed her on some of her escapades, and when she realized it she wanted to put him off, shooing him away and acting like she was crazy. Those snubs didn't scare him, and he kept following her every step. Later he would tell her that he followed her to watch after her—so that nobody would hurt her, so that no brute could try to take advantage of the desperation of that little lady, the one with her black hair tied into a thin braid, with that strange tattoo running up her arm, with that charming birthmark under her eye and that sparkling gaze that lit up the earth when combined with her wide smile of perfect teeth. And even though at the beginning she tried to run him off like he was a dog that threatened her, in time she also started to get interested in that stubborn fellow. Convinced that it would be better to disappear so she wouldn't keep killing people, she decided she'd prefer to let that guy steal her away. She was tired of wandering around through the town like a madwoman. So that's how they ended up taking up in an abandoned house on the outskirts of town, where nobody would happen upon them. My abuelo Güero was in charge of bringing food, doing whatever work he could find to provide a pillow to rest their heads on and a table to fill their bellies at. But the visions didn't subside. Exactly the opposite—when she slipped into the depths of sleep, Mamá Lochi was expulsed by the return of the terrifying images of what was eating her mother from inside.

"I was real stupid," she told me one day, while we climbed down the mountain together. "If instead of being afraid, I had taken her to be cured, maybe you would still have a great-grandmother." And she wiped away the tears that trailed down to her chin.

It was strange to see my abuela cry. Though on those occasions she let loose, and her tears burst forth like a waterfall in a storm.

"It took me a while to discover that I wasn't killing anyone with my dreams. I was just gettin' ahead of what was comin'. But the things that the spirits announce, Emilia, can change sometimes. It's hard work—but it's possible, as long as people want to. That's taken me a lifetime to understand."

One of her uncles went to tell her that her mother had gotten sick, that she was asking for her. When she saw her, she knew she only had hours left: Her skin was yellow and her eyes, sunken between her bony cheekbones, looked out at her from a distant border.

"Go with Don Jacinto, stubborn kid," she said to her before going quiet forever, before closing her old-little-girl eyes.

She says that around then she was tempted to go looking for the curandero because she didn't want to go against her mother's wishes. But something stronger stopped her. That man produced such a fear in her that she couldn't ignore.

He had attended the burial, and like always, invited her to visit him. My abuela was already pregnant with her first son, though she didn't know it.

"You have light in your belly, chamaca. Come see me if you don't want it to go out," he said as he stepped away, chewing his reed pipe. "And stop being so afraid of me already."

That first baby was born dead, and she dreamed that a blindfolded man was stabbing her in the womb.

The second, she birthed a few months before she should have: It had teeth, and its toes were stuck to each other. It wasn't until the death of the third, a little one named Ángel, who was a year old and was just starting to walk when he got pneumonia and died, that she started to consider going to look for Don Jacinto. At that time, my father was growing inside her, though she didn't know it.

"It took giving birth to your father for me to draw up the courage to go visit Don Jacinto. I was out of options. I waited 'til the last moment. And that very day I saw her in my dreams . . . her, my mother," Mamá Lochi told me one day. "I could even smell her scent of fennel, as clear as you can smell mine. She was standin' near the unlit stove, wearin' the apron she used every day, and she said to me: *I'm glad you're going to cook, Lochi. It was about time, stubborn kid.*' And she kept lookin' at me with those watchful eyes, like she was waitin' for me to add the firewood and put the herbs in the pot. I was really stupid, Emilia. I should've paid attention to her—a different sun would've set on me." And she kept looking at me intently, before adding, "Life is a mystery, Calandrita, you shouldn't try to solve it, just live it and that's all."

A question nagged at me since that day, though I took a while to work up the courage to ask my abuela. Always with that fear of making her angry for being nosey.

"So how was it when you visited Don Jacinto, mamita?"

My soul burned to know about it. She'd resisted the witch doctor for so long. I saw a plea in her eyes. She didn't want the question and didn't answer me. All the way up on the mountain, on top of a boulder from where you could see the whole town and the villages on the other side of the mountain, she simply stayed quiet. I knew it was best not to interrupt her thoughts. She could become furious and, like I'd committed an unforgivable offense, lash at me with the branches of the ocote trees, looking at me fixedly like she didn't recognize me, punctuating her swings with words I couldn't comprehend. This time none of that happened. This time she took a deep, deep breath and simply said:

"Hold your horses, chamaca. We'll get there eventually. Because I was stubborn—just like you with your questions, like a dog with a bone."

And that evening we went down the mountain without her saying a single other word.

The man was around thirty years old. His brown face was halfway obscured by a faded gray hat. He had half-closed eyes and a naked torso, and his arms fell at his side like his body had abandoned them. Goyo observed his big and calloused hands, turned up to the sky, almost imploring. He had his shirt tied around one leg, heavily stained with blood. There was a dusty backpack at his feet. One of his shoes lay upside down beside him, like it was saying: *What are you lookin' at.* The other one looked distracted, peering out—it still had a foot inside it. It crossed Gregorio's mind that the man could be someone he'd known from before, one of the men who had crossed the line with them. He approached the body stealthily, but with an incipient happiness that climbed up to excitement. To be with someone. To be able to talk. To not feel so lost in the middle of that soulless wasteland. He was still breathing. When Goyo was a few centimeters away, he heard a moan, and then, the sound of the rattle. It came from a snake covered in huge brown diamonds, an enormous monster that made him retreat a few steps.

It was slithering close enough to make his nerves tense. Goyo stayed still as a stick, breathing slowly. From the monster's skin, luminous ripples burst forth like sparks. And then it stopped just like that, suddenly. It lifted its head and turned to look at him.

"Ah, you bastard. What're you lookin' at, fuckin' animal," the teenager mused to himself. A long, forked tongue danced from the mouth of the serpent. It emitted a strange rumbling and sounded its rattle.

The idea came to Gregorio at once. A simple idea, a motor that moves the body without asking for anything but its immediate execution. Goyo let out that high-pitched whistle he had learned from Mamá Lochi. When she let it sound, the heads of all the tiny serpents in their nests would poke out. As he whistled, the animal raised its head even more toward him. He breathed in and whistled again. Pushed forward by that same motor, he got closer. Slowly. Leaving aside any thought that would bring forth fear, just that sharp impulse, persevering and focused, moving his legs, tensing his body. That force managed the energy that guided him with precision. Maybe it was his hunger. Maybe it was his desire to die. He controlled his breath until finally he was standing next to the reptile that was on the verge of leaping forward. Goyo took in another breath. With the same smoothness of rhythm he had in his approach, he emitted a new whistle. There was something enveloping about the sound—it created an invisible force that tied together his humanity with the life of the animal. Not even one thought. He kept whistling, coming closer with short steps and, balancing himself gracefully, took the knife out of his back pocket. As soon as he was just a step away, he kneeled down before the reptile, which submitted to his whistling, stopping its rattling and lowering its head until it rested on the flat ground. With one calm and firm movement, Gregorio Ventura pierced the flesh and held it to the ground. And he threw himself backward. The monster's tail whipped through the air. A cold sweat, accelerated heartbeat, and sudden terror returned Goyo to this world. Then he remembered the words that his abuela said, in a trembling and throbbing voice, whenever she killed an animal:

"Your flesh, from the earth, to the earth."

He kneeled down, pressed his head to the ground, covering the snake with his body. The creature twisted rapidly under him then slowed down. At last the agitated breath turned into a measured rhythm. When Gregorio lifted his face, the snake was dead.

"I'm a fuckin' lunatic," he heard himself say.

A few steps away, the dying man let out a whimper. He had his shirt knotted below his knee to stop the flow of the venom from where the snake had bitten him. Goyo moved the rag to look at the wound on his heel. It was still bleeding. The swollen flesh was a deformed mass. The man was in a cold sweat, just barely breathing. A bloody foam fell from his mouth and Goyo took off the man's hat, thinking he might recognize him as one of the migrants, but he had never seen that face before.

"It's gonna be fuckin' tough for me to be able to help you, mister." The man regarded him with a pair of glassy eyes, filled by an unsettling distance. The other world was already looking out from his trembling pupils. He wanted to say something. A scapular hung around his neck. The teenager cleaned his mouth and looked inside his backpack where, in addition to a rolled up sweatshirt, a T-shirt, and a pair of pants, he found a canteen of water and a few cans of beans. Goyo drank and then tried to give the dying man something to drink. He barely managed to taste a little bit, but most of it dribbled over the edges of his cracked lips. The teenager took his turn and drank eagerly. He wanted to gulp it all down and even suck the final drops from the bottle cap's edge, but managed to stop himself from emptying the canteen.

"Photo," he heard the man say in a whisper. The life was evaporating from him and the word was a spiral of itself, disappearing in the air.

"Photo? I don't understand you, mister."

His brains were probably cooking in the heat, Goyo thought. How was he going to take a picture of him. And what for.

"Photo," he repeated, his voice a stream of vapor.

"But how do you want me to take a photo of you."

"Pocket," he murmured at an almost inaudible volume.

"Ah. You want me to find it. I'm a dumbass."

He rummaged through the pants. There were some bills and a folded piece of paper. Some phone numbers and names written in childish handwriting. He spilled out all the backpack's contents—nothing that looked like a photo. It was when he stuck his hand into the shirt tied around the man's leg that he found it. A woman with a wide smile and big and brilliant eyes looked at him. She was hugging two kids, both sitting at her side, smiling, protected by her maternal cuddle. Goyo considered the image. And he brought it up to the dying man.

"This must be the one."

He helped him lift his head. The man opened his eyelids

a millimeter more. Viewing the image separated him from his invisible beyond. His opaque eyes radiated light for an instant and filled with tears. That was all he needed to jump over the old stone wall to the other world. A second before he did, a tremble shot through him that contorted him from head to toe, leaving him vanquished in a strange position. Gregorio Ventura witnessed the escape of the last remains of life beneath his skin.

Who knows how long he stayed looking at the cadaver. He waited for him to take a breath, to open his eyes, to hear him say a word from this world. Nothing—only shadows, stillness, and silence.

Evening fell. And he didn't have even a name for the unknown dead man. Many times he'd heard Mamá Lochi say that when someone helps, or keeps a dying person company in their journey to the other side, their spirit will stay with them forever. What was he going to call that spirit if it came to him. He didn't even know where he was from. He didn't know anything about anything. He looked through his belongings; he didn't find anything that could identify him, just that paper with numbers and phone numbers that he'd kept in his pocket.

"I promise you, Mr. Departed, that if I come out of this alive and kicking, I'll call your family and tell them what happened to you."

He gathered rocks and shrubs to cover the body and prayed for his soul. He looked at the photograph. Questions ran through him—the evening and the sunset had refreshed his mind. Where could that woman, those kids be. Maybe in a town, a city, a countryside, absorbed in their daily lives without suspecting that their father, their husband, their brother, whoever he might be, lay dead in the middle of that nowhere. He imagined them by a stove, flipping tortillas, heating up beans, eating some tacos. He imagined a warm night, the contentedness of being together with close words and known sounds. He asked himself if the spirit of that dead man would also travel to find them again. If in situations like that, the spirit of the dead could divide itself up, be in many places at the same time. Maybe one part was already with the family, making them feel his presence in some way. Maybe he was also nearby. Looking around, Goyo's eyes passed over the growing darkness. Hoping to find him, and to be able to talk for a little bit, even if it was with a dead man. He thought about loneliness, about time, about how far away his life from before was. And he thought of his own death. It might be circling him now.

"What a fucking shitty-ass sadness."

And he uncurled one of the dead man's hands, rigid now, and stuck the photograph between his fingers.

"That way, when they find you, sir, maybe they'll identify you," and as soon as he said it, he heard his own sigh. "Like that could happen. I'm a real idiot."

He finished covering up the grave with a pair of rocks that he dragged from far away. He intertwined two sticks into the shape of a cross to put on the makeshift headstone. He prayed an Our Father, on his knees, by its side.

The jacket, the hat, the couple cans of beans, and the canteen he'd found in the backpack, plus his own lighter, were going to be useful to him. He put on the hat and the jacket: The cold would descend as soon as the night fell over the desert. He pulled the knife out of the now dull body of the snake. Its color was gone. A sad pale skin. The light had drained from it and decomposition waited to take over the rest. While he skinned it to rescue the meat, Goyo asked himself where the life that used to be in that flesh could be. But maybe it was nowhere. He started a bonfire and roasted the remains of the animal while he devoured beans from a can. When the meat was cooked, he chewed it eagerly. He hadn't forgotten the eyes of the snake right before he pinned it down with the dagger.

"What a fuckin' shitty-ass hunger," he heard himself say, breaking through the emptiness that surrounded him. He couldn't remember ever having felt so much. And he wrapped a piece of the meat in a shirt, for the road, fighting against his desire to devour it, too.

The *tic, tac, tac* at a distance shook him from his drowsy thoughts. The hare, rose-colored in the sunset, gleamed between a clump of bushes no more than a hundred meters away.

"Fuckin' animal, what's your problem." And he saw it jump away until it became an ignited spot running far in the distance.

Gregorio Ventura lay down next to the embers and, even though he made an effort to stay awake, soon the weight of his exhaustion trapped him in a sleep that ended up breaking down his discernment.

"Emilia, where are you," his tired voice wondered aloud.

First she was a diffuse shadow wandering around him, until he was able to distinguish the characteristics of his sister standing amid the haze.

I don't know. I'm going to the mountains.

"Emilia. Tell me where you are. Take strong steps. Leave something along the way."

I can see you kinda blurry.

"Take strong steps, Emilia."

Caco, I'm going to the mountains.

"Something tells me you're close. That I'm gonna find you real soon, Calandrita."

Caco, I'm hungry and thirsty.

"Hold on, Calandria. I'm gonna catch up to you real soon."

The girl's blurry silhouette shimmered. Behind her, a bright specter came and went at her back, above her head, at her side.

"And, Emilia, watch out: Something's circling you."

He waited for her response for a few moments, but she wasn't there anymore.

A distant boom shot him out of his sleep, and he opened his eyes. What could that be. The night fell onto him and none of his surroundings could tell him where he was. He was shivering. It was a cutting cold, breaking through his skin. He wrapped himself in whatever he could find so he wouldn't end up frozen by it. He didn't have enough energy to look for a way to start a fire so he curled up on the remains of the embers, afraid of being discovered at a distance. Phosphorescences shone from the rocks on the neighboring grave. Not enough time had passed for that to happen. And yet they were the same kind that tended to appear on the tombs in the cemetery in Amatlán. He raised his eyes to the sky. To the silhouette of the haughty mountains. It would be best to start walking—with some food and rest in him, he could walk to temper the cold that weakened his bones.

Emilia's voice still echoed in his head, coming from the

depths of his sleep that was not yet gone. He put on the backpack and decided to keep going—to wherever his heart and his crooked step led him.

Ever since I can remember, on the Day of the Dead Mamá Lochi would get Goyo and me gussied up, fill a basket with fruit, bread, and sweets, lay out flowers and light candles and take us to the graveyard. There she made us say prayers for the soul of my Mamita Estela, for my abuelo Güero, for my great-grandfather Emilio, for Mamá Goyita, for the little chamacos who died on her. We'd kneel down before the tombs to make them their altars, murmuring our repeating prayers, talking with whoever else was also visiting their departed. The cemetery was covered with a yellow blanket, a soft tapestry made of marigolds, and the air was pregnant with a sweet smell mixed with copal, the tree resin that sometimes made my stomach turn. The tombs covered in sweet pastries, sugar skulls, fruits, flowers, and candles. A lively sight at nightfall, like the other world was revived in this one. We were there for an hour, and when we left, we went straight to Tomasa's house, right next to the graveyard, to have some hot chocolate with a piece of pan de muerto. For years I thought pan de muerto was really made of dead people, but I liked it so much that I didn't get picky and I'd eat two or even three. At bedtime I'd be taken over by nerves: What if the dead person I'd wolfed down was a good person, or what if they weren't. Sometimes if I was in a bad mood or felt like doing something I wasn't supposed to, I put it down to the dead person in my intestines being a bad one, and it scared me so much I'd get them out of me by puking.

My papá also went to the graveyard, but always dragging along his broken face. He didn't like to think of my Mamita Estela. Whenever Mamá Lochi talked about her or we asked him about her, his mouth twisted up like a juiced lemon and he wouldn't answer us. It was pitiful, seeing him with so much blame on his shoulders. He'd leave a bunch of flowers, give a quick walk through the tombs, and then, in a whisper we could hardly hear, he would say he was going to go see his compadre Pancho. We wouldn't see him again for two or three days. He'd arrive all disheveled and smelling of liquor, his eyes deep red. He'd hug me tight and would say that I looked a lot like her, that he missed her. Then he'd go to the mountain and work for hours under the sun's rays without having even a bite of a taco—that was the only way he could lighten his soul.

For my abuelo Güero, dead from a heart attack when I was one, my abuela put a bottle of aguardiente and a little box of unfiltered cigarettes on his tomb.

"I'm leaving this for you, viejo, so you can enjoy it. And in a little while I'll come back to put you in order," she'd say after crossing herself. Then she'd quickly wipe away the tear that rolled down her face. My abuelos loved each other. Their eyes had lit up just seeing each other.

The visits to the graveyard put Mamá Lochi in a gray

mood almost like rain. Not only when she left the gifts for her Güero, but also when she left her pots of flowers, candies, and toys from the market for the three children that had died on her.

It was after one of those visits that she told me about the day she buried her third chamaco. She clearly remembered the glassy and fulminant eyes of Jacinto Estrella looking at her, with that gaze of his like a sleepless owl's, while she was on her way out of the cemetery, dragging her soul along.

"Stop with the stubbornness, Eloísa, soon enough nobody is going to be able to help you even if you repent. You'd better make a plan for it, before the one that's on his way ends up with the same fate." He turned around and disappeared down the road. Mamá Lochi says that a fear entered her then, the kind that can't be calmed, when she saw how Don Jacinto's pupils shone. Just two black holes about to swallow her up, she told me as she remembered it. In the days that followed, he appeared to her wherever she went. Around a corner, on the mountain, in her dreams. Mamá Lochi started to feel one of those fears that twists up your guts. Fear that makes you jump at your own breath. Mamá Lochi was afraid of the revenge that the beings from the other world would exact on her if they felt rejected. Afraid that now a lightning strike would really kill her. Afraid that the son she had in her womb would be ruined or they'd come back to snatch him. But her obstinacy was enormous. And she still put off going to him.

I think that's why my Mamá Lochi adored my father—because with his birth, she also gave birth to herself as a curandera. Both of them were difficult labors. He was the first child of her womb to really survive, after three pregnancies. Beno and Isidro came after, but for her there was nobody like her little chaparro. Giving birth to him took a lot out of her, like he was an enormous and spiny chayote plant. I think she knew that by giving birth to him she wasn't far from giving birth to herself and taking charge of accepting her destiny.

She was pushing for a full day, but the chamaco just didn't want to come out. My abuelo Güero had gone off to get drunk with one of his friends, sure that this time he wouldn't only lose the child but that he'd also lose his wife. In the middle of the labor, when she was pushing and pushing without getting the chamaco to come out, Jacinto Estrella appeared to her as a phantasm, and my abuela's insides trembled. The voice sounded hoarse, like it was coming right out of his liver. Don Jacinto warned her harshly that her time was running out—that this was her last chance. That she needed to accept the tools before she'd have to reap what she'd sown and it left her in ruins. That she wasn't going to have a son or grandkids if she didn't accept her destiny.

Between her pains, pushes, and screams, Mamá Lochi stopped her breath to gather up her strength and, with a wild look in her eye, she turned to her comadre Tomasa, who was praying nonstop at her side:

"Go and get Jacinto Estrella. Run." She said it with a faltering but decisive voice and an energy that surprised her friend. Tomasa remembered that the request even scared her.

"Are you sure, comadrita?"

"Run! I'm telling you to run!"

Tomasa left her with the midwife, Sofía, who had arrived to help her along, and took off running to find the witch doctor. But imagine her fright when she just barely opened the door and the man was there. Tomasa crossed herself like he was an apparition.

"I heard someone asked for me," Tomasa recalled Jacinto Estrella saying, with that snide smile that made your skin crawl, always with his reed pipe between his lips.

Don Jacinto entered without asking for permission, lit a fire in the middle of the room, prepared an herbal tea, set out incense, and sang and spoke in that distinct tongue, whispering words to Mamá Lochi's womb and her ear. Three pushes later, the whole town could hear the cry of the giant baby that was my father, announcing his arrival to the earth.

"He wasn't far from suffocating," the witch doctor pronounced after cutting the cord, while he held the baby in his hands to smell him and look at his eyes up close. He looked inside his mouth, and, according to Tomasa, at that moment, the baby stopped crying and considered the man with his ocelot eyes, like he sensed something.

"Well, did you lose somethin', chamaco?" Mamá Lochi said he joked. "They're going to call you Emilio," he declared. "And you're going to be as bullheaded as your mother. You're not going to listen to anybody, not even her, and that's gonna take you far," he concluded, laughing, before handing the little creature over to the midwife to be washed off.

"I'll see you in a few days, Eloísa," he told my abuela before disappearing.

The light still rippled out between the logs on the stove when the midwife put my father in my abuela's arms. She held him tight to her chest before putting a nipple in his mouth. "Just look at those big ol' eyes. Emilio. That's just what your name will be. Emilio, like my father."

A few days had passed when, fresh from having given birth and burdened by the idea that her stubbornness would bring some misfortune to her baby or to one of her loved ones again, Mamá Lochi presented herself before Jacinto Estrella. As soon as she entered it, the dark room became illuminated with the light of the candles distributed from wall to wall. Jacinto Estrella was sitting in the middle of the place on a palm mat, contemplating his hands. Mamá Lochi wondered how he'd gotten all the candles to light and looked for someone hiding in the corners. But there was nobody but the two of them in the room.

"Nobody visible to the plain eye," she insisted when she told me, "because just a little later I noticed the spirits that were all over the place."

Don Jacinto sang in a whisper and, without lifting his face, he asked her, "Did you get the visitors I sent?" His voice seemed to bounce off the adobe walls. Mamá Lochi responded no. That nobody had visited her.

"Don't be a liar," he responded sharply. "They did get to you. They never fail me." In that moment, Mamá Lochi decided to lower her guard definitively. There was no way to get anything past that man. If she saw his phantasms and intuited his thoughts, surely he could do the same to her. There was no place to hide from his vision, so she took a few steps toward the center of the room and sat down facing him.

"Yes, Don Jacinto. They haven't stopped visiting me. Every night, ever since the lightning hit me."

The shadows projected on the floor gathered around to embrace her, and Mamá Lochi said that was when she felt a deep sense of relief like she couldn't remember feeling in years. And which she received with complete gratitude.

A dizzying dust storm spun around inside her. Where was she. She heard voices, like they were coming from far away—others were speaking in whispers. Sometimes shouting, or a radio: grupera music, the voice of an announcer, the ring of a phone, or the rhythmic pinging of an electronic game. Sometimes, she could hear the rumble of a car passing by. Crackling earth, birds that chirped as they flew past. Every now and then a deep wail crossed through the space, calling out three times, leaving a choppy and metallic echo floating through the air.

A brash voice, belonging to a woman, sounded out near her, then there was a jolt, shaking her. Emilia felt this contact from her beyond, which she tried to return from in vain. The disoriented images visited her like gusts of an unexpected wind: old, broken-down cars, armed men, and crying children ran through those fractured visions.

Between slow blinks, she was able to observe what surrounded her. She saw walls and a roof made of sheet metal, a dirty lightbulb hanging from exposed cables that twisted through holes in the ceiling, metal shelves full of bottles, the filthy mat where she lay, the rags that covered her. She sniffed the air: sweaty bodies, food, strange scents. Maybe alcohol, or medicine.

Between one awakening and another, she dozed. A jumble of images: the mountains of Amatlán, the desert in its soullessness, her Mamá Lochi, pain, Caco, the dryness and cracking of her skin. An endless wandering, without knowing what she was wandering through. She awoke with a start. Maybe she had died. She took some time to convince herself that no, she was alive, even though she didn't know where. The voice of the woman who shook her sometimes, who stuck water and food in her mouth, became more and more clear. Still blinking her eyes open and shut, she made her out. A huge face with small and hostile eyes. Jowls that hung from her chin. Acidic breath, a wild roughness. Hands grabbing, turning and checking her over, sticking a bitter liquid in her mouth. Then, silence. An expectant stillness, bracing for the movement to come and go again at its own relentless impulse.

Bit by bit she remembered: the mesquite tree, the walking, the bird. Then the clouding of the world and her nosedive to the ground. A crumbling into pieces, a detachment from herself until she ended up facedown, embracing the dust. She remembered more: casting aside the bag, the money, the gun.

I sure am stupid, she thought, with that interior voice that was hers, but sounded far away.

That's when she felt the gaze locked on her back and sensed a measured breathing at her side. When she turned she met the wild, dilated pupils of a girl no older than ten years old. They observed each other in silence for a few moments. Farther off, on the other side of that little girl, she intuited other presences submerged in an anxious sleep.

"We need to escape," the girl with the wide eyes told her with a barely audible whisper, sounding like a puppy in a slaughterhouse. "When the fat lady goes away." The sharp voice sounded like it was coming from another world.

"Where are we. What is this place," Emilia asked, turning her head to take a peek around her at a cramped room, which she didn't know to recognize as the inside of a mobile home. A refrigerator in one corner, a narrow table with two folding chairs off to the side, bottles on a nearby shelf. And them, the four girls that occupied the dirty mats, pushed deep into a corner of the trailer.

"Spit out the bitter stuff. She's coming. Go to sleep." And the girl closed her eyes after a shadow of fear passed over them.

Emilia heard the singing coming from a woman's voice. And her skin crawled. Why this fear. *Who is she,* she asked herself, peeking at the door that was opening with a creak. First the obese leg, wrapped in a dark legging, appeared on the step. Then a hand full of rings, one on every finger. Then came the body that barely fit through the narrow door.

When she sensed that the woman's head was turning to look at her, Emilia closed her eyes.

The woman shot them a quick glance and sat at the table at the entrance to the trailer. Emilia half-opened her eyes. She watched the woman take a deck of cards from inside a brass box and then start to play. The radio sounded and she hummed to herself. Sometimes she interrupted herself to stick a fistful of popcorn into her mouth. Emilia saw the woman flip through a magazine, look out the window, smoke, and get up to open the refrigerator and take out a soda. At the slightest hint that she might be seen, Emilia closed her eyes, only to reopen them cautiously. The woman's greasy hair was held back tight against her skull with a clip. Her dark eyes, small and ratlike. Her mouth found no rest: She chewed, hummed, smoked, drank.

Emilia asked herself how she'd arrived there, how long she'd been in that place. She wanted to ask, speak, but a feeling advised her to wait. Wait and watch. She felt lost. In the world. In time. Where was Caco. And sleep overtook her again.

Some men came up to the door, smoked a cigarette, and asked the woman for a beer, which she took out of the refrigerator. They called her Vaca. They talked about shipments, about the arrival and departure of merchandise, about if the girls were ready yet, about the fucking vicious heat. Later, the woman returned to her chair and dozed with measured snores. One of the girls started to complain—she mewled, asked her mother for water. Vaca stood up and came down on the girl with fists, then made her swallow a spoonful of the bitter syrup. A silence returned, only interrupted by the last dregs of a whimper. When it started to get dark, she threw them some pieces of bread. Emilia grabbed hers and scarfed it down. She realized that her hands were tied together with a tight rope.

The woman looked at her with her dark rodent eyes and addressed her in a mix of English and Spanish:

"So you're up now, new girl. . . . You must be hungry, pinche piglet. That's right, todas son little pinches pigs, don't you forget it, because if you do I'll be happy to remind you, comprendes?" And she passed out spoonfuls of the bitter-tasting liquid that all the girls drank without a sound, except for the one who was already in a deep sleep. Emilia held it back in her mouth—she needed to spit it out, the girl beside her had said so, but the lady didn't take her little rat eyes off her.

"Swallow it, new girl. No me chingues." And the liquid passed down her throat all at once. Emilia didn't know half the words she was saying, but she understood enough.

"Hurry up and heal up, piggies, so you can get the hell out of here already," the woman spat. "And you, new girl: You're one of the lucky ones. Tienes suerte, you hear me? So get yourself together, so you can go have a good time with the jefe y no me chingues ya."

Emilia tasted the bitter remains still on her tongue and felt nauseated. She wanted to vomit. Where was she going, she asked herself from within an echo of unsettling thoughts. But then something happened after a little while—the dizziness of the world turning over and not knowing which way was up again. She looked at the fat body seated in the chair. Black butterflies with huge wings came in through the window, and she saw their faces: Sharp fangs came out of their little mouths and dove into the woman's body, but she gave no sign of a disturbance.

I hope they really come, she managed to think before sleeping.

When she woke, she tried to sit up, but her body was a heap of cement. Vaca wasn't there.

"What's up with me," she heard herself say.

The girls slept like her. She shook the one next to her.

"What is this, where are we?"

The girl's pupils shook. She didn't know.

"What's going on with you . . . why are you looking at me like that?"

"It's that stuff they give us. Spit it out: It's a drug." With effort, the girl lifted a corner of the filthy mat and stuck her finger into her mouth. A green liquid came out from inside her. Emilia tried to do the same, but she didn't have much in her stomach. She looked over the rest of the girls—one of them, the smallest, was drooling from her open mouth. Her bewildered eyes were wide-open. The other was sleeping deeply. And there was that headache of hers, like something grinding in her skull.

"We need to escape," the one at her side finally babbled.

"But she's watchin' us."

The one beside her chewed at the ties around her hands. It would be difficult to get out of them.

"She leaves a lot."

And in just a little bit the dizziness came back to Emilia, setting off her equilibrium and pushing her into a heavy sleep.

There were drifting voices outside, shouts, like someone giving orders. At intervals, others, incomprehensible: no louder than whispers. Then the disconsolate begging, painful wails that seemed to come from far away. Emilia opened her eyes again, she felt goose bumps from the pure hopelessness of the situation. There was nothing good there, nobody who would care if she lived or died. The girl next to her dozed again, her mouth open. Emilia wanted to stand up to look out, but she was pulled down by an exhaustion, a sluggish fatigue that didn't allow her to move, and besides . . . those ropes. Not only on her hands, but her feet were also tied together. The ropes hurt her. She was overcome by a who-knows-what: a desire to kick, to cry out, to take off running.

She needed to get out, to find a way.

"Caco . . . where are you?" She felt the squeeze of her throat, the nausea, the desire to let herself break into tears and hide in some place that nobody would ever find her.

Calandria, a woman has to be brave. Find some way, you'll know.

"If I just knew, mamita."

Mamá Lochi's voice rang out right from her insides. Crying wasn't worth it. What for. Better to figure out what to do.

The girl next to her opened her eyes again. "Who are you talking to."

Emilia just looked at her and then said, "I'll try to untie your ropes, and then you get mine."

And she scooted her body closer, to see if they could— but that unraveling exhaustion. That dizziness. The vomit threatening to rise up. Her body felt heavy. Her head spun and images came like she had a screen before her. She curled up again on the busted mat and couldn't resist that sleep that pulled her into a dark abyss. There she lay, with nothing to hold onto. It was a while before she woke up, startled, to realize with worry that the other girls weren't beside her anymore. When could they have taken them?

From the trailer's half-open door came the fat woman's voice, speaking to someone else: "Las girls que vivieron van pa'l boss, but this fuckin' pendeja still needs time pa componerse. I'm gettin' her ready. Uno o dos días, le calculo. She's real cute. She doesn't even have hair down there yet. Ya sabes los tastes del jefe, that's just how he likes 'em. La girl tiene suerte."

"Ah, how about that jefe. He could open a kindergarten

with all those pinche niñas."

And they laughed so hard they shook.

"But don't give them so much of that pinche chingadera, you're damagin' the merchandise, you already killed dos o tres, Vaquita."

"Les voy a dar whatever the fuck I want, Taquero. No me chingues."

There was a silence. Then, faraway whistles. In the distance, a ranchera song played.

"You'll see. I'm gonna give him this one lookin' like a pinche reina." Another silence. "I wannna get rid of her quick 'cause me dicen que vienen more," Vaca's voice broke in again. "That set's goin' to the guys in California."

"Eso dicen."

"Pero tengo un bad feeling, Taquerito. You know how they already caught Chivo's shipment. Espero que a estos cabrones no les de cold feet. If they get scared and rat us out, nos sacan de aquí a puro plomazo."

A loss of hope, a hatred like Emilia couldn't remember ever feeling before, chewed at her from inside. She thought of Goyo, of Mamá Lochi, of her house, of what she had been, and she started to cry. Very softly. Quietly. So they couldn't hear her. And she ended up falling back asleep, without wanting to, into that grief that pushed her to get lost in her visions. The world came and went in her mind, distorting, sinking into bottomless holes, falling until she woke with a start. Then she'd feel the abyss again: *This is really happening and there's no dream that will free you.*

Over a couple days she received the food that Vaca gave her without complaints. She gave her bread, but also rice and even some pieces of meat. She stopped giving her the nauseating syrup and helped her stand up to use the toilet. She rubbed cream into her body, she cut her fingernails, her hair. Emilia started feeling better and, on the third day, dared to ask: "Where are you going to take me?"

Vaca hooked her rat eyes on the girl's fearful eyes. Then she was off her chair and beating her in a second, lashing her on the head with a stick and pulling at her hair, grabbing her by the neck. "¡Cállate! Here, you only talk if I give you permission. Comprendes, fucking pendeja? If you open your trap without me telling you to, I'll fucking kill you y me vale madre el pinche jefe y sus fucking tastes." Vaca strangled her, pressing into her neck with force. "Got it?" hissed the woman, before she threw her harshly onto the cot.

Emilia swallowed her wail. Then she squeezed her eyes shut and wished with all her might that an army of fanged butterflies would swarm the fat woman and eat her up entirely. What a nice banquet they would have. The only problem was that all of them would die from the fucking indigestion.

The ravine, with its carpet of little pebbles, forced Gregorio Ventura to lift his feet as he walked, as they tended to lightly sink down every step. The moon emerged from its refuge of clouds embedded in a pale sky, drawing lines over the mountains and illuminating his way. For several hours now his hip and foot had been torturing him, and he decided to stop. On the way he had eaten half a can of beans, used up his reserve of water, and stopped a couple times to doze off.

Hours before, he'd reached the shade of the mesquite tree his sister had pointed out to him with the little towers of rocks she'd left along the way. But he was caught off guard when he got there to find a hundred-dollar bill under a pair of rocks, with the words in Emilia's own handwriting:

To the split in the mountains.

"Órale, Calandria. Where the fuck did you get this, we were all out of cash." He looked at both sides of the bill and saved it in his pocket.

He followed her trail for several hours, headed for the split in the mountains. As the night came in, he thought he heard a boom—a firework or a gunshot from far away. The full moon allowed him to keep following the signs she'd left here and there. He kept going and it wasn't long before he came across the bag. Illuminating the inside with the lighter, he pulled out the cash without counting it. He looked around. Whose could it be? He smelled the marijuana and chewed a pinch of it. He looked around again. Except for the cold darkness and the silhouettes illuminated by the moonlight, nothing moved around him. Just his growing thirst and that loneliness, all his own. He remembered the men who had killed Vaquero—they were looking for money.

"Fuckin' Calandria, you jacked their cash." He laughed. And then that discomfort in his soul swooped in real quick. Emilia. Where was she? The sudden fear: What could have happened to her to make her drop this bag of cash in the middle of her journey.

He found the cigarettes, then lit one. On the second drag he coughed. He never smoked and it didn't even taste good. But it calmed his nerves, and he kept walking. A few steps ahead, he noticed something shining under the moon: the other sneaker. And a little farther than that, a gun. It was loaded and smelled of gunpowder.

"This was the boom from a while ago."

He sniffed it. Many hands had come into contact with it. He saved it in the back pocket of his pants. He tossed the sneaker into his backpack, with the other one. He shone the lighter over the ground. Tire marks.

"They took her." He kept sniffing at the ridges the tires had left on the dirt, but it was difficult even with the moon and the lighter. His sister's signals were gone—he looked for the little towers, the sticks stacked on top of each other to point out a particular direction. He didn't find a single one.

"Ay, Calandrita. That car took you. They better not be some fuckin' sons of bitches, that's all I can hope," he heard himself say, his nerves tying up his intestines.

Later, when he was in the ravine, his feet sinking into the pebbles, he lost sight of the car's tracks. There was no way for it to leave a mark there. He pressed forward, toward the mountains that soon divided, and went deeper into the ravine between them. At some point, he looked up: a slight slope, then a curve—beyond that, the heart of the mountains.

His skin told him that Emilia was alive.

He looked back: the immense desert. He continued for a while, and when he couldn't anymore he allowed himself to doze off. Then he felt her close to him again and that calmed him.

When they played hide and seek in Amatlán, no matter how lost and distant they were, they always found each other. All it took was for Emilia to tightly grasp a rock, a tree trunk, a fistful of dirt on the path. Just touching them with some oomph, giving them a lick, or spitting out a little bit of saliva, and that was all it took. The things would be impregnated with her, and it was enough for him to know that she'd passed through there. A code of rocks and branches. Of aromas and the tiny invisible bits that a body leaves behind as it moves forward. It worked backward, too. Gregorio would leave her piled towers of pebbles on both sides of the trail, indicating a direction. Sometimes they used branches from jocote or guava trees. Or, farther up on the mountain peaks, oak leaves that they pulled from the trees and stuck into the ground, like uncertain sprouts. They'd run into each other's clues—with their silence, those things spoke to them, playful accomplices to their games. Mamá Lochi would always say that they were united by their secret matters, invisible ties.

And in the middle of the desert, his heart wrenched, something told Gregorio Ventura that she was nearby.

"I'm gonna find you, even if it's that very last thing I do in this fucking bullshit life."

Since before the afternoon, the hare had kept him company. It appeared suddenly, with its unmistakable *tic, tac, tac*. Then it distracted him, jumping, disappearing into the dust and the sun's glare. He was overcome by the desire to hunt it again. The desire to suck the juicy meat off its bones. He'd take off its skin covered in soft hair to give it to Emilia. So that it would bring her luck and nothing bad would happen to her ever again. He wasn't going to use the gun. He didn't want to alert anyone—better to arm himself with fist-size rocks. Well-trained when it came to target practice, he trusted himself to find the right moment to get close enough to look in its eyes, lightly lift the rock and throw the projectile that would knock it down. One good throw would do it. He came within few steps of the hare, threw the rock and hit the bull's-eye. The animal yelped and jumped before disappearing from view. Gregorio didn't see it again and, when the night came, he felt sorry. He missed it, like there had been a link between them. Its absence made his loneliness grow wider.

Sitting on the rocks illuminated by the moonlight, the young man took the rest of the snake meat from his backpack and devoured it hungrily, forgetting his resolution to save it for his sister.

He didn't even want to think about her fate. Maybe she was hungry. Thirsty. There was only a can and a half of beans left. He'd save as much as possible for her. As he ate, he was attacked again by that thought: What if those talks with Emilia in his dreams, that feeling he had that she was nearby, were just stories he was telling himself. It was more likely that somebody had stolen her, or that those death-gobblers were eating her. He hated himself for having those thoughts. Feeling her presence nearby meant that she was alive. Maybe the badmouthing snake he was eating was getting its revenge by invading him with those ideas. He spit out the bite he had between his teeth. What the fuck were they thinking when they decided to leave their town and go look for their father, their uncles, all so detached from them. An intense rage squeezed his insides, and he wanted to turn back the hours. But even more rage engulfed him when he felt that if he didn't find Emilia, soon enough he himself would want to be dead.

"Hell fucking no. I'd rather die than die. . . ." He laughed at his unintended humor. "Fuckin' blabbermouth snake. Just making me say stupid shit."

He opened the bag and took out bundles of money.

"What a fuckton of cash."

Nobody let go of this much money just like that. They must be looking for it. And he turned over that idea, trying to imagine if it was really Emilia who'd carried it. Or someone else. And if it was her, why had she let go of it? He sniffed it and had the impression that Emilia's hands had dug around inside there. He decided to stop thinking about that. He wasn't going to get very far.

He spit again to get rid of the remains of the snake meat and half-closed his eyelids: Emilia appeared to him, floating over the mountains, beside the moon. Her hair was down. Her body, slim, light, did somersaults in the air. A lively, penetrating luminosity sprouted from her dark and lively eyes, uneasy and restless, like a river in a storm. A bird's caw shook him from his dream state. When he lifted his head, he saw a large bird flying over the ravine that disappeared into the split between two mountains.

"If I only had wings. Life's a bitch."

He set off walking again on the small boulders that shifted under his steps, when the familiar *tic, tac, tac* made him lift his head. There was the hare: the white pelt shining in the moonlight. *It could be a different one*, he thought, but it was the same as before. He was sure. He stopped. He didn't want to scare it away. He could beg it not to go, to not leave him alone, to keep him company on that absurd journey that was leading him to nowhere. He watched it duck its head under a bunch of bushes on the edge of a ridge, and chew on the grass.

"Forgive me. Don't go," his voice called out, and he was surprised to see it take in his words. He started to walk toward the hare, but it kept a distance between them with its repeated leaps. This time Goyo gave in to the work of pursuing her without giving any thought to where he was going. He came out of the ravine to climb through the crags, following the white and gleaming mass that slipped just a few meters ahead of him, stopping every now and then to chew at the few bushes on the way. Hoping to not end up without his companion, he followed it in its climb up the mountain. He saw it vanish and then return to view more than once, until finally it disappeared definitively into what seemed like a cave on the mountain peak. Goyo approached it cautiously, looking into the hole's dark for the unmistakable shine of the hare, without finding the smallest hint of it. He faced a dark void of uncertain depth, about a meter and a half tall and wide enough for him to fit through.

When he looked back the way he'd come, he saw the ravine with its white pebbles. Beyond it, only the soulless desert.

He had climbed up enough to have an overview of his surroundings, but he would need to wait for sunlight to continue the search for his sister. He felt around for a space to pass the hours that separated him from the dawn. He wrapped himself in the rags he was carrying that had protected him from the icy night, and he curled up as best he could in that hard and rocky spot, until he slipped over the cliffs of his own sleep.

He was shaken from a nightmare by another caw of a bird flying overhead. In his dreams, he had seen Emilia being devoured by the vultures—dozens of scavengers surrounding her body, tearing her flesh with their hooked beaks. Through a dense fog, he'd tried to get closer, to stop them from devouring her, but the birds pecked at him, while even more touched down on the ground until they created a somber and uncrossable river. Once he was awake, he shook his head to get rid of the fatigue of the bad dream.

"Fuck me. No, that's not going to happen," he said to himself and looked up to the sky.

The moon hung low. It wasn't long until morning, and he shivered.

With the spreading of the dawn's light, Gregorio thought of continuing forward and peeked into the hole where the hare had disappeared. Nothing was moving in that landscape of slopes.

"Where does this fuckin' hole lead?" He heard his voice sink into the concavity, like the morning light sunk into the earth. He looked in his backpack for the lighter and went into the cave, lighting it up at intervals. The cavern widened like his steps were activating some secret mechanism. He barely needed to crouch over now to keep going forward. It was a tunnel. Maybe it would lead him right to hell itself.

"Don't be a wimp," he told himself, and the echo of his voice traveled until it was lost in that dense darkness.

The room Don Jacinto Estrella lived in was a place with dirt floors and adobe walls, with a fireplace in the middle and a palm mat alongside the only window, which looked out onto the river. In a corner he had a table where he put his instruments, and farther away there was another palm mat where his curados could lie while he treated them, and a chair that he never used. He placed the clay pots where he prepared his concoctions on the hot plate with two wide burners. The utensils and pots looked like they were always waiting for the moment they'd be put to work. There, he cooked powerful substances, my abuela insisted on reminding me, with ingredients nobody could imagine.

The morning that she decided to visit him, my father hadn't even been in this world for five days. But Mamá Lochi was already more than convinced. She wouldn't be able to bear it if he also jumped over the old stone wall, all because of her. That morning, a dense haze wandered calmly through the roads. A rainstorm had fallen the night before and the day began with sprinkles. The clouds lowered and covered the mountain in pieces, leaving only their peaks visible like floating islands. Then those same clouds went on lowering, and soon the density of the fog didn't allow for anyone to see more than ten steps ahead, and the town's roads were now of some other world.

Don Jacinto was sitting on the palm mat. When the dark room lit up with candles as soon as Mamá Lochi placed a single foot inside, she knew why the witch doctor had insisted with such vehemence for all those years. He wasn't the only one who wanted her to take up the instruments: The presences that filled that dirt room exhaled a celebratory energy when they sensed her near. Mamá Lochi said that she understood later that she was going to be a bridge, a union, a link between this world and the others.

When she confessed to Don Jacinto that she had received the messengers he'd sent her to her dreams throughout all those years, the shadows swarmed around her, hugging her, whispering airy words into her ear, encouraging her to give herself over.

"And there was that look in Don Jacinto's eyes. It was like when you stand on the edge of the cliff, ready to launch forward and fly, sure that nothing bad will happen to you."

She told him about her dreams, and he listened in silence. She felt like he knew her. And she even thought, *What am I tellin' him this for, he probably knows it already.*

They spent two or three hours like that. Her chichis, full of milk, started to ache, and she felt like her son was hungry.

"Go feed him, Eloísa, and come back," he told her.

He knew it all. He sensed it all.

Mamá Lochi told me how she ran home. She felt light from having been able to share the dreams she had never before been able to tell anyone. She felt truly grateful, full of affection for that man who had been so scary a few days before.

At the door to the house, her Güero was waiting with my father in his arms and crying as hard as his lungs could let him. Baby Emilio latched onto her chichi like a little calf and sucked until he fell asleep.

"I'll come back in a bit," she told my abuelo. "It'll be a while." He just looked at her suspiciously because he didn't really understand what she was up to. Güero was different from the other men in town who didn't let their women out on their own. He knew about her strangeness. About what tortured her. And with their son in his arms, he kept watching her as she went farther down the way.

Don Jacinto hadn't moved from where she'd left him. The candlelight waved over the adobe walls and the shadows danced like they were at a party. He sang quietly, like he didn't want them to hear him. He told her to take off her clothes and put on a loose robe that he handed her. My abuela stayed there, standing still. How was she going to get undressed like that, right in front of him. But he turned, lit his reed pipe, and held his gaze looking out the window.

"There, Don Jacinto."

He turned around calmly without setting an eye on her and went straight to the table. On it were three unlit candles, a clay basin with copal, a drum, a palm leaf, a seed necklace, a crucifix, a knife in a leather sheath, a blanket embroidered with wool yarn in various colors that covered an object she couldn't see, and a bowl filled with roots and fungus. Don Jacinto gave her a bitter tea to drink and then lit the copal. He sat down to sing and wait.

"The light interrupted the shadows," Mamá Lochi recalled, "the shadows the light, and the lights and shadows came into me through my pores until a song sprouted from my chest, in that tongue I spoke without knowing."

And there they were. Don Jacinto played the drum, and he himself sang until their voices floated through the smoke and the darkness sprinkled with the pallid evening. Between his intonations, Mamá Lochi heard the trill of a bird that at first she thought was circling around outside. But soon she realized that wasn't it. Don Jacinto stood before the table and pulled the blanket off a cage where he kept a calandria with a white chest. Without disturbing the bird, he took it out of the cage, whispering some words to it. And he put it in my abuela's hands.

It stayed there until he took it from her hands, placed it feet-up on the table and opened its chest with the knife. A river of blood flowed from its front. My abuela told me she was surprised that not even a small chirp had come out from inside it. With his thick fingers, he pulled out a tiny, red, still-warm heart and gave it to my Mamá Lochi to eat.

"He didn't tell me to do it, Emilia. But just as sure as I am that my name is Eloísa, I was sure I had to eat it right there and then. I didn't even feel a little grossed out. It's what had to happen, and that's it."

When she swallowed, one of those deep trembles shook her. She says that even her hair was shaking. The room was spinning, and she thought her body was going to explode. When she wanted to scream, only a trill poured out of her throat, just like the bird's, and no matter how much she tried to say something, there were no longer any words for her to grab onto. The room grew. The ceiling, the floor, the walls were far away. Everything was immense.

"After that I started to fly, Emilia. Just what it sounds like. I was a bird, and I was whizzin' around in circles, bumpin' myself against the walls, because I really wanted to get out of there, to get lost in the air. I stayed like that for a while, until I was out of energy, because I just couldn't find my way out. It was Don Jacinto's loud laughter that brought me back. But he was made of smoke and laughed with his big ol' mouth wide open. When I looked, I realized he had a river running inside. Really. I'm not lyin' to you. That was my way out and I flew to his mouth and crossed over. When I looked around again, I was flyin' through the country, between trees, mountains, and rivers—I flew over all of it, feelin' a huge sense of freedom, a happiness that I'd never felt before and I've never felt again. A lightning bolt flashed over the horizon. It was a moment that made me remember who I was. I really wasn't me, but the lightning reminded me. I knew that I needed to go home before the storm. I couldn't let the rain get me, much less the lightning. But where to go. I was flying away from the storm clouds that were following me, and at a distance I heard some cacklin'. I thought it must be Don Jacinto, that he hadn't stopped laughin'. I hurried to get there before he got tired and closed his mouth, because if he did, I wouldn't be able to return anymore. I was pushed forward by a force that came from inside me, just like that, without words. In the distance, I finally made out a dark hole. First I thought that it was another storm gettin' close, but then I realized that no, it was the exit. As I got closer, I started to recognize the walls of the house, and I saw myself, sittin', watchin' myself return in my bird body."

The trembling and Don Jacinto's laughter had already

stopped and she felt a prickling throughout her body that wouldn't leave her in peace. Right away she turned to see her hands, the arms that poked out from the hems of the tunic. She saw real clear how, from the small holes in her skin, thousands of larvae wriggled out, tiny worms.

"When I was about shake off that nastiness, I saw that the larvae, as soon as they tasted the air, turned into butterflies. Real quick, the room was full of them. Butterflies with huge wings."

Don Jacinto placed the embroidered tunic that he had used to cover the birdcage over her shoulders, and a seed necklace around her neck. He handed her a palm leaf, a handful of copal, a clay basin to burn it in, and said some words in his language. Then she curled up on the palm mat where she'd been sitting and slept deeply.

She was awoken by the cry of Emilio, her baby. In the darkness she made out Güero, my abuelo, sitting beside her with the chamaco in his arms.

Don Jacinto exited the room with his cane and his sack. From the window they watched him walk away until he disappeared into the mountain. By the time they got back to their house, he still hadn't returned.

The limestone walls bulged in sections and, more than once, when he flicked on the lighter, he saw the light spook the tiny creatures in the concavities. The metal hood on the lighter got hot—the intervals of light grew more distant from each other and soon Gregorio Ventura was left in darkness.

"I better not run into some fuckin' poisonous animal. Or something from another world."

He was tempted to retreat, but when he turned around he saw the complete darkness—not a single beam of the incipient dawn was visible from the way he'd come.

"Might as well keep goin'." And led almost by his intuition alone, careful not to put his hands on the rock where a critter could catch him off guard, he walked for a while before some luminescences shone from below, suggesting an exit.

A powerful light received him at the end of the tunnel, and he covered his eyes before taking a look around. The dawn had arrived. The tunnel was in a deep, wide incision in the middle of the mountain. The neighboring mountains and the continuity of the desert expanded in zigzags framed by tall peaks. He'd imagined that when he emerged from the cavern he would find a city, like those he'd seen in the movies: big buildings, innumerable windows, antennae shining in the sun or a lively and costly electrical illumination that didn't leave a single corner of darkness. He'd imagined finding a grocery store, eating and drinking until he burst. None of that. Just a bunch of rocks, dry and arid. Just unpopulated land, just abandonment. He sat on the edge of that unknown peak to look out on the emptiness.

"Would've been better to die." And he felt a jab of sadness in his chest.

There were inscriptions in the tall walls formed by rocks and dirt: human figures, animals, names.

"Where did I end up." He fixed his gaze on the distance.

A deep, wailing horn cut through the air and rang out three times with a metallic and choppy echo. By the last sound, Goyo was already flat on the ground. He tried to make out something in the distance that would reveal where that sound was coming from. Maybe they were following him—waiting for the moment to trap him, skin him, devour him. Maybe they'd seen him, they were letting each other know, and they would grab him at any moment. His chest pressed onto the earth, he looked out into the distance, crawling along the edge of the ridges. The mountains closed into each other in that landscape, forming a wide extension of curves and twists, making it difficult to see much from the peaks. After a certain point, and as the morning grew over the land, something shone at a distance: a burst of gleaming lights unfolding far away. He tried to figure out what it could be. To the naked eye, and with that uncertain and deceiving stretch of land between the lights and him, he noticed that the gleaming covered a portion of the land right at the base of one of the distant mountains. He guessed they were separated by at least a two-hour walk, though he couldn't be sure. Not a single blade of grass moved around him. Just the heat progressing in contemptuous strides. He made out a route down the mountain and started to walk, trying to avoid the clumps of creosote bushes, the saguaros, the declines of the land and the pebbles that, after a time in the sun, turned invisible, rolling under his sneakers and making him slip. A white bird with wide wings cawed as it flew over him. He saw it take off in the same direction he was going, until it disappeared into the mountains.

"What a weird fuckin' bird."

As he came down the mountain, he noticed a change in the air. As the sun moved up the sky, the mountains created kindly shadows and a light veil lay over the shapes of the world. Suddenly, that haze that had surrounded him for a couple hours cleared up and he discovered that what he'd seen shining from up high was an immense cemetery of scrap metal. Wrecked cars, trains, and buses sparkled under the growing sun in a junkyard in the middle of all that nothing. The enormous lot was surrounded by a tall chain-link fence.

He approached it cautiously. Soon he discovered a man pacing around inside the fence, looking one way and the other, the sounds of his walkie-talkie reaching Goyo's ears. He crouched between two nearby boulders—he would stay there until the man turned the corner and was lost from view. When he thought nobody was around, he took off running, half crouched over, to the chain-link fence and made it to the other side with a jump. He quickly slipped away between two gutted cars whose remains were roasting under the beams of the unrelenting sun.

The junkyard was big enough that it took a while for him to explore it and figure out what kind of people inhabited it. He circled a particular area near the metal fence where at least a half-dozen train cars lay prostrate, like bodies on death's door. He stayed down, chest on the dirt, under the scrap metal that slept as though that was as far as time could reach. A cemetery of metallic remains. So many halted journeys. What were those inconsolable trains doing in the middle of the desert, smack dab at the end of the world, in the middle of a nothing bordering on more nothing—dozens and dozens of them, like the sad remains of extinct animals. The bastard sun slammed against his back after being facedown for so long. He decided to crawl, slowly, silently, to check out more of the surroundings. He felt the threads that connected him to Emilia palpitate. He ran stealthily and ducked under the wheels of a train car when he heard distant shouts. He felt protected and hidden there under the wagon's frame, pressed against the metal supports holding it to the ground. He tucked his backpack and the bag of money into the corner of the car—if he wanted to explore that place, better not to carry all that. Lighter now, he slipped between the cars, aiming to not be seen, and went about checking out the lot. He spotted three pacing men, busily entering and exiting a sheet metal barracks in the middle of the boneyard. There was another one a few meters away and two trailer homes next to that. He saw an enormous woman come out from one of the trailers and walk a few steps to a barrel, from which she extracted a bucket of water.

Goyo wanted to run and throw himself face-first into that

container, but he waited until he was sure that nobody was nearby. Then he made a break for it, shielding himself with the metal cadavers until he reached the barrel and stuck his face in, drinking like a dog until he was satisfied.

"Who's out there?" he heard someone shout from inside the barracks, a few meters away. It was a man's voice, followed by the creak of a door.

Gregorio made a quick getaway to a neighboring trio of jumbled cars, where he hid and spied on the figure that came out of one of the nearby barracks. The man had a gun hanging from one shoulder and walked toward him, his heavy and loud boots bringing up dust with each step, his wide eyes looking from one side to the other. Gregorio felt the sweat run down his forehead. He felt something ice-cold inside him. He closed his eyes. He couldn't concentrate enough to melt into his surroundings and disappear. He was tired. "Concentrate," he murmured to himself. The dirty boots came toward him—he could hear the gun brushing against the man's clothes. There he was, just two steps away, when Goyo heard a car motor and a honk that echoed into the sky.

"Fuck." He heard the guy's hoarse voice coming from a meter away, on the other side of the metal scraps that kept him hidden. "Ya llegaron las new bitches."

The boots went back the way they came, and Goyo took a deep breath.

He watched from a distance. A truck approached from an adjacent road he hadn't seen before. The car stopped in front of the barracks, and he watched a tall white man step down, wearing a sleeveless shirt, military pants, and thick boots. Another man, this one dark-skinned, had just come out of the barracks dressed in jeans, cowboy boots, and a cap.

They exchanged greetings, pounding each other's backs, laughing. Then Goyo noticed the presence of those heads in the back of the truck: women and children, blindfolded and tied up with rope. They unloaded them with shoves, knocks, pistol-whips. They lined them up against the car, and the guard examined them with words that Gregorio couldn't make out. He looked the other way: The enormous woman was coming out of one of the trailers, and Goyo hid inside an old car.

A bitter, turbid feeling settled into the insides, the very heart of Gregorio Ventura. The growing laughter made him look back toward the truck. When he saw that one of the men grabbed a girl from the back, he felt like there was a hole opening under his feet that would swallow him mercilessly. Despite the meters separating them and the glare off the sheet metal and cars, he could tell the chamaca wasn't moving. Her legs hung over the man's shoulder and her small feet encased in colorful sneakers stood out from that distance.

"It's not Emilia," he heard himself say in a relieved whisper. He wanted to run out, to ask them where his sister was. Surely they had her. He could offer them the money he had in the bag under the train—but he thought better of it and restrained himself.

"Calm down," he told himself. "Better to get your bearings first. You need to know your fucking enemy."

The doors to the barracks closed, and he decided to stay huddled inside the car to wait for the arrival of the night. He was hungry, but he didn't want to go back by the train cars to eat the last of his provisions. He tried to keep himself on guard by observing the movements around him. The fat woman returned to the trailer and much later came out and sat in a chair in front of the door. She put down an umbrella and a radio on a metallic table and sat to leaf through a magazine. She went in and out a couple times. Gregorio saw various armed men come and go. He saw them take a woman out of the barracks and beat her. He saw a man use a long tube to make a sound and recognized the metallic wailing that he had heard before, when he was high up the mountain. Immediately, as a response to that call, several men came to the barracks and disappeared into the building. Finally, his exhaustion won out: pressing himself into a corner of the old car, with a hunger and thirst that had no end in sight, he curled up as best he could under the seats and instantly fell into a deep sleep.

When Emilia woke up, Vaca was walking out the door. She made an effort to sit up and slowly considered the ropes tied around her hands—they were twisted into crude knots. She started to chew on them and was working on that when Goyo appeared at the door, sneakily, his finger over his mouth asking for silence. She gazed at her brother like he was an apparition. The sunburned face, cracked lips, bulging yellowed eyes. His hair a rat's nest. And Emilia, all pure bewildered happiness—she wanted to hug him, to jump up, to let her calandria inside sing out its joy.

"Don't make a sound," Goyo whispered into her ear. And then: "I'm going to get you out of here, but you have to do what I tell you." And his eyes, alert, flashed with determination. He set himself to untying the ropes around her feet and hands, continually glancing toward the door.

"She didn't go far, but if we don't manage to get out before she comes back, don't let her see that you're untied. Can you walk?"

Emilia nodded her head as she stood up. Even if her

legs had felt weak the times the woman had yanked her to the bathroom, her yearning to get the hell out of that place brought back her strength.

They could hear Vaca's raucous voice in the distance. The siblings looked at each other.

"I'm gonna distract her," Gregorio whispered. "When you see her leave, you stand up and you run to hide by all the cars—look for the busted-up old trains. They're straight ahead, but far, all the way to the back. We'll meet there," he finished, pointing to a spot in the distance.

Goyo signaled for silence with his hand. The woman's yells announced her approach: "You're a pain in the ass, fucking hijo de la chingada! ¡Te voy a partir tu pinche madre!" There was also the sound of a man's brash laughter in the distance.

The woman would enter the trailer in a minute—Emilia lay down again. Her calandria was banging on her chest now, and she had to shove her mouth into the bend of her arm to quiet it, keeping her scared eyes on her brother who was looking for somewhere to hide.

She saw him hole up between the mini fridge and a piece of furniture alongside it, close to where the woman usually sat. He did everything he could to make himself into a ball, adjusting his limbs, sticking his head between his legs to erase his presence. He hadn't finished erasing himself when Vaca took her labored steps up into the trailer.

The woman threw a distracted glance at the girl, who closed her eyelids just in time. Then she put her legs up on the same chair as always, without noticing the presence of the teenage boy. Her hand went in and out of a bag of popcorn. Then she started to play cards, lit a cigarette, and searched on the portable radio for a station playing music.

A half hour passed before her deep snores resounded. Gregorio slipped toward the door with that feline stealthiness of his, and, before Vaca could see him, he managed to get out and disappear.

The ropes were loose now. She finished untying them, taking advantage of Vaca's nap, though she left them on her wrists to pretend she was still tied up. The woman woke up, stretched, drank a soda, and left the trailer again. Emilia went to look out the window but saw she was already walking back, this time with company: a man with a gun over his shoulder and a cigarette between his lips.

As soon as they got into the trailer, the man uncovered the girl.

"She doesn't look so used up. You know he was pissed when we sent him the last group. He killed 'em just 'cause they weren't how he wanted. We'll see if he likes this one. When will she be ready?"

And he lifted up the shirt she was wearing.

"Stop creeping around, cabrón! Te digo que ahí viene otro delivery, in a little while. You can take whoever you want from that group—party time. But deja de chingar aquí cabrón, it's not yours . . . al boss no le gusta cuando meten los pinches fingers into what's his."

"Cálmate, fucking Vaca. A little touch won't do anythin' to her. Just to warm her up a bit, you won't even notice it."

"Shut up already, pendejo. Get out of here and tell los de repartición que they'll get it tomorrow at the latest. Did they come for the others yet?"

"No, in a bit. Perdimos a una. Who knows when the fuck she disappeared."

"Ah, if you guys aren't fuckin' pendejos. But diles que es

sábado, so they can use the permitted merchandise today."
She looked at the girl like she was a dog that she wanted to
kick but was obligated to care for. "Esta se va tomorrow at
the latest. I want her to go already. . . . I feel like she doesn't
like me. She gives me a bad feeling. And anyway, she goes
separate, 'cause you're takin' her directito al boss.'"

"What'd the kid do to give you a bad feeling, Vaca? No me
digas que you're afraid of a little baby. You're fuckin' kidding,
mi vaquita bonita. If the guys could hear you . . ." said the
man, starting to laugh.

She gave him one of those wide-eyed looks, like she was
afraid. "De veras. She doesn't like me. No sé qué es but stay
here for a minute and you'll see. Actually, get the hell out of
here already." And she snapped her fingers at him. "By the
way, Perra has the other ones. Ve y dile a esa bitch que they
gotta be ready for tomorrow. Got it, pinche hijo de puta?"

The man hurried to leave the trailer, leaving dust in his
wake without a look back.

Emilia half-opened her eyes and saw the woman's back
rising and falling—she had fallen asleep and was snoring
scandalously. The girl felt a dizzying, gnawing hatred. She
wanted to get off the cushion and grind her up with her teeth.
And right then an intense pain like she'd never felt before
swept through her head: a thousand wasps stinging at her
insides, stabbing her brain with such a zeal that she almost
needed to scream. She squeezed her eyes shut and grabbed
her forehead, when the buzzing forced her to open them and
look up.

"Fuck! What's going on?" the woman shouted suddenly.
She was surrounded by a cloud of swarming insects. Small
and dark, they buzzed frantically, diving into the woman's

flesh, her face. She jerked around and waved her hands from side to side trying to get them off her. Emilia stood up. She pressed a hand into the center of her forehead, to see if that would relieve the pain. But the pain was still there and yet, in spite of it, she was overcome by an uncontainable laughter, mixed with the spontaneous trill of her calandria, as she watched the woman trip over one piece of furniture, and another, until she fell on her back, shouting and unable to stop waving her hands around against the swarm that wanted to devour her. After her laughter, Emilia's vision clouded up and those images came before her eyes.

First, she saw Vaca step toward the exit of the trailer and fall down face-first on the steps. Then came a chase between kids, between men, then that wandering in search of Caco, that hiding, and then sitting in a rickety car, half-heartedly moving forward. In the next image, a man appeared at the steering wheel of a truck, looking at her fixedly with his bicolored eyes, one blue and the other brown. Short and straight hair. On his head, a wide-brimmed hat—around his neck, a shining crucifix that covered part of his chest. Beside him there was a woman with long hair, dark and straight, looking at Emilia with incisive eyes framed by her brown and weathered skin. She, too, had a sparkling crucifix hanging over her chest, identical to the man's. The image made way for another: her, with Caco and others, sitting in that same truck, making their way forward, skirting the desert. Suddenly, the flood of images stopped and she saw Vaca come her way, grab her by the hair, and throw her onto the filthy cushion to shake her with fury.

"Fuck you! It was you! ¡Lo sabía! I don't give a fuck about el pinche jefe! I'll kill you, pinche marrana!" And with a shove that nearly burst her head open, she threw her on the mat. "You think it's funny, huh? ¿Quieres ver que te puedo hacer, pinche marrana?" And she went to the kitchen to get a knife, the force of her steps echoing in the trailer.

She stopped short when she heard the scattered bangs on the outside of the mobile home.

"What the fuck . . ." She looked at Emilia with her rat-like eyes lit up with rage. That's when the girl noticed the stings Vaca had all over her face. The insects had eaten her up . . . and Emilia remembered the fanged butterflies her abuela talked about. Mamá Lochi had sent them.

"Thanks, mamita," the girl whispered.

The woman came back and grabbed her by the neck, lifting her with one hand. "What did you say, fucking bitch? Vas a ver, pinche cabrona." And she threw her down onto the mat before walking out the door. More bangs on one part of the trailer and then another—a rain of pebbles was falling on its outer walls.

"Goyo, Goyo," she murmured through her stinging tears and the remains of the pain waving through her head. "I'm getting out of here, now," she said, and she stood up with effort and looked out one of the windows. It was getting late and the sun was falling over the mountains, pieces of metal, strewn-out tires, motors and car parts of all sizes. Outside Vaca was screaming her head off. There was a vacant lot farther away, and Emilia managed to make out two barracks where people went in and out. She looked for a nearby hiding spot, for the first stop on her escape route. She looked for her brother, in case he was close by. And she saw that, on the other side of the wasteland, there was an endless maze of scrap metal. No trace of the trains. A few meters away, Vaca flashed around her flashlight—the daylight was out. Farther away, Emilia could just make out a very small boy, lost among the scraps.

"Who the fuck me está jodiendo? Is it you, pinche Josué?" she heard the woman say, flashing her light. Farther away, Goyo ran to hide between the cars. The fat woman whistled, one, two, three times, without stepping away from the entrance to the trailer.

There was the sound of steps approaching, and men's voices: "It's got to be the pinche baby, the one that escaped. Quién sabe what's his fuckin' problem."

"It's not just one, it's two. Uno chico y uno grande. The big one is a cripple, o algo trae. If you see them, just shoot."

"We don't have a cripple, Vaca, you must have seen wrong."

"I don't see wrong, pendejo. Si te digo que he's a cripple, it means he's a cripple, fucker. Vete a la chingada, güey. Get out of here! Lárguense ya cabrones, you only think about fucking around, that's all you're good for." And after spitting, the woman went back up into the mobile home.

When Emilia heard those steps on the stairs, she hurried to throw herself on the mat, tangle herself up in the ropes and act like she was asleep.

When she entered, Vaca grabbed the knife and walked over to her. "Now you're gonna see what's good, pinche marranita." She brought the blade up to her face first, then shoved her forward and pressed the point to the sole of Emilia's foot. Emilia didn't want to open her eyes, she could hardly contain the cries of her calandria, which were bursting out of her from the fear. The pointed tip started to drive into her heel and soon she felt the pain and the thread of blood running over her skin.

"Nobody will notice it here, fucking marrana. Not the pinche boss, no tiene ojos pa esto." And she buried the tip into the other heel. Emilia tried to break free, but the woman overpowered her easily and she started to laugh as she listened to Emilia chirp and scream.

"Pinche chicken . . . calm down, chingaos, if you don't want me to stick it in your pretty little mug, too. . . ." And she stopped. She threw the knife on the table and pushed Emilia's feet to the side. "Thank your lucky stars that I'm not gonna keep going. Pero te quiero cortar la pinche lengua, and take out your fucking eyes, too, fucking marrana."

Then she sat down and tossed Emilia a rag to clean herself up. She started to sing a romantic song under her breath. One that Emilia had heard on the radio all the time in Amatlán, because her abuela's comadre Tomasa liked it a whole bunch and sang it all the time. And before then, Emilia had also liked it.

I wish the butterflies had taken out your guts, Emilia Ventura thought, her eyes still moist while she soaked up her blood with the dirty rag. And she made a silent promise: If she and Goyo got out of there, she'd never sing that song again. Or any other song that sounded like it, for the rest of her life. And she hated that fucking asshole Vaca with a rage that burned, above all, in her wounded heels.

From the day Mamá Lochi took up the instruments until that day that Jacinto Estrella vanished from the face of the earth, not one day passed without my abuela going to see him, to keep learning his ways of curing people and seeing the world. Every day, at least a dozen people waited at the door to his house, asking to be attended by him and, soon enough, by Mamá Lochi, too, who took no time to make a name for herself as a great healer. Though at the beginning my abuela only assisted him, I think that they plunged into a relationship that she never wanted to talk to me about. People said things about them. My abuelo Güero never objected to his wife spending many hours every day dedicated to working for that man. They said that the witch doctor had enchanted him so that he wouldn't get mad that he was stealing away his wife. Mamá Lochi just laughed. "That's all just talk," she'd say as she burst into laughter. Nobody understood what threads wove together the relationship between her and Don Jacinto Estrella.

"He was a father to me, Emilia. Respectful and wise.

My Güero knew that real, real well, because he saved his life on one occasion, too."

Mamá Lochi would go to find Don Jacinto the necessary herbs for his concoctions, the mushrooms to bring him closer to the spirit of things, the animals whose lives they used for cures. And she cleaned the room where he treated the sick. Jacinto Estrella never tired of telling her that she had a good hand, not only for remedies but also for rubbing the salves they made onto their curaditos. Mamá Lochi said that hours could pass, or days, or even weeks, before he let out a single word, and he spent those lapses looking at the mountain, at the entrance to the forest, smoking his reed pipe or carving a piece of wood with his knife. My abuela didn't know where that man had come from, but she did know where he'd gone. There was some secret pact between them, which she had a hard time sharing even with me, her confessor, her hope that death wouldn't relegate her to oblivion.

Now I know what she wanted me to know. Back then I would just get tangled up in whatever I could bring myself to understand. Now that I'm grown up I know that's why she taught me, that's why she took me along on her journeys up the mountain, that's why she told me her stories and showed me those she couldn't tell me—so that I could give it all a name. But how did she want me to name the mystery if she never stopped telling me that it was best to consider mystery in silence? Or maybe you could sing it if you had a nice voice and a poet's soul. She always said that the mystery is like a fleeting breath, one that leaves a feeling of absence in its wake.

After his disappearance it was said that Jacinto Estrella had been killed by gunfire, by a pissed-off drunk who got revenge on him for not having saved his wife. That they had buried him on the mountain pass in a place that wasn't easy to access. They also said that a lightning bolt had hit him and turned him to dust, as a punishment from the heavens for handling the elements like he was God. Others whispered that the very same spaceship that had dropped him off on Earth had come to take him back to some other world. Mamá Lochi laughed and laughed when she heard those stories. Like she did know. But she kept her cards close to her chest. The only times I didn't see her laugh when people talked about Don Jacinto's disappearance was when they brought up the place they called the Cave of the Voices. She would get very serious. Listening to what was said about that place. About whether he had passed to the other world there. About whether the spirits had taken him. About whether he had entered and couldn't find the way back. About this or that.

"Shut up already. Don't spread gossip about what you don't understand," she protested on those occasions, real angry. Then everyone who was talking would go quiet—an order from my abuela, given in that tone of voice, was like an order spoken in God's own voice. We all wanted Mamá Lochi to talk, to tell us what we intuited she knew, but nothing. Not a single word from those lips. If she didn't get upset, she'd just keep looking and shaking her head, like that was all she could say about the matter. What I realized, ever since I had use of logic, was that in our house they suspected that Jacinto Estrella was alive—that he had, in some sense, retired and that Mamá Lochi would visit him whenever she could.

Who knows what made me feel so comfortable with my abuela that, on one of those occasions that I saw her get ready to go out, I dared to follow her. It was a little bit before my father went to the other side, after she started to tell me all those things she told me about. I felt I had the right to know what nobody else knew. They said that whenever she put Jacinto Estrella's clothes in her sack, she went out to the Cave of Voices, but nobody had ever stumbled upon the place. It was known that it was a long trench that passed between two steep mountains where three white amate trees grew. That it was the way to another world, that only those who knew how to use its force and understood its powers were able to go there and return without getting lost on the way. The stories they told, always in low voices, mentioned the people that had accidentally stumbled upon the Cave, gone in, and been lost forever. Those that found their way out tended to come out crazed, like Chucho, who every once in a while came down the mountain half-naked, barely wrapped up in old rags, with his indecencies out in the open, and talking with animals. But beyond all the claims of this and that and the other, what was repeated most was that it was a tunnel to the beyond.

In the house we suspected that whenever my abuela went off to the mountain without saying, "I'll be back soon," it was because she was going to do something related to Jacinto Estrella. Nobody knew exactly what. It was just mumbled speculation. In those times, she'd retreat into a silence that nobody dared to break. She'd take the curandero's clothes from the wooden box she saved them in and throw them into her bag, capture a snake to keep alive in a jar, and gather food, water, and her instruments. She'd take off without saying a word and woe to anyone who tried to ask her questions or stop her—she rained blows down on anyone who came close to her, like she was possessed by a pissed-off demon.

On the rare occasions that one of her sons or the kids from town dared to follow her despite the blows, it didn't go well for them. She would realize and set some misfortune upon them along the way to teach them a lesson—or she simply disappeared, suddenly, without leaving any trace of where she'd gone.

The morning that I followed Mamá Lochi, I did it from a considerable distance. She didn't turn around to see me a single time. She paused at the point where we had to climb over the roots of the amate trees, but she didn't allow herself even a tiny look back. I was pretty dumb—I didn't suspect that that, in itself, was a sign that she knew I was following her. It took a fair bit of effort for me to climb over those white trunks and roots before we got to the peak, their extensions embracing the world, with the constant risk that I might slip and roll down to the riverbed that ran below. As tall as ten men standing on each other's shoulders, the trees spread their roots through the rocks, clinging to the stone in their desperation. I saw her approach the entrance to the cave, a black and unsettling hole. I stayed on the edge of the mountain slope, barely peeking my head out so she wouldn't see and get pissed at me for following after her and being a chismosa.

"You'll stay right here, Calandria." She didn't even turn to look at me. There she stood, sticking her hand into her sack to take things out from inside it—Jacinto Estrella's clothes, the live snake, a gourd she had filled with water—and then she started to walk toward the hole.

"I'll be back soon."

When she said that to me, I felt my insides turn over.

"But, mamita . . ." I managed in response.

"You heard me, chismosa. I'll be back soon."

I stood there like a stone in a wall. So the gossip was true. But I couldn't even think of asking her about it, because she was already walking in with her copal burning, shaking her gourd of water. When I finished getting up the peak and came closer to the cave, I just barely made out my abuela disappearing. I was inching closer, little by little, when I heard the echo of a bird's wings flapping. It came from inside the cave. The trills and ululations of an owl. It made a racket at the start, but over time it quieted down. I was a step from entering now, but the stories I'd heard about the cave returned to me and I stopped short, feeling a tremble run through me without any compassion.

"Mamita!" I started to scream like I'd lost my mind when I imagined my abuela stuck in a monster's mouth. I felt palpitations in my heart, the calandria that wanted to escape my chest, and between those chirps of fear I kept shouting, "Mamita!"

I was frozen still. I didn't even dare to take a step. I was so convinced that my abuela wasn't going to return that I didn't care about letting my chicken wails free. I looked around. I had never hiked so high. I could barely distinguish the trees on the mountain below. Its paths were no longer visible, much less the town. I was grabbed by that strange feeling that always took me when my abuela invited me to consider the unexpected parts of her world. How could this be, if we had just climbed for about fifteen minutes. It wasn't long enough to make this landscape look as though we were up in the clouds. If Mamá Lochi didn't appear again, how was I going to climb down from there? And what if the monster that just swallowed her up came out soon, and, not satisfied, stuck out its big ugly head with its trap wide open and full of sharp teeth, to swallow me up in one bite, too.

I had just enough time to shut up and wipe away my boogers and tears before Mamá Lochi started to appear in the depths of that blackness. It was little by little, and at the start I didn't even recognize her. Like they'd changed her inside there. She came with her silver hair shining in the sun— loose, which I'd never seen before—and a smile. Behind her, submerged in darkness, I could just make out a brief glow, but before I could look into it better, she had already blocked my view with her body.

"Chamaca chismosa. I told you not to come up here."

"Mamita! It's just that I was worried about you!"

She had Don Jacinto Estrella's white clothes hanging over her shoulder. She looked like she was in another world, and all she said as she hurried to rebraid her hair and shake the leaves and feathers off her clothes was: "Let's go back, chamaca."

Without even flashing a glance my way, she hurried to descend, grabbing onto the roots and branches of the steep mountain. And there I followed, behind her, at my fastest because I didn't want to end up alone on that fearful peak. Of course I couldn't wheedle a single word out of her. A barrier formed between us and it asked for my silence.

When we were close to the house, Mamá Lochi sent me back along another path and warned me not to tell anyone about this visit, because nobody would believe me—better to save it in secret until she died. I managed for a couple days, but then it came out of me and I told Caco. He listened to me quietly, and I watched him furrow his brow and scrunch up his nose. His lips pursed and when I begged him not to tell our abuela or anyone else what I'd told him, he said: "I'm only gonna believe you if you take me there. I bet it's just one of those fairy tales, the kind you like."

I swore and swore to him that it wasn't made up.

"So take me. If you don't, I'll ask Mamá Lochi and see what she has to say."

I begged him not to tell her, and he made me promise that I'd take him.

We took advantage of a day that our abuela went to Santiatepec, while our father was with his friends, to go into the mountain. I always had a good sense for walking along the ridges. I remembered every tree, every ravine, the turns, the rises, the dips. On the climb to the cave I had opened my eyes real wide so I wouldn't forget the way, because I sensed that it was a special occasion and would never happen again. I remembered the first part very well and it didn't take much for me to recognize the route, but when we arrived at a certain altitude, where I was sure the ascent to the cliffs with the amate trees would begin, we only found a small peak filled with maguey and nopal cacti. There was no mountain up above those and no peak that went as high as the altitude that I'd felt that day. That's where I started getting mixed up. We climbed the hill and arrived at another path that I didn't recognize, and then we had to climb down before night caught us. Mamá Lochi saw us arrive, and she just threw us one of those looks that said that she knew everything. We tried a couple more times and every time we ended up at the very same place, until Goyo, sick of it, told me:

"You're a big storyteller, Calandria. I'm not going to say or ask Mamá Lochi anything, but only 'cause I gave you my word. Don't want her to get pissed at you."

It wasn't until weeks after that time I followed her in the climb up to the Cave that, one evening, she told me about the moment that Jacinto Estrella vanished from the world. The words came straight from her hoarse chest.

It was on a morning that she came to his house, just like every day. But nobody opened the door. Mamá Lochi usually arrived before the dawn—before the coming and going of curaditos seeking help began—to start preparing salves, broths, and infusions. As soon as she put one foot inside that day, she knew something was off. For a few weeks she'd been having dreams where he would say goodbye—she saw him surrounded by feathers that had fallen from his body, with an unmoored look in his eyes, like he was lost in another world. He had recently been insisting on reminding her what to do when he wasn't there anymore.

"Well, where are you goin', Don Jacinto," my abuela asked him.

"Well, wherever I need to go," he replied to her, without any further explanations.

That day, as she entered the curandero's house, she saw that his white robe, his sandals, and his handkerchief were on the table, alongside the copal burner, the candlestick, and the vessels where they stored herbs. A very distinct odor floated through the air. My abuela took a while to see the man, naked, huddled into a dark corner, hugging his own body and trembling like a beaten animal. Surrounding him were a bunch of fallen feathers and the sound that came from right inside him made Mamá Lochi realize the gravity of the situation. She helped him lay out on a palm mat, covered him in various blankets, and made him some infusions. She shooed away the people who started knocking early, and spent various days tending to him. But he just wouldn't get better. He didn't say a word. He just looked at her with the eyes of a harmed animal.

"There's some events in life that change you. He was never gonna be himself again, Emilia. Somethin' dark and powerful had beaten him. Who knows what he was gettin' into, but he didn't really come out of it all the way."

One day, Mamá Lochi woke up early to go give him his infusions and something to eat, to rub him with ointments, but she couldn't find him in the house anymore. He had gone without a trace. Even his white clothes and sandals were left behind, forgotten.

Mamá Lochi says that she was inconsolable for the next several months. That her days went in a fog that didn't let her see life. At night, she was accosted by nightmares and she sleeplessly asked herself where Don Jacinto had gone without ever finding an answer. Until the day that a white owl entered through her window, sat itself atop the stove where she was making an atole, and watched her. Mamá Lochi says that's when she knew that Don Jacinto Estrella was somewhere. And that there would be no way to return him to this earth. He didn't take long to appear in her dreams, but if she really wanted to see him, she was going to have to go to find him exactly where he was hiding himself from the world.

Before he found his sister, Gregorio Ventura spent three days and nights slipping through the scrap metal, staying alert so he wouldn't get caught off guard. The men who paced through the junkyard's twists and turns passed by closely. They smelled him at a distance, but he succeeded in disorienting them. In his explorations he found a way into a wrecked car, barely visible under the heaps of junk piled on top of it. He entered through a smashed window, one that only a tiny child could get through, or someone with elasticity like his. Through the peepholes of that hiding spot he watched their movements—the order, the mannerisms, the routines of the junkyard's inhabitants. Once it became night, he managed to get into their food storage and grab some cooked rice, sugar, bread, and water. When he discovered Emilia was alive, his soul came back to his body. By then, a few things were clear to him: The junkyard served as a temporary storage space for merchandise—he had seen a truck arrive full of sacks that they moved into one of the barracks—and that, more than anything, it stored young women and children. The girls who arrived injured or ill they put into the parked trailers separate from the barracks, one a few meters from his own hideout, another farther away. The rest they put to work at various tasks, watching them very closely, before loading them back up on a truck and taking them who knows where. The horn howled out every four hours, announcing shift changes. With the exception of the prisoners, everyone there was armed.

Gregorio looked for his sister, careful not to be seen, sneaking along the barracks' walls when the guards' distraction allowed it. He watched them transfer a group of girls from the mobile home and put them in a truck that disappeared through one of the entrances to the junkyard. He saw a car leave with six women and two kids, and another arrive with more people. Finally, he managed to look into the trailer. There she was, his Calandria—thin, trembling, curled up in a corner like a dog. He waited for another opportunity to make her aware of his presence. It was important to act with caution, and from his hiding spot he could make out every movement.

"Fuck. As sure as my name is Gregorio Ventura, I'm gonna bust us the hell out of here ASAP," he whispered, curled up in his hideout.

He didn't stop looking over and considering the gun he had in his pocket. If it came down to it, he would get his sister out of there by gunfire. The only times in his life he had shot a gun were when he used the old buckshot rifle that his father hunted with. How would it work with a teeny little gun like this—what if it didn't shoot?

At least I'll scare the bastards. And that thought calmed him down.

After he got into the mobile home, untied Emilia, and

succeeded in getting out of there without being caught by the fat woman, he looked for munitions: pebbles, screws, small remains of metal and glass that he saved in his pockets. Whatever he could throw at the trailer to distract the woman, forcing her to come out. He looked around—he needed an angle of attack. And there he stood, vigilant, tense. From outside, he saw a cloud of insects pass by, headed toward the mobile home. Only Emilia could call in an army like that. Suddenly, he was surprised by the furtive passing of a small and evasive figure. He hadn't seen him arrive—it was a small boy, half-naked and very skinny, running around looking for a place to hide. As he passed close by, Goyo saw the signs of a beating on his face and body: a swollen eye, a split lip, bruises here and there. With his good eye, he threw a terrified look at Gregorio. The harsh steps approaching and sweeping gaze of one of the armed men forced Goyo to crouch into his hiding spot, but not before signaling to the boy to go into the tiny hole and stay quiet. Soon, the watchman, whose military boots echoed on the dust, came close to them, making sounds like he was calling for a dog. His soulless features moved with the ferocity of an expert hunter.

"Shh," Goyo whispered to the boy. A few minutes later, he peeked out one of the holes. The man was a good distance away from them now. His head and body bobbed in and out of the scrap metal a few meters from where they were.

"Ven, pinche bebe. I'm not gonna do nothin' to you. C'mon, niñito. Ven."

The man delayed his return to the barracks. He cursed as he poked around.

"Get him, c'mon already!" he ordered the other men to join him in searching. They looked through the nearby junk, poked sticks into the car windows and the gaps inside and under the sheet metal.

"He must be in there somewhere. Ándale . . . hunt's on," one said to another. After half an hour, they abandoned the search.

"What's your name?"

The boy trembled, looking at Gregorio with an indecipherable turbulence. He didn't open his mouth, and they stayed like that for a long while. It was getting late.

"You alone or with your mom?" The responding sob came with such force that Goyo was afraid they'd be heard. "Don't cry. Calm down." And he offered him a piece of bread he had in his pocket. He watched him devour it.

They didn't dare come out of the hiding spot. Gregorio thought they couldn't wait too long. They might take his sister away from there at any moment.

"How good's your aim?" he asked the boy, and showed him the debris he pulled out of his pockets. "Will you help me? And then we'll get out of here." He explained what to do.

An amber light, leaning toward darkness, slid over the scrap metal. Gregorio took advantage of the shadows that dissipated through the corners, nooks, and bends in all the sad scrap to run and duck under the trailer. Over his head, Goyo heard steps, the movements of the woman inside the trailer. He heard her shout, and then the terrified calandria.

"What's goin' on?" He returned to the hiding spot and the little boy: "Go, right now, get out and do what I told you," and he repeated what he had explained. "So my sister can get out of there, you understand? Then hide, I'm going to let her see me, so she follows me."

And they both got out of the smashed car. They waited, crouched beside the mobile home for a couple minutes before the boy threw one, two, three projectiles made of pebbles and screws.

He kept it up until the woman's voice broke out, "Who the fuck me está jodiendo? Is it you, pinche Josué?" he heard the woman say, lighting up her flashlight. And then Goyo left and started to run so she would see him. She came down the steps, shining her light here, there, farther away, even though night hadn't fallen yet. The beam met the silhouette of the boy who ran with agility and disappeared among the scrap.

Rather than go out and look for him, she whistled three times without moving too much. In moments, three armed men arrived to where she was. He heard their steps running to approach, and then their voices: "It's got to be the pinche baby, the one that escaped. Quién sabe what's his fuckin' problem."

"It's not just one, it's two. Uno chico y uno grande. The big one is a cripple, o algo trae. If you see them, just shoot."

"We don't have a cripple, Vaca, you must have seen wrong."

"I don't see wrong, pendejo. Si te digo que he's a cripple, it means he's a cripple, fucker. Vete a la chingada, güey. Get out of here! Lárguense ya, cabrones, you only think about fucking around. That's all you're good for." And after spitting, the woman went back up into the mobile home.

"Fucking hell," Gregorio murmured, tucked away in his hiding spot.

He waited a sensible amount of time for the men to distance themselves and then slipped under the trailer, hiding himself behind a tire. He heard the woman issuing new threats and then heard her sing, like nothing was up.

The sun was rising when he woke up, startled by the sound of a truck—sleep had overpowered him. The boy was at his side and stared at him. He hated himself for letting his exhaustion win out. There were no sounds coming from above. For a few seconds he worried that they had taken her away. But then he heard steps overhead and the fat woman's voice, talking to his sister.

"That fucking hag's never comin' out of there." Movements from the barracks stole his attention—something was happening over there, and he decided to go see what it was.

"I'll be right back. Don't let them see you," he told the boy.

Gregorio Ventura left the hiding spot and ducked through the scrap until he was near the barracks. They were unloading a truckful of women at one of the entrances. They were young and gagged, their hands tied. The early light allowed him to see their wounded faces.

"Review of merchandise!" shouted out the same guard who had been looking for the boy the night before. A smattering of laughter and voices brought about the opening of bottles, the music booming out—a party was starting. Six guards came out of their dens, accompanied by contaminated laughter. They took more women out of the barracks, trembling, frightened, pressed against each other with that fear that set their teeth chattering. Amid gropes, squeezes, and blows, they made them get undressed and walk through the men, who pinched, bit, slapped at the women as they passed. The women were sobbing, pleading, which only worked the guards up more. The men took off their guns and leaned them from one side to the other, without much order, then took their picks.

In the center of the lot: sobs, wails, and gasps for air. A concert to set the skin crawling.

"Fucking sons of bitches." Gregorio Ventura was filled with a fiery rage, disheartened and sudden. His mind a blank, his heart and entire soul entered into an open, dark acceleration. One of the guards was on lookout, watching the discordant chaos in front of him. The cries, the deafening laughter.

Goyo took the gun out of his pocket and crawled out of his hiding spot. He had reviewed the cartridges: five bullets. He had no thoughts, no head at all, just an infuriated body, with that enraged burning climbing, rising and falling, leaving him breathless.

"I'm going to fuck these bastards up, even if it kills me" was all that he managed to say to himself, not considering the consequences or obstacles it might bring.

A few meters from the pileup of violated bodies, just barely hidden by a barrel of junk, he lifted the gun to point it at a guard absorbed in his solitary pleasure, and shot. And then he shot again—two, three, four times—aiming to hit the men but not the women they were shoving themselves onto. The shouting built up, the loss of control, panic, shoving.

"Attack! Attack!" one of the injured screamed. One of the women threw a dead man's body off of her and ran, naked, to grab one of the machine guns. And she shot with a fury without end, until she was out of bullets.

Gregorio Ventura, shaken by the unexpected outburst, took off running through the maze of scrap metal until he reached a hiding place where he stopped to listen to the chaos he had unleashed: gunshots, voices, running.

A bullet hit Vaca's head as she stood at the door of the mobile home. She fell facedown onto the trailer steps without a word.

As she heard the commotion, Emilia pulled herself to her feet with effort—the wounds in her heels ached. She looked out the entrance of the trailer. Her splayed-out guard blocked her path and, without hesitation, she jumped over her, landing in the puddle of blood that was already flowing down the steps. She walked on her toes, to not touch her heels to the ground, and as she left that place she launched a heavy mouthful of spit onto Vaca's open-mouthed face.

"I hope you're real dead," she told her before slipping away into the maze of tin.

Goyo poked his head out of his hiding spot. A man passed close by, gushing blood, running to the edges of the wasteland. In the distance he saw the inert mass of the watchwoman. That was when he caught sight of his sister, disoriented, looking side to side, searching for somewhere to hide. She was walking strangely. He saw her crawl into some old junk just a few steps from where he was.

Gregorio was about to call to her when he heard the order, "Stop! ¡Alto! Fucking bitch!" It came from one of the guards, a guy with an unkempt beard, tall as a mountain. Goyo didn't remember seeing him before. Maybe he had, at the entrance. He looked at the mid-calf boots, the pants tucked into them. He was in a T-shirt. One of his arms was bleeding and he pointed his gun at Emilia.

She stopped. And her calandria trill broke out.

"¡Cállate! Or I'll kill you!" the man shouted, and shoved

her to the ground. Pointing the gun at her, he kicked her. Gregorio stood up and without a thought to get in his way, he aimed at the man's back, shot his last bullet, and watched the man's body fall immediately.

"Grab the gun!"

Emilia rushed forward to get the machine gun that was as heavy as a corpse, then took off running with her painful steps through the hallways of the junkyard, headed for the train cars. At her back, continued shouts, distant groans, running feet. Several gunshots still rang out. Emilia and Gregorio Ventura pressed together, well-hidden under the iron of the train where Goyo had stowed away the backpack and bag.

"We'll wait a while and then see what—" The joy of seeing her rose in him, and he hugged his sister. "What's up with your feet? Why are you walkin' so weird?"

Emilia showed him her injuries. "It was the fucking fat lady."

"Fucking hell . . . Well, now she's dead. It's what she gets, fucking asshole. Look at you. You're practically naked." His sister was only wearing an old T-shirt.

He pulled an enormous pair of pants from his backpack, and Emilia put them on, though she had to roll up the legs. She was overjoyed when she saw the pair of sneakers Goyo put before her.

"See, I'm a real badass. Even found your fuckin' shoes."

They laughed. Quietly, covering their mouths. The harder they tried to be quiet the more they wanted to laugh.

A few hours passed, still as a graveyard's stone walls, as they sheltered under the old iron of that broken-down train. At the start, they heard shouts, gunshots, people running, and car motors that continued until they gave way to the uncertain tension of a silence. The evening was falling. They waited until it got dark, first eating from the cans of beans and then curling up against each other for warmth when the cold fell upon them.

It had been dark for a while when Gregorio said, "I'm gonna do a quick look. I'll be back soon."

"I'm going with you."

"No, Calandria. I'll be back soon. We need to go. Gotta figure out how. Really, I'm gonna look for just a second and I'll be back."

"Don't go."

"Nothing's going to happen to me. Plus, I have this." He took out the machine gun they had taken from the guard with the beard. Then he paused, looking at it. "Actually never mind. I'll leave it for you." And he put it in his sister's hands.

"It's super heavy, I don't even know how to use it."

"Just squeeze this"—he pointed to the trigger—"and take everyone out."

"What if they get you?"

In the middle of the traitorous dark, her eyes were opaque marbles.

"I'm not going to leave you, Calandria. Don't be a wimp." He knew that would shut her up. "I promise I'll go real quick and be back. And if any of those assholes comes here, you rain lead and take 'em out. I already told you, do it like this." He explained again how to fire.

He left the gun over her legs and slipped out of the train.

"Count until a half hour. Slow. If I take longer, count another half. And if I don't get back by then, get out of here, grab our stuff and hightail it to the desert. Look for a road and someone to help you."

And Emilia watched the darkness swallow him as she nodded yes, even though she wanted to shout, "No, don't go."

She put the gun on the ground, hugged her jacket, and started to count: *One. Two. Three.* She didn't want to think about anything else, or imagine. She just focused on counting. Every sixty she lifted a finger. When she finished her fingers, she counted memorizing each of her toes.

She'd been going for twenty minutes when she heard a car motor and stopped short with the numbers—just that damn tremble made her teeth chatter. The ground, beneath the trains, lit up as the car approached.

"Uy," she whispered in panic. The calandria started to belt out, and she had to cover her mouth with both hands.

She pressed up against a wheel of the train car and felt up above her head, but she couldn't find a place to hang from so they wouldn't find her. The lights were just a few steps away—the car had stopped close by. Emilia grabbed the gun with difficulty, it was so heavy. And she pointed it. She heard the car door open and closed her eyes, begging Mamá Lochi to make sure that they wouldn't discover her, that nothing bad was happening to Goyo.

"Emilia, come out. It's me!"

Simply hearing his voice, she dropped the weight of the machine gun and let her calandria break free.

"Shh. Don't start with that. Come out!"

And she came out from under the wagon.

"¡Ándale! Hurry up! Throw me the bag and the backpack. C'mon! We need to get out of here!"

She tossed out their things, dragged herself out from under the train car, and got into the car. Her brother climbed into the driver's seat.

"But you don't even know how to drive," she told him. Still, he managed to get them moving forward, even though it was in fits and starts.

Turning around to look, Emilia realized that there were two little kids in the backseat. One of the girls she'd talked to in the trailer and a little boy who looked like five years old, half-naked with a wounded face.

"And these two?"

"He escaped yesterday. She was out there, hidden, too."

"There are more," the girl said.

"But where are the men?" Emilia asked, with a leftover tremble in her voice.

"They're dead all over the place. And I think the rest must have run off, because their cars are gone."

"Just one took off," the girl said. "I saw him. He was injured."

"And all the girls? And the rest of the ladies who were there?" Gregorio interrogated.

"They took off toward the desert . . . in one of the cars. They were all naked." They looked at the junk around them.

"Emilia, if any of those assholes is still alive, you shoot. We're gonna see if there are kids or women who haven't gotten out of here yet."

Emilia lowered her window, lifted the gun with all her strength, and pointed it outside.

The car advanced through the cramped hallways of total abandon. They found the lifeless bodies of several watchmen by the barracks. Vaca's body was still strewn across the entrance to the trailer, a trail of cold flesh hanging over the steps. Emilia felt the urge to spit on her again.

"Stay here. Get at the wheel, Calandria. Hit the gas if anything happens."

There they stayed, waiting, as he disappeared into one of the sheet metal rooms.

It wasn't long before he came back out. He was carrying packages, bags, and a jug of water.

"This'll be useful later," he said, and threw it into the trunk.

They made a few circles. In case there were more kids.

"I don't think there's anybody left." Goyo looked around as the car lurched along.

"Yeah, there are. I saw them," the girl insisted. "They're here somewhere."

They circled through the halls of the enormous labyrinth a couple times. The dark, dry, barren silence bit at their skin. There didn't seem to be a soul around.

"I don't think there's anyone else."

"There's one!" the girl yelled, looking out the window, and she pointed ahead.

There were two feet poking out from under a car. They stopped beside it.

"Come out, let's get out of here," Goyo said, but the boy didn't want to come out—he curled into a ball, trying to tuck in his telltale feet.

"The bad guys are gone. They're dead," the girl informed him from the back seat. A tearful and dirty face looked out from under the rusting tin. Then he stood and got into the car. In a little while they found two more: a boy and a girl, up on the roof of one of the trains.

"Don't be scared," the girl in the car whispered to them. "Are there more?" They just lifted their shoulders: Who knows.

"Let's get out of here already. I don't want those fucking assholes to come back."

At the exit to the junkyard, there was a woman splayed out in the middle of the road, cold and naked. They had to get out of the car and move her off the road to not run over her. When they turned her over, Goyo recognized her as the one who had shot all the guards with the machine gun—a bullet had gone right through her brains. Everyone got out of the car. The headlights illuminated her body.

"What a shitshow." They put a shirt over the woman's face before getting back in the car and out of the junkyard.

When they went out, Gregorio turned off the lights. Once they were out on the open land he turned them on again. They bounced over potholes, and every now and then the motor turned off.

"What if they catch up with us, Goyo?"

"Just calm down. They won't catch us. They're already real cold."

"But more will come," one of the kids said. "There's always more."

"If they catch up with us, they'll get what's coming to them," Goyo said, motioning at the machine gun.

As they moved forward, everyone turned around to see the path they'd left behind: the open mouth of a hungry coyote. No light. No shadows. Not a single thing.

We knew that Mamá Lochi wouldn't go back up to the Cave again the day she incinerated the white robe, sandals, and the rest of Jacinto Estrella's belongings. It wasn't much after I'd followed her steps. After that time, I saw her go up at least a couple more times, but she lost me along the way when I tried to keep up.

"Rest in peace, Don Jacinto," I heard her say in the cemetery the day that I went with her to place the ashes of the curandero's belongings. "Now he really is planted deep in the other world." And she was so down in the dumps that not even the sun could brighten her up.

The Day of the Dead was approaching, and I asked her to tell me what to do so I could see the dead, but she didn't even respond. I wanted to see my Mamita Estela, who I hardly remembered anymore. All I had of her was a photo with Caco and me, each of us sitting on one of our mamá's legs. She was real pretty. With her long, dark hair, her small mouth, her white teeth that contrasted with that deep sadness in her eyes. In the photo my brother is crying, with a pout that always makes me laugh. And I'm less than a year old, looking at her like I already knew she was going to leave us soon and I didn't want to lose even a second of her presence. I don't know where we were. I imagine that the photo was taken by one of those photographers who arrive in town on special occasions, along with the festival cars full of mechanic games and the vendors of toys, candies, and bread. I imagine it must have been just before she got sick, or maybe she was already, because she looked sad, downcast, distant.

Just one year after I arrived to this world, my Mamita Estela got sick and entrusted me to my abuela. So Mamá Lochi stepped in as our mother. Obviously, I don't remember any of it. Mamá Lochi told me that as soon as they took me off my mamá's chichi I started to run, like I wanted to go far away, and a few days after that my Mamita Estela got into bed. She could barely get up, just to take a few steps to the toilet on the other side of the backyard. She wouldn't even try the tiny spoonfuls of chicken broth my abuela would bring up to her lips. The incense, the prayers, the herbs, and the meals that Mamá Lochi made to cure her didn't work.

"C'mon, chamaca, eat something. Just look how bony you are," they say Mamá Lochi would repeat over and over again. My mamita would just turn her face, looking out the window, like she wanted to fly away. But yes, silently, she let herself be rubbed with salves and let her body be scrubbed everyday with the treatments Mamá Lochi made from herbs and lard. But not even that, which never failed with the rest of the family, brought back her spirit. Mamá Lochi said that sickness that grabbed my mamita like that, so suddenly, was pure sadness. A sadness deeper than a dry well. One of those that kills whoever it grabs, and there's no incense or salve that works against it.

"I bet that witch Rosina cursed her with a hummingbird. They say she keeps a dried one in her pocket, in a red bag with rosemary, horse shit, and Estelita's hair. And everyone knows that'll fill whoever it's dedicated to with sadness. I bet she paid Norberto to fuck her over, that man only does evil. Fucking cradle-robbing hag," my abuela would say as she waved copal smoke through the house or smudged the room's corners with ocotillo branches.

Speaking of Rosina. She was a widow, older than forty, and she was my father's lover. She was a powerful witch who grabbed onto the young so they would do her evil bidding. But no matter how hard Mamá Lochi worked to weave together defenses against the curses, Rosina found weak threads she could break with a touch. The sorrows that beat down on my Mamita Estela's soul ended up killing her. My brother, Goyo, was really attached to her. He would get under the covers and hug her, crying the whole time. It was like he smelled what was coming. Who would guess that he would become so brave with the years, despite that crooked foot he was born with, which hurt him often but he almost never complained about. Even though I don't remember much about my Mamita Estela, not even her face, I remember Caco's crying when they took him out of the bed where she lay totally dead. Stiff as an adobe. I touched her still-warm body while Mamá Lochi dressed her for the wake, and her black eyes looked at me from the beyond, like they wanted to tell me something. And Goyo cried until our ears hurt. He clung to her body. It was like he wanted our mamita to take him with her. They had to send him out of the room and shut him in the bathroom until he calmed down.

Years later on the Day of the Dead, around the time that Mamá Lochi burned the belongings of Jacinto Estrella, we went to the cemetery to leave our altar of offerings to our departed. On the way home, I told Goyo that we were coming back when night fell, when everyone was sleeping, to spy on the dead. I don't know if I wanted to act like I was brave with my brother or what. Or if I really wanted to see my Mamita Estela.

"All right, Calandria. But you better not back out later, okay?"

When the night was already grown, with everyone nice and asleep, Goyo yanked the covers off me and pulled me out of bed.

"Ándale," he said in my ear. "It's time."

Because it took me a while to open my eyes, he shook me. "Don't be a wimp. Did you chicken out already?"

"No, 'course not. I'm not a wimp, Caco," I whispered as I stood up and stuck my feet in my sandals. On tiptoes, we crossed the room where everyone else was snoring, until we were out on the street. The air glowed with so much moon. The tree's shadows moved with the wind, and I asked myself if they could be the departed, standing just over there. I was holding tight to Goyo, and even though he was pretending to be brave, he was on edge, too. We approached the graveyard's gate. They'd put a lock on it. The two of us trembled like a lizard's tail that had just been chopped off.

"We should probably go back," he said, and who knows

what got into me but I told him no, that if we were already there, we couldn't chicken out. And like a soul led by the devil, I let go of his arm and started to climb the cemetery's stone wall.

Goyo couldn't be shown up. He wasn't going to let his sister, who was three years younger than him, have bigger balls than he did. If he let his fear overpower him and backed out, Armando and Cheque, the neighbors we were always running around with, would never let it go—that right when the moment of truth came and it was time to get real brave, the older one, the boy, had chickened out. So he followed me, and also climbed the stone wall. It was when we were already on the other side that I realized that the calandria in my chest was jumping up and down. The graveyard glowed. The tombs full of flowers were covered in a silver veil, like moondust had rained down on them. I felt really clearly that I had entered the world of the dead. The branches of the jocote trees swayed and they let down a rain of tiny leaves on us that murmured in a strange language. I stood stock-still, thinking that maybe I had started to understand the language of the plants, like my abuela. Standing in a corner, against the stone wall, hardly breathing, I didn't dare to move a finger, much less take a step. Goyo was the same or worse than me. Neither of us dared to say we should to put our sandals to good use and scram—leave the departed in peace so that they would leave us in peace, too.

There was the sound of an owl and the clicking of insects, when, to our shock, we saw a shadow move deep in the graveyard.

"I see one there," I said. And Goyo responded, with a trembling voice:

"Motherfucker. Me too. Now we're really in it. . . ."

Carefully, trying not to make a sound, we ducked down and pressed ourselves low against the shadow of the stone wall.

"What do we do, Caco?" I whispered into his ear.

"What if it's our abuelo Güero?" he told me.

"Or our Mamita Estela, here to give us a hug," I added, both hopeful and scared to death.

Our feet were glued to the earth by our fear. In the distance, the shadow moved through the tombs. It was murmuring and, every now and then, it sang in a dragging voice. The moonlight gleamed. I was so scared I peed myself. I begged dear God that Goyo wouldn't notice. That day he didn't say anything, and he wasn't the type not to say something when he had the opportunity to wind me up, so I thought that I was safe. It was later, much later, when we were walking through the desert, totally lost, that we reminded ourselves of that scary night to lift our spirits. There, he told me that on that night in the graveyard, when everything got scarier with the spirit, he felt a little warm liquid seep into his sandals. He didn't say anything, just to not alert the dead. And he confessed to me, as we walked, all needled and scratched by the creosote and cacti, that that night in the cemetery he begged the blessed Virgencita to make sure the spirit wouldn't see us, wouldn't take us. And he promised her that, no matter what, he'd never tease me about how I had peed my pants that night.

The departed spirit was just a few small steps away from us. We heard his voice, and it got me thinking that there might be more dead spirits around him that were invisible to our eyes. I pulled Goyo to stick our backs against the wall, so that no more of the dead could appear from behind us. The tug made us fall against the stones, and one that was loose rolled to the ground, landing on my brother's foot. Goyo let out a cry and that departed spirit, who we were almost touching at this point, quickly turned toward us while still murmuring. "¡Ay, nanita!" he shouted, his voice coming from the beyond, and then he took off running, truly scared to death. And who knows what got into us that made us run after him, even though Goyo was still complaining about the pain from the rock falling on him. The departed spirit yelled, screamed, and jumped over graves as he went, carrying as much stuff as he could in his arms.

It wasn't until we saw him trip and fall that I started to ask myself why he didn't use his powers from the other world to start flying or disappear like the dead do. We stopped short two steps from him. We heard him say things we couldn't understand. He laughed and sobbed, and I was thinking he was speaking the language of the departed, when Goyo all of a sudden said, "It's not a spook! It's fuckin' Chucho!"

I wouldn't know how to describe how we felt about Chucho. He was a guy who tended to wander through the town. They said that he had lost his mind from going into the Cave of the Voices. When we saw him on the street, a mixture of curiosity, teasing, fear, and laughter possessed us, like a demon. We threw rocks at him so he would chase us, but even with all that, we had some respect for him. Mamá Lochi said that we should be considerate with him. That because of a curse, a malicious spirit had entered him when he was a newborn baby. That he had been born with teeth and saying strange things. That he knew more things about the other world than this one. He would disappear from sight for months and then appear in town asking for food. There was always someone who would give him a taco or offer him a plate of rice and beans. He would sit in the plaza and the dogs would surround him like they felt understood when they were with him. Mamá Lochi said that he, too, understood the language of the animals, though the language of men just entered in one of his ears and came out the other. Just as suddenly as he would appear in town, he would also hole up on the mountain and weeks could pass before he returned, with his filthy rags hanging off his body and his private parts showing. He only covered up when someone, cursing and threatening him, tossed him an old cloth and told him to.

Under the moonlight, that Day of the Dead, Chucho looked like a phantasm. He had thrown a white cloth over himself and he was eating the food we'd left out for the dead. He wouldn't let go of the bottle of aguardiente that Mamá Lochi had left on our abuelo Güero's grave.

"You're real fucked," Goyo said. "Just wait 'til I tell my abuela that you messed with the drink she left our abuelo. You'll really have it comin'," my brother spat at him. I was scared to hear him because I couldn't forget how many times they'd told us it was better not to talk to Chucho, to not even look him in the eyes if we didn't want him to pass his curse on to us.

When he heard Goyo, Chucho got on his knees and started to howl right there, like a coyote. He howled and let out a cackle that gave me goose bumps—if the fear from earlier had gone, his yelling brought it back. We took off running like wildcats, me chirping like a calandria, leaping over the tombs until we jumped over the stone wall and, faster than my memory of the last time we made that journey, arrived at the house.

Mamá Lochi was waiting for us at the door, with a candle in her hand.

"Well where were you, demon chamacos?" Her rough voice announced her anger. I could see her eyes shining in the darkness. "Don't be stupid. You can't be playin' games with the dead."

Some time later, when Goyo and I sat down to rest with the other travelers, before we lost each other, before crossing the line, we were even happy remembering that night. We returned to that day and looked for details that we had forgotten. We laughed until our stomachs hurt and forgot for a bit how lost, how alone we were in that immense desert, so far from our home and our dead.

They had been driving for more than two hours when the car gave out.

"Well, now we're fucked," Gregorio Ventura mumbled, and he turned on the lights to see what they could make out— just wasteland in every direction they turned their sleepless eyes. He tried to start up the engine, lifted up the hood to see if he understood anything in it, poked at it here and there just to see if something worked out. Finally, he got back in the driver's seat, placed his head on the steering wheel, and slept for a while. The others, except Emilia, followed his example and slept, not having the strength to do anything but give in to that other uncertain world.

"C'mon, Caco. Ándale, wake up. I don't want them to find us." Not even a half hour had passed, and Gregorio lifted his head. In the middle of the wild darkness, he looked at his sister like she was a being from another planet:

"We gotta go on foot."

He woke everyone up, and they got out of the car. He put the machine gun and the marijuana in the trunk and put the car keys in his pocket. He split the money between the backpack and the bag. He pulled out the provisions and water and distributed the burden among everyone.

"What if the bad guys come back?" they heard the bruised boy say.

"I thought you were mute," Emilia said.

"I'm not *mute*, I'm Simón Aguilar."

"Well, we can't carry it around everywhere, Simón Aguilar. It'd even be dangerous. What if the police get us . . . we'd be fucked. The handgun is enough. And it's easier to hide." He took it out of his pants to show the boy and then stowed it away again. Though he didn't tell them that it didn't have any bullets. He didn't want to scare them.

Two boys weren't wearing shoes. Goyo took the knife out of his backpack and tore out four pieces of the tire. He tied them around their feet with the rags they had left. They had to tighten them up every now and then because they'd loosen as they walked. After a while, Simón climbed up onto Goyo's back, and Lupita, one of the girls, picked up Emilia's hand and held it so tightly that it made her fingers fall asleep, so she had to keep switching the girl from side to side. The other three went one behind the other, following each other's steps, pressed together like a little trail of ants. The cold cut the air, so they couldn't stay still, and they couldn't do anything with their exhaustion other than leave it to the side.

The lights in the distance were closer by the minute. They came and went, then some time passed and nothing. They couldn't guess how much longer before they arrived who knows where.

The day broke as they came across an untraveled highway surrounded by desert. Here and there the saguaros stood with their twisting limbs, and Emilia, as she considered them, thought that she would never again see any landscape that wasn't this one. She thought of Mamá Lochi, that thankless sadness weighing heavily inside her. How long had it been since she heard her voice. Maybe she'd gotten stuck on the way. Could just be that she really hadn't wanted to cross the line with them. She tried to call her forth—all she heard was a gloomy silence. Then she shut her eyes and tried to remember her face, her hands, her scent of wet earth, of ocotillo, of fresh herbs, of tender corn. Nothing at all. She started to cry out of pure frustration. How could she leave her just like that, without even saying goodbye.

"What's going on, Calandria. What're you cryin' for now."

The sun came out from behind the mountains. The asphalt was freezing. They didn't want to walk any more. Emilia's boogers ran down her face along with her tears, a waterfall without an end in sight. And Simón at her side, hugging her.

"Don't cry," he told her, and she looked into his glossy eye, surrounded by a swollen bruise.

She dried her face with the edge of her shirt.

They took up their forward march again, stepping on the asphalt that the first rays of the morning would soon warm. Emilia's injuries on her feet forced her to walk on her toes. Or to tilt her step so that the wounds wouldn't open. She had wrapped them in some rags that somewhat relieved the pain. The sun, and its heat, rose. Not a soul was near. An hour passed before they saw the silhouette of a car coming toward them from a distance and they ran to hide in a ditch, flat on the ground, heads down. They were terrified by the idea of running into police or anyone from the junkyard who might have been looking for them. They saw a truck pass and it braked right beside them. They didn't want to get out and stayed deep in the ditch.

They heard the motor start up and once it was far away, they stood up. They managed to read the words written on the back of the car: *God helps the travelers.*

"I wish," Gregorio grumbled.

"They saw us," said one of the girls, in a thread of a voice.

And they set off walking, stumbling over the asphalt.

"I'm thirsty," one of the other girls said. Hours had passed since they'd run out of water.

"Hold on. We'll find something real soon," Goyo said, his eyes fixed on the horizon.

After another half hour of walking, Goyo took six little piles of bills out of the bag and handed them out. The kids stared at the money.

"Save it in your clothes. In case we're separated. It'll get you somethin'. Don't tell anyone you have it."

The truck that had stopped earlier was coming back. Goyo stopped, ahead of the group.

"We have to risk it. If we don't, we'll die here."

And there they stood: a line of children, like stones in a wall, one against the other, looking at the car in the distance as it came closer. The front had the same words painted on it: *God helps the travelers.* As it approached, they saw that the man at the steering wheel wore a hat. There was a woman beside him. They had two travelers in the back camper, who hadn't been there, or they hadn't seen earlier. It was clear they were also lost. When it finally stopped, the children no longer had the strength to even be afraid.

The man at the wheel observed them with his bicolored

eyes: blue and brown. On his head, a wide-brimmed hat. Around his neck, a crucifix that covered part of his chest. At his side, a woman, looking at them with incisive eyes framed by her brown and weathered skin.

"I've seen 'em before," Emilia whispered, remembering her visions.

They looked at them for a long time. He bit into a piece of jerky.

Those in the back, a man and a woman, looked worn down—like them, they had crossed.

"Where are you going, kids?" The man with the hat and bicolored eyes had a hoarse voice and spoke his Spanish with a gringo accent. Goyo searched for the answer he didn't have. He looked at his sister and glanced at the two people in the truck's bed.

"We're going to Colorado Springs," Emilia stepped forward, remembering the place where their father lived.

The man was silent. The seconds stretched.

"It's far from here," he finally said in English.

Gregorio and Emilia looked at each other. They hadn't understood.

The man addressed the children in broken Spanish: "Who want work, get in. Work in field. Good pay."

All the kids except the brother, sister, and Simón got into the back of the truck, which pulled forward before they had a chance to say goodbye. And they didn't even have enough time to feel upset about the quick farewell before the car, which had gone forward fewer than fifty meters, returned in reverse.

"Get in," the man said, and he punctuated the foreign words with a gesture, before elaborating in Spanish. "I can take close to bus." Without a beat, the three climbed up.

The sun was dancing high when the truck stopped. Emilia was startled awake by a hand shaking her shoulders. She'd fallen asleep after the woman up front had given them water and a bunch of bananas that they'd devoured in minutes.

"Wake up, Calandria."

"Where is this?" Emilia asked as she stepped out with Goyo and Simón onto a sidewalk. Around them there were buildings, wide roads, and flowing traffic.

"Here are in Tucson, Arizona. Up there," the man at the wheel said in Spanish, and pointed to a building a few steps away, "is bus station. There look for Colorado. Can you pay?"

Gregorio nodded.

"Okay. Inside, telephones. Have number to call?" Goyo nodded. "Put this"—he reached out a hand with coins in it— "and dial. So your people tell what to do." And he threw them a warning look. "Careful with police. Good luck," he finished before kissing the cross on his chest. He, the woman, and the rest of the kids raised their hands to say goodbye as they drove away down a busy avenue.

The three entered an endless maze of hallways, windows, people running side to side.

"And you, what's your deal?" Goyo said, looking at Simón, who appeared to have no intention of leaving them. "You have someone to call? Who's expectin' you?"

From the swelling of his eyes, Simón looked out at him before shrugging. Emilia looked at his bare, dirty, injured feet.

"Let's get him some sandals, at least." Emilia kept her eyes on the floor.

"Wait a second, Calandria, first we should figure out what

we're gonna do with him," Gregorio insisted. "Your mom . . . she's back there?" Goyo crouched down to talk to him more closely. He couldn't remember what the boy had told him in the junkyard.

"I already told you. She's back there . . . she died." He blinked quickly, unceasingly.

The brother and sister looked at each other and felt a shattering inside that no word could get through. Goyo tried to continue. "But you gotta have other family—someone who was waitin' for you on this side?"

Simón lifted his shoulders, then shook his head.

Emilia and Goyo's eyes found each other again.

"Well, fine. We can't just leave you here all alone. Come with us," the older brother said, finally. "What else can we do. Our dad can go fuck himself."

He managed, after several attempts and with the help of a man nearby who spoke Spanish, to get through to his father.

"Well, we're here now, boss," he stammered, a knot building in his throat upon hearing the voice on the other side of the line. Emilia stuck her ear against the speaker that her brother leaned toward her.

"Come over, then. We'll see what we can figure out."

"But we don't know how."

"What do you mean you don't know how—don't be dumb, if you already crossed, it's real easy here. Look for a bus to Colorado Springs. When you get here, call me." And he hung up.

Gregorio and Emilia looked at each other, with that dry sadness of total abandonment. And Emilia thought that her abuela was right: Women bewitched Emilio Ventura, to the point that he forgot his true loves.

"Fuckin' Dad," Goyo said, "I don't even wanna go see him. What if we take off somewhere else, Emilia? We're finally here."

Emilia felt that heartbreak that turned into lead in her chest. Despite that feeling weighing down inside her, she couldn't imagine being so close to her father and not seeing him with her eyes, even just once.

"We should go, Goyo. Even if it's just to see him for a little while. Then later we can look for somewhere to go."

They considered each other in silence for a few seconds.

"Fine, then," the young man said, without any excitement. "I hope we don't regret it later."

"Me too, Caco. Really, me too."

Mamá Lochi said that the best herbs, the purest ones, are found close to the heavens. Although back then, when my father was about to leave, she didn't even talk to me about that. She was lost in depths difficult to reach, even more so to understand. Now I know that she did everything she could so that her son wouldn't go. I saw her prepare salves that she rubbed on his hands or in his hair when he wasn't looking, I saw her add dry herb powders to his coffee or his atole, I saw her beg her saints and the Virgin, light candles, burn incenses. But even with all her efforts to get her chaparro to stay at her side, she couldn't keep my father back.

"Don Jacinto used to tell me: That chamaco is going to make you pay for all your stubbornness, Eloísa." She knew that once he left, she would never see him again. She dreamed it often, but she didn't want to accept it and wanted to believe that she could change that destiny. She knew his fortune, and ours, long before any of us did. The spirits spoke to her in dreams, in low voices and right in her ear.

The morning my father left to the other side, between

darkness and daybreak, I was awake. Like I could smell it coming. Because nobody really came straight out and told us anything about his departure. We heard talk of it, sure, but neither he nor anyone else approached Caco and me to communicate that we weren't going to see him until who knows when. Beno had left already, and a little while later Isidro and his wife, Magda, took off. Finally, he accepted that there was no other choice. Mamá Lochi thought that with the money they'd send back she could build a bigger house so we wouldn't be so cramped up. Some people had built new ones in town, but the majority of them ended up abandoned. Caco and I would sneak in, hide, wander through the empty rooms. I liked the smell of new cement. We used the broken toilets, their handles stolen, and we would tell each other stories about apparitions when night came in.

When my uncle Beno left, it took me like two days to realize he was gone.

"And Beno?" I asked my abuela. She was serving me a mushroom soup and placed it on the table. When she was distracted, she didn't answer. It wasn't until night, when we were drinking an atole by the wood fire, that she told us.

"Well, Beno must be lookin' at the lights up north by now. God willing he arrived safely, because it's been days since I've seen his shadow."

It made me angry that they didn't say anything to us. But that's how they were. And we didn't even notice. Always running up and down the mountain.

A month passed before we had news of Beno. One day, the neighbor who had a phone sent a chamaco as a messenger so that Mamá Lochi would go answer a call. She returned smiling, light as a butterfly. It seemed like someone had taken a sack of logs off her shoulders.

"So Beno hasn't gotten himself job yet, but he arrived safely and my godson took him in. He asked me to send a little help from here so a path can open up for him and he can find work soon. Tomorrow first thing we'll go to the mountain to get herbs, Emilia. I want to send smoke up to my saints. That damn kid will see that I do my part from here too."

Months later, Isidro and Magda decided to go. A day before they left, Magda was real nervous about whether she was going or whether she wouldn't after all. Isidro argued that there was no point in losing the cash they'd already paid, that the rest was already tied up in debt, that why would they do all that for nothing and who knows what else they said to each other. I left them bickering and fell asleep. When I opened my eyes, they were already walking out of town.

That was still about a year before the night my papá came up to my cot to give me a goodbye kiss on the forehead. That's how I knew he was going, because he wasn't one to give me kisses in the middle of the night. He didn't even give me a little word of farewell. I acted like I was asleep, but I can't forget the feeling, a gut punch that climbed into me and stayed stuck there. I wish I had grabbed tight to his neck and held strong so he wouldn't go. I don't know what anger I had inside that made me stay quiet as a skeleton and I let him go, just like that, without saying goodbye.

It was hard for me to get used to my father's absence. There were days that I would sit on the side of the road up the mountain to wait for him, like he was coming back home. That's the path he'd take to come back from working in the field, with his hoe, his burlap sack full of sticks, and his straw hat. With the dogs splayed out beside me, I stared up the path and concentrated on thinking that when the evening fell, I would see him emerge with his long steps. He would take off his hat to dry his brow and wave it above his head to greet me. The dogs would run and jump with joy at seeing him again, and I would run to hug him and convince him to promise me that he'd never go again. Or at least that if he left, he would take me with him.

Goyo, Mamá Lochi, and I got used to being alone. We went to school, helped with chores around the house, looked for lumber and herbs on the mountain and gave the animals food to eat. In the evenings, Mamá Lochi would sit to embroider by the fire and talk to us about everything that came to her memory. About how she met her Güero at the town festival, about when they killed my great-grandfather, about when her Güero stole her away, about how they had hidden for several days until Mamá Goyita got sick. So many stories. It didn't seem to matter to her that we were just chamacos. Mamá Lochi was born to tell stories, and we could spend hours listening to her talk, while she embroidered and embroidered those enormous cloths full of flowers or birds that she never got the chance to use in a celebration.

Now I ask myself how it could have been that I loved my papá so much. How could I miss him like I missed him, if he almost never paid attention to me when he lived with us. I'm not saying that he didn't even look at us, because it wasn't like that. But he was almost always occupied in his things, and who knows what his things were. And then, in his free time, he'd go off to see his compadre Pancho. Or at least that's what he said, because my abuela always looked at him like she didn't believe him:

"You're goin' to see Pancho, huh? And you think I was born yesterday, chaparro? Don't lie to me, Emilio, I know you're going to see that witch. . . . You should hate her, but there you go runnin' off to her. You better watch out, that tricky bitch is real powerful." Mamá Lochi didn't like to argue much, so she would hit the brakes herself when she was on that path—she would turn around and start to do some chore, because there always was one to do.

But, to be honest, whenever my papá decided to play with us, we always had a blast.

"Chamacos, get your sandals and something to dry off with, we're goin' to the river."

Whenever he would announce that, we'd jump up like grasshoppers, and in the blink of an eye, we were already standing next to him, ready to follow him through the mountain and throw ourselves into the puddles that formed during the summer storms. We'd get into the cold water and never grow tired of kicking from one side the other, fishing bottles out of the river and diving in from a boulder tangled into the roots of an amate tree. My father would come into the water and teach us how to float—he told us about how when he was a kid he swam in the same swimming holes. Afterward we would gather the guayabas scattered along the riverbed and eat them while the sun warmed our skin. It wasn't anything fancy, but on days like those, I felt very fortunate that he was my father and he was with me.

After he left and weeks passed without any news from him, I watched my abuela's hair become more white and the lines on her face, which were barely visible before, started to sharpen like they had finally found the opportunity to make themselves seen. Her gaze became opaque, and even though she never stopped embroidering her cloths, after a while she stopped telling us her stories. It was like she preferred to plunge into the solitude of her memories, but without talking about them so that they wouldn't run out.

When the neighbor with the telephone came to tell her that one of her sons was calling, my abuela would take off running and would return in a little while with her chin stuck to her chest, dragging her sandals like it hurt her to walk. "It was Beno," she'd tell us, like that wasn't good news. "He just sent a little money, I have to go get it there at the bank in Pueblo Grande." And she'd do a half turn from us, to hide her sad eyes. Neither Goyo nor I dared to ask any questions, because we knew how much it hurt her to not receive a message from her chaparro. I think we never said anything to her or asked her about it because of the terror it gave us to think that she, the strongest, wisest, and toughest woman in the universe could get swept away from us by tears, a river running downhill—that she could leave us all alone as she drowned in her sadness.

From my father, not a peep. Neither my uncle Beno nor my uncle Isidro nor Magda had news of him. Emilio Ventura had disappeared in a distant land, like a cloud that the wind takes away.

A year passed before we knew anything of him. He lived with Lucrecia in Colorado Springs, and like my abuela always said, that hag had him under a spell. He couldn't even send a message to say "I'm alive," at least, so she could sleep soundly.

He had some affection left for us still, because suddenly he'd remember to send us a little money to keep going.

It sounds bad to say it, but, sometimes, in my rage, I even thought it would be better if he had died. I felt so bad for having those ideas that I would punish myself with no food or water for a full day so that God would forgive me. It was even worse when I found out that I was going to have another brother. I got so angry it was like they had sliced my guts open and filled them with chile and lime. I grumbled to Mamá Lochi about it like I'd never complained before, from daybreak to nightfall. I blamed her for letting him go. I told her that he didn't love us even a little bit, that he had killed my Mamita Estela, that we weren't worth shit to him, and asked why had he brought us into the world if he was going to push us off to the side just like that.

My abuela listened to me complain, looking at me with her sweet, harsh eyes, and she'd say, "Calm down, chamaca, stop sayin' dumb things. That's just how life is. And I'm sure that even with everything going on, my chaparro loves us very much and he'll treat us right soon enough."

I have no idea what Mamá Lochi was thinking when she said that, or if she just said it to calm me down or calm herself down. The fact is that I would end up angry with her and more than once I stormed up the mountain to climb to the highest point, and when I ran out of breath, I would splay out right there on the earth and watch the clouds pass over the branches of the oak trees. On many of those trips I would start to speak with the insects that were near, and when a butterfly came by, I would ask her to do me the favor of letting her sisters up north know that that fucking witch Lucrecia was saying they were ugly, ugly—to make them angry enough to stick their fangs into her and take out her eyes.

That rage in me dissolved with the months. Mamá Lochi never stopped saying that, no matter what, her son was alive and healthy, and that was what mattered. I started to reconcile myself with his absence, to the point that I was happy to speak to him the time he called. Though he didn't say almost anything: "how are you kiddo, what's going on with you. . . ." And that was it.

Another year passed and, around the time I turned twelve, my abuela got sick. From one day to the next I simply noticed that she had shrunk. She didn't have an appetite, and it was difficult for her to get out of bed.

"Your abuela's doin' real bad," Tomasa told me. "I hope God doesn't take her yet."

But she was dimming like a candle. The mere idea sunk me into a sorrow and sent me back to racing through the mountain. Not even that could calm me. How could it be that Mamá Lochi, my dear mamita, was being taken away by Death herself? If God allowed that to happen, I told myself as I climbed the boulders high up on the mountain, I would never again pay attention to anything that guy had to say.

Tomasa came daily to help us for a while. She gave Goyo and me recommendations for how to take care of my abuela, who lay prostrate on the bed, almost unmoving, every day more thin and shrunken. Even the scar that the lightning had left her was shrinking. The little leaves of the reddish fern that crisscrossed her arm sunk in as the days passed.

Back then, a young curandero from Santiatepec would visit us. He had trained with Mamá Lochi and loved her very much. He said he couldn't do more than what he was doing, and she didn't want to go to a clinic. All that pain, gathered in her soul, had come out onto her skin. She couldn't even get words out anymore. Though she kept trying to tell us something whenever the sun was highest in the sky.

"Emilia, gather your strength," she'd repeat, every time more quietly.

One morning when I went to give her her coffee and bread before I went to school, I found her sitting next to the window in her room, where she could see the mountain. The dawn was foggy and cold, you could barely make out the trees growing up the ridges. She was shivering, and I put a blanket over her shoulders. As I came close, I saw her eyes were moist. She turned to me and grabbed one of my arms, softly but firmly. From her lips came that hoarse and serene voice, clear in a way I hadn't heard in weeks.

"Calandria, when I'm gone, you have to go look for my chaparro on the other side. There's nothing for you here and you don't have anything to do."

"But, where are you going, mamita? Don't go. Don't leave us all alone." My voice was like a thin glass, about to break at any moment. Mamá Lochi kept silent, one of those silences with no end in sight.

"Bury me with your abuelo and my little ones. I'll be in good company there" was what she added. It was real clear that she wasn't capable of shouldering any drama from me. After she said it, she went back to the silence with her gaze embedded in who knows what distant lands.

"But, mamita"—I drew up the courage to respond—"you can't leave us. Where are we gonna go. And we're not gonna leave you here all alone."

She returned from the beyond where she was and told

me, with her harsh tenderness:

"Don't you ever forget that you were born right here, Calandria. Your dead are here." And she looked at me intently, not moving a single eyelash, digging into my thoughts. Without taking her eyes off me, she gestured toward her bed.

"Look under the mattress. You need to make it work with what's there so you can go look for my chaparro. Right there I've written down the address where he lives. And the telephone number. And you know the rest, Emilia. You're a brave woman, even though you're still a chamaca. And when you're on the other side, when you think that you lost it all, just remember that you came to the world to tell the story. Your story, my story, the stories of our dead. However many fit in your memory, whoever they are. . . ."

I don't know where she got the breath to tell me all that. Right after she said it, she put her thin, wrinkled arm, decorated with shrunken ferns, around me and, unexpectedly pulled me to her chest. She breathed in deeply, like she had used up all the air she had left. I felt that old knot that every now and then rose in my gut, and to stop myself from crying, I fully breathed in that scent—of ocotillo, herbs, wet earth, like after an intense and liberating rain—that her body always carried.

Emilia noticed that her father didn't try to hide either his happiness or his suffering when he hugged them. Once they arrived in Colorado, he told them what to do over the phone and they agreed to meet at the street corner he said. And the brother and sister waited for him with that unraveling, that tearing feeling inside them.

"Just look at you. Almost didn't recognize you so covered in dirt," he said, glancing them over and pulling them in for another hug.

Their doubts vanquished, they hugged him too—Emilia grabbed onto his waist, pressed herself against his body and shamelessly let free the wails of her calandria.

"Stop it already. Well, who told you to come all on your own like this. As soon as I could, I was gonna send for you."

They stood, silent, wanting to tell him their thoughts.

Don't be a liar, Papá. You'd forgotten all about us. But not a word came out. They didn't want to make him angry.

A fresh breeze blew, and Emilia lifted her gaze and saw the trees with big leaves that were starting to fall because it was the beginning of autumn.

"C'mon, then. We need to walk a bit before we get to the house."

They still felt the rattling of the bus that brought them. Before boarding, they'd gone to the station bathroom to wash themselves off, when they noticed the looks from the surrounding people and a man who spoke Spanish approached them.

"Wash off and fix up your clothes if you don't want the border patrol to get you."

In a bathroom, Gregorio had taken the opportunity to throw the gun in the trash can.

"If they find it, they won't even know whose it is."

The Guatemalan man told them where to go, what to do to get to Colorado. Once they were on the bus, they were alert, nervous—what if the border patrol, the police, any of them captured them without any papers. Luckily, they got to their destination without a single disturbance.

When she saw her father, Emilia felt like the crossing had been a bad dream.

They started to walk, but Emilio Ventura stopped suddenly when he noticed the chamaco clinging to them.

"And what's the deal with this one?" He looked him over from his head, with its bruises and marks, down to his toes. Those plastic sandals that were a bit big on him, and a sweatshirt that reached down below his waist.

"He's with us," Emilia piped up. "He doesn't have anyone."

"What do you mean he doesn't have anyone? That's not possible. Everybody has someone."

Simón linked his hands together and raised his elbows, like he wanted to fly away. It made Goyo feel who-knows-what when he saw how he scrunched up his toes, still filthy, inside his sandals.

"He really doesn't have anyone—he says that they killed his old lady. And his dad, he doesn't even know who he is. And he doesn't have family on this side."

Emilio Ventura's glassy and unwelcoming eyes landed on the little one. He took a deep breath, like he was building up strength.

"How can you think I'm gonna keep him. If I barely have enough to give you two something to eat. Plus, you have two brothers now. And the third is comin'. And to make things worse, I got canned. I don't know when I'll get work again," he said with a thread of shame mixing in with his anger. His head's movement showed that something was fighting him behind his words: "He needs to go back. I'm sure someone is lookin' for him."

"What are you talkin' about, boss. There's nowhere to return him to," Goyo said. "Really, there's nobody. Don't be like that. We've been with him for a while. He doesn't have anyone, Dad. Really."

Simón held on tight to Emilia. A poorly hidden pout broke onto his face. Emilia put an arm over his shoulders. Goyo stood at his side.

"If he goes, so do I." Emilia didn't know where those words had come from.

"We'll go, then," added Goyo.

"Don't stay stupid shit," the father snapped, and he considered them in silence. Who knows what he was thinking. "Let's go, then. We'll see how we manage."

The room in the house they shared with other families was dark—a discolored living room, a big, blaring television, a table, and some chairs gathered here and there. On a wall, a dozen family photos. Emilia noticed that there wasn't a single one of them.

Lucrecia barely nodded her head as a greeting. She just stood there, holding a child, looking at them from the back of a miniscule kitchen. A grimace was stuck on her face—it was like she'd been born with it.

They settled into some chairs. And they spent a while arguing over the destiny of Simón, who appeared to be glued to Emilia's body, like the cold had frozen him there.

"Leave it, Emilio. We'll figure it out." And the four turned to look at Lucrecia.

The father considered her like he was saying: "Now what are you talking about. . . ." And then he looked back at his children and this unknown little chamaco. Finally, he lowered his gaze to observe his own hands, folded together on his lap.

The daylight hardly illuminated the inside of the room. Emilio Ventura switched on the electric light. Goyo placed the bag on the table. Then he looked at his sister.

"Boss, this is for you. So you don't have to worry anymore."

And right there, the teenager half-opened the zipper to make the cash inside visible. The father sat up and the pallor of the dead settled onto his face—more than just money, it seemed like he was looking at a dead man who was speaking to him. Lucrecia and the chamaco she carried looked in, too.

"Well, where did you get this. . . . What did you get yourselves into?" he whispered, and raised his eyes to face his children.

"We found it, Papá."

"I also have some. . . ." Simón piped up, excited, and

pulled out the wad of dollars in his clothes.

Goyo was surprised, he had forgotten that he'd given it out.

"What do you mean you found it—tell me the truth. What are you mixed up in?"

"Really. We're not mixed up in anything, boss. We'll tell you right now, but we're hungry. Are you gonna offer us a taco?"

A suspicious look flitted over the father's face.

"But what did you get yourselves into. . . . Really, you didn't steal this? Or are you getting mixed up with narcos?"

Emilia and her brother looked at each other again.

"What are you sayin', Papá. They're the ones that stole from us," Goyo spoke up first.

The father grabbed the money that Simón held out to him, calculated how much there was in each stack and counted the number of stacks.

"There must be more than fifteen thousand dollars here. Where did you get all this cash?"

"It's ours, Papá, I'm telling you. We found it and there was nobody around to ask. We'll tell you everything in a little while."

An ambulance's siren traveled down the street.

"Okay," Emilio Ventura said at last, when the sound stopped. "We can work with this for a while. We're going to need to find a bigger place so we can all fit. . . ." he conceded, with a content smile that he could no longer hide.

Lucrecia had poured out the contents of the bag after leaving the boy atop the bed. She couldn't stop exclaiming as she took the stacks of bills out to look at them up close: "And they're really real?"

"Yeah, they're really real," Emilia said, feeling an angry stab moving around her insides. Her abuela's words about Lucrecia came to mind, that there was nobody but that woman to blame for the fact that her chaparro wouldn't even give her a little call.

"This will last us. But we need to be smart with it, to get the most we can out of it. And no matter what, you're gonna have to get to work," the father continued, and he considered his children like he had just seen them for the first time.

"You must be hungry. Ándale, Lucre, don't just stand there, offer us some of yesterday's leftovers."

They sat around the table to eat hungrily. To tell about where they'd been. To tell about how Mamá Lochi had gone, always missing her chaparro. Outside, the murmurs of the cars, the voices of the people passing down the street, the chirps of the birds gathering at the top of a nearby tree told them that the sun was falling—for the first time at the beginning of that new life, in that new world.

I can't imagine how Mamá Lochi must have felt when she almost couldn't talk anymore and could only follow us with her eyes from her bed. More than once I sat beside her and tried to guess what she must have been thinking, what she thought of me. I tried to do things the way she would have, if she could have, so that way I could keep a piece of her soul for myself. But she was already far away. She was leaving and there was nothing I could do to stop it.

The morning she died, in the hours between darkness and daybreak, I was laying out on a palm mat by the fireplace, trying to warm myself up a little by the embers. I had fallen asleep squashed under that dull anxiety that awaits everything we don't want to arrive. The calandria inside me shook like it was sensing a storm. *Ven, chamaca*, I heard her voice clearly, calling me, just as I had heard her so many times before. I stood right up and went to see her. The moon filtered through the windows, illuminating the adobe walls. A glow fell over her face. She was sleeping and just barely breathing. Outside, the tops of the jocote trees shone, filled with fruit. Their shadows sketched onto the whitewashed walls like they'd been drawn with charcoal. I don't know what it was exactly that I felt, but it sent me to go wake Goyo, who got up without protest, and the two of us quietly watched her thin, bony figure, her smooth white hair spread over the pillow that she had embroidered herself and filled with cotton from the mountain. Even though I didn't remember what it was like to see someone right before they're about to jump over the old stone wall—I had already seen my Mamita Estela die, but I could barely remember it—I understood very clearly that Mamá Lochi was dying. Her breathing was barely audible, like she no longer had the willpower to pull in air. The light that fell over her face made her bones poke out more, her flesh look prunier. I brought myself up to her chest. I could hear a distant beat, of a heart that's shutting down. I wished she would open her eyes, to give me a final look, a wink, so that I could see whatever she could tell me with those two windows to her soul. But she kept them closed until her last breath, and I had to console myself with the memory of when they were alive, never letting go of their amazement at the world.

No more than five minutes had passed as we stood there by her side, watching her vanquished body, when we heard her final breath. Even in that she was generous: She called for us in a secret whisper to give us her last breath. She warned us that she was leaving, so we could have the time to tell her something or, at least, time to let our hearts beat alongside hers. To press ourselves against her chest, to feel the final embers of warmth that were left in her body.

When the light of daybreak bathed the dirt floor, Caco and I were still at her side, glued to her chest, not fully taking in the idea that she had left us forever.

Beside her I felt a sadness of the sort that can't be put into words. I didn't have the strength to bear that she was gone from me. And I was holding those heavy thoughts, laid out on the mat, when I closed my eyes. Then I saw myself, like I was outside my body, with that pain on my shoulders. And there I was, looking at myself, when I saw a light cloth, like a veil, a membrane, wrapping around me, covering me completely. As it advanced over my skin, I advanced into relaxation until I entered into a deep sleep, and when I emerged from it I was rested and fresh with the strength to face what was coming.

"That happened to me, too. I dreamed that she was wrapping something around me, and it was Mamá Lochi herself. . . ." Caco told me when I went to wake him, and we looked at my abuela's immobile body, resting on the bed.

We buried her next to our abuelo Güero and her two little ones, as she'd asked. If the other world really does exist, well, they'll have been together since then. That idea gave me peace. What worried me most was to think of her alone with a bunch of unknown spirits. But I've never stopped feeling her close by, except for those days after crossing the border, when I'd lost her. Even though I suffered her absence then, I think deep down I knew that she would return sooner or later. And that's what happened: After we found my father and started another life in another world, she came back to manifest in my thoughts. And she let me know that she wasn't going to finish saying goodbye to me until I finished telling this story, which she charged me with sharing so many years ago.

Calandria, when you're real, real far away, don't forget to draw out on paper the story you carry inside: the story of your homeland, of your dead.

At Mamá Lochi's burial, we had visitors from Cerro Gordo, from Ocotitlán, from Pueblo Grande, from Amatlán itself—her curaditos came from all over. A ton of people respected her and came to honor her: They brought candles, flowers, songs, and memories sweetened by the aroma of the copal to keep her company. There was a procession to the graveyard. The curanderas who came to say goodbye to their friend sang their prayers, said words. Once she was buried there wasn't a single person who didn't tell me and Caco to give them a shout if we needed anything. But to be honest the two of us knew that that was just parrot's talk. That even though many people admired our abuela, they'd end up forgetting about us. That now we really were alone in the world. It was my abuela's comadre Tomasa who told our uncles the news. When she told them, she says they started to sob over the phone. That they said they were putting Goyo in charge of making sure nobody came to live in the house. That they were going to tell my papá to come back or to come get us. Weeks passed with no news. My brother and I took care of ourselves as best we could. We made use of the comal and went out for tortillas and beans. We did little jobs here and there to be able to afford a plate of food. Goyo hunted volcano rabbits or turtledoves that we cooked over the fireplace, or we climbed up the mountain to look for mushrooms. We gobbled down grilled grasshoppers when they came in swarms.

It took me a while to remember: Mamá Lochi had hidden away some money. When I searched and found a rusting metal box filled with a bunch of bills, I almost fell back on my butt. There were also documents, the addresses and the phone numbers of my papá and my uncles. There was a photo of her and her Güero at a fair when they were young. And another of my papá with my Mamita Estela, carrying a baby that I didn't know if it was Caco or me myself. The money was much more than I had ever seen at once in my whole life. Fear entered me. What if we got robbed. We took out a bit to buy some food and hid the rest under the partition wall to the kitchen. Better to do that while we figured out what to do, and we decided to keep living on the goodwill of Tomasa, of the others in the town who shared their food with us, of the insects, fungi, herbs, and birds that we found on the mountain. Tomasa insisted almost daily that we come live with her while we waited for my papá to arrive. She herself talked to my uncles more than once, but they stalled—they said that it was real hard, that my papá didn't have work and was tangled up in who-knows-what with Lucrecia. That they were going to save up some money for us so we could get ourselves something to eat.

Neither Caco nor I could bring ourselves to move around much. We went to school one day and didn't go another—we went up the mountain to gather firewood, to hunt whatever animal or to collect plants or fruit. We did the same chores as always, and when we had some time, we sat on the steps at the entrance to the house and threw rocks into the patio or watched how the rain fell as we threw glances up the sidewalk to see if, maybe, just maybe, we'd see our papá walking down it to return to us. We didn't say anything, but I knew that we both were hoping for the same thing. I had already told him about Mamá Lochi's final wish. That we leave. He had his doubts. I, every day that passed, felt that maybe we should pay attention to her and figure out how to go and look for my papá and my uncles. Though that idea, of grabbing my junk and taking off without even knowing where to, wasn't the sort of thing to make me say *get out of my way here I come.* After a few months even comadre Tomasa started to grumble about how our relatives had left us to God's will and how she had to feed us.

One evening as I came down from looking for wood on the mountain, I ran into a guy that I knew connected people with trucks that went to the border. A lot of people had gone with him and they said he offered a safe service. That after the drive north they took charge of putting you in the hands of guys who would help you cross. He was there leaning against a boulder, on the sidewalk back into town, chewing at a piece of straw, I don't know if he was waiting for someone or what. He was older than Caco, four or maybe even six years. Darío. He was known for his scowling face. He never took off a dirty blue hat that said *California* in red lettering with a white dove drawn on the front. I remembered that he owed Mamá Lochi a big favor, and I told myself that it was time for him to pay it. I approached him with my bundle of firewood hanging from my shoulder, not really thinking anything, but knowing what I had to do. I remember that he made a movement with his head, like *what do you want,* continuing to chew that piece of straw between his teeth. I took the rope holding the firewood down off my shoulder and talked to him. I told him that my brother and I wanted to get to the border and cross, and how much would it cost for him to get us on our way. He looked at me like he was sizing me up. He didn't have a good look on his face, and I wondered to myself whether he remembered the favor he owed my abuela and me.

It happened like two years before my uncles and my papá left, one day that Mamá Lochi and I were walking through the mountain looking for herbs. We were walking up a long path and she was telling me who knows what, when suddenly she went silent and stiff, looking fixedly ahead, like when a spirit was speaking with her. I thought that she had seen one of the creatures that appeared to her sometimes, because she put a finger on her lips to ask for silence. I perked my ears up but didn't hear anything. Then, suddenly, I heard a whimper from the ravine. She took a few steps to look over the steep slope that went along the edge of the path and, with a leap, jumped onto the dry leaves that covered the earth below. My abuela was really agile. She didn't seem the age that she was. With her strong legs, with that skin that not even the barbs from the harshest plants on the mountain could break. I was shocked to see her jump, but I followed after her, coming down the slope in slides. When I reached her, she was leaning over a body, half-covered in leaves, like he'd been laid out there for a long while. It was Darío, the very same guy I'd talk to years later. No matter how much my abuela shook him, he only let out a few moans that I could barely hear.

"He's alive," I heard her say, "but his spirit wants to leave him. There's lots of shadows around him."

I prayed to God that he wouldn't kick the bucket. It was best not to get tangled in the troubles of the dead by watching them die.

"Let me see if something stung you, chamaco," I heard my abuela say, like Darío could hear her, and she searched him all over. Then she pulled up his eyelids, brought her ear up to his heart, to his stomach, touched his head all over, opened his mouth, sniffed him, and rolled his pant legs up to his knees.

"This is bad, Calandria," she said, and she hurried to tear up the chamaco's shirt and looked in her sack for some of the herbs she had just gathered. She tied a tough knot at his knee, another low down by his ankle, took out her knife, and opened the skin at the center of the bump that was just below his knee. It oozed enough to make you want to yack. But my abuela didn't stop there: She lowered her undies and urinated on it. Darío, in his unconsciousness, moved his leg like it was hurting him. She lifted her undies back up and waited a bit and then, with another piece of cloth, covered the wound with herbs and started to sing. Then she went quiet and told him:

"Hold on, chamaco, we'll get you out of here soon." She gave him two or three tough presses on the chest, and Darío gulped in a mouthful of air like he hadn't breathed in a while.

Mamá Lochi tossed him over her shoulder and I don't know how she did it, but she managed to get him up the slope and onto the path. Once we were up there, she ordered me to run like lightning to get help. When I came back with a mule and its driver that I'd found on the way, she was coming down the path with the chamaco on her back like a pile of lumber, still unconscious.

As I looked at Darío there in front of me, with his foggy eyes, chewing that piece of straw, I didn't know if he had ever been told that it was Mamá Lochi who had saved him from dying from that coral snake's bite.

"Well, if you have cash, I'll take you to the trucks going to the border," he told me, as he spit out the pieces of straw stuck to his tongue. "In two weeks I'm takin' a group. Ten thousand a head, and you have to give me at least half before we go."

"Ten thousand?" shot out of my mouth. "That's too much!" My blood went to my feet like the earth was sucking it out of me. I didn't know exactly how much money my abuela had left under the mattress, but I knew it wasn't that much. And despite that, something deep inside me lit up and I asked him, straight up, if he remembered the favor that Mamá Lochi had done him when that snake bit him on the mountain. He looked at me intensely, the bastard. His face even changed.

"Your abuela? Don't fucking lie! It was a mule driver and his mule that found me knocked out and brought me down the mountain! What are you talking about, your abuela. Your abuela didn't have anything to do with it, nosy little brat."

So ungrateful! With all that it took us to get him to the path, and my Mamá Lochi, as old as she was, carrying him on her back!

"No," I said, with all the serenity I could manage. "I went to get the mule and the driver. It was my abuela that saved you. If she hadn't found you and done those cures on you, you'd be dead by now. Go ask your papá, he'll tell you. I'll see you later." And pulling the wood back over my shoulder, I headed back home with the hope that the memory would soften his heart.

Goyo didn't take it well that I had talked to Darío. As soon as I opened my mouth to tell him, he got very red, like the blood wanted to come out his nostrils. He started to scold me that I hadn't made good on my word that I wouldn't say anything until we were sure of what we were doing, for not consulting him, that he was older and he was the man, that I had to pay attention to him.

"You're not my boss and you can't tell me what to do and make me ask permission to do whatever I want," I told him. And I turned around, left the house, and took off for the mountain. I wandered for a good while, and when I came back, we still spent another two hours mad at each other, not speaking. At the end of the day, I was the one who approached him.

"We should go, Caco. What are we waitin' for? It's been almost six months since Mamá Lochi left and I don't see anyone coming to get us. I'm gettin' embarrassed of asking Tomasa for food. And it'd be better if we used the money to go. Let's go. Listen, I think we can get Darío to charge us less than what he asked for."

"What are you talking about, Emilia. It's a fuckton," he told me. And because we read each other's minds, we both headed to the kitchen, lifted the block where we'd hidden the money and started to count the bills. It was almost enough to pay for one complete trip. Who knows how much Mamá Lochi had deprived herself of to save up all those pesos.

I proposed that we save a part and tell Darío that we only had enough to pay half. That when we found our family, we could pay him the rest.

"Are you sure?"

"Yeah. I'm sure."

Really, really, I wasn't sure of anything. But we had to try. Caco didn't stop looking at me.

"It's gonna cost us a ton to find them." And he thought for a minute, but then he said, "You're right, we don't have any other choice."

The sun had barely climbed over the mountain when he himself went to negotiate with Darío. I guessed that Darío had talked with his papá and he had told him that Mamá Lochi had saved him and not the mule driver, because he agreed that we could give him just a part, but he wanted to come by our house and see what he wanted from it. In the afternoon, he showed up with a little cart to carry away whatever thing looked good to him. The bastard didn't even leave a single outlet.

We decided not to tell Tomasa anything, but the evening before we left she came to see us, and just by looking in her eyes I knew that she already knew. In a small town even the rocks pass on what they hear. Tomasa put an envelope with some pesos and an image of the Virgin in my brother's hands. She told Goyo to take care of me, and if he could, to call her when we had arrived somewhere safe. That she was going to keep trying to get through to my uncles and my papá to tell them we were coming. That she would take care of the house until we returned, and that she was sure our abuela was going to guide us along a safe path. My brother and I stood in the door and watched her walk down the road. She walked with her head down like it was heavy. My abuela's comadrita Tomasa was a good person and she appreciated us. If she had more to help us with, I know she would have.

That same night, Caco and I dug a hole in the backyard. After putting some photos in plastic bags, we buried them under a tree and put our faith in it not raining much before we could come back to rescue them. We still believed we were going to come back soon. I don't even know what we were thinking. Maybe about our papá, about finding him, about the excitement of the adventure of going to the other side.

One October morning, in the dark hours before dawn, we took off down the path with an old backpack, a bit of food, and three things to wear each, until we reached the graveyard where we'd agreed to meet Darío. Caco and I were trembling, I don't know if from the cold or the nervous excitement that we were carrying. There was no moon. We looked toward the cemetery, and for a moment I squeezed my eyes shut, asking Mamá Lochi to appear, even though she was dead, and hug us to stop our trembling. Then Darío arrived in the pickup truck that he used to haul the bundles of harvest. He told us to get up in the back where there were other people from our town that I had barely ever spoken to. I watched the houses, with their streets and the cemetery, shrink as my own heart shrunk in my chest.

"Adiós, mamita. Adiós, Mamá Lochi," I said in my thoughts, before the daybreak began to tinge the distant mountains with its light.

Caco, Simón, and I weren't with our father for long, because Lucrecia's bad side didn't take long to come out, and she did what she could to get rid of us. For all the good intentions she had at the beginning, her jealousy won out in the end. She couldn't handle us there, reminding our father of his past loves. My two half-brothers were real irritating and then the third one arrived and there was no space for us. Even though we had moved to a bigger place soon after we'd arrived, thanks to the money we brought, we still got in the way. The money lasted a while, but ended up running out. My papá defended us as much he could, but the screaming fights got worse every time and there was nothing left to do but send us to live with our uncles, in another city. They were carpenters, and they made it easy for us to move in with them. They didn't have kids and always loved us very much. If I'm being honest, I did feel resentful, I wished our father had fought more for us, but with the passing of time my rage faded. When he died a few years ago, I finished forgiving him, and, even though I couldn't be by him in his final moments, sometimes I go to the church where we left his ashes. Who knows where his spirit went off to rest.

Caco learned the carpenter's trade and that's been his work, with its highs and lows. He had two kids and has taken to drinking. He hardly speaks Spanish now, he says what for, if he's never going to return and nobody understands it here. He doesn't like it either when I call him Goyo, much less Caco. He says I should call him Gregory, that it sounds better. But I don't pay that any mind. He sleeps badly, and he's turned bitter in his character. Simón, he went to live with a woman. He works in the woodshop with my brother and my uncles, who are quite old now, and he's a good carpenter. He doesn't drink, because he's very religious. He always wanted Caco and me to convert to his beliefs, but with little luck.

Ever since I arrived in this country, the grasshoppers in my feet have made me jump from city to city, from job to job, until I decided to settle down as an assistant in a small public library while I got myself papers and studied to be a teacher. I tell the stories that live in me to whoever lets me, especially all those kids that I see daily and that come from my homeland. Sometimes I write them down, drawing the words over the paper, like Mamá Lochi liked to say. Even though I learned English, I always repeat those phrases to myself, the ones that I have deep inside and I've known since I was a girl—I remember their music, I write them down, I read them and reread them so that way they can't go ahead and abandon me.

Just a few weeks ago, my abuela's comadre Tomasa, who is ninety years old now but still kicking, sent me the package of photos and documents that Caco and I buried under the amate tree before we left. She sent them to us with a three-line letter handwritten by one of her grandchildren, where she said that she missed us, that she missed her comadre, though she knew that her spirit was near her. That she hoped to see us soon. It filled me with hope to read that, but I think she'll jump over the old stone wall before we return to our homeland. The photos that she sent us are dirty, but not so bad. After all that, they were in good shape because we went to great pains to wrap them in plastic so the rain wouldn't ruin them.

I don't know what it was that I felt when I saw my abuela in a picture, given the only photo I'd brought I lost when I crossed the line. I kept looking at it, with those tears that didn't have any end running down my face. There she was, standing at the entrance to the house, in her checkered apron, her fingers linked over her abdomen, her burlap sack crossed over her body, her tree made of lightning shining from her arm, her long braid falling over her shoulder. The only thing you learn with the years is that what you've lived—its undeniable tangles, its secret and incorruptible ways—who knows how, but it becomes recorded in memory without you even realizing. All it takes is a piece of a memory to jump forward for the rest to rise to the surface completely. But then sometimes, no matter how much we dig with our picks and shovels, it just doesn't give in. There's no way to bring back a face, a gesture, a moment, a voice.

When I saw the photos, I realized that all I remembered of Mamá Lochi was the smell of her skin and her voice, which I recovered in the days we were with my father, after I lost it for a while there in the desert. But she always came to me without a face, a gaze, much less a body. And though I've never stopped hearing her since then, in those unexpected but certain ways of hers, with time I discovered that she especially let herself be heard when I most needed her—in moments of doubt, of sadness or heartache. For years I held her close like that, but when I looked at her in that photo, I felt that the sound of her words united with that body in the image. Then I started to hear her more softly, like she needed me to connect them in my head so she could start saying her farewell. A few nights ago I saw her in my dreams, my abuela, entirely silent. She said goodbye to me with that gesture that was so hers, raising her open hand as the marks that traced over her arm flashed, like the lightning that etched them into her skin was a living inhabitant of her body also saying its farewell.

Sometimes I believe that I have a path and a destination. Sometimes I also feel really lost, as lost as I was when I was adrift in the middle of the desert. And a feeling comes to me like everything that happened just happened, even though in reality it's been twenty-something years now since I left Amatlán. And I ask myself when they stop happening, those things that mark you like a scalding ember buried deep in the skin. It feels like yesterday was the day my father gave me a goodbye kiss and walked up the path in the middle of the night. Or that evening of the downpour, when Mamá Lochi took me up the mountain to her secret cave where we sheltered ourselves from the rain. I hear the big old drops falling onto the rock. That evening that she started to tell me her stories, partly to make me her accomplice and partly so I would bring them with me forever and they would arrive wherever my steps did. Or that day she stopped breathing, with her soul already floating up to her mountain, through the branches of the jocote trees, through the amate trees, through her sky.

Lately, at night, when I get under the covers and turn off the light, when I close my eyes and slide down the mudslides of sleep, when I cross the line to that other world, I still feel my abuela. Her scent of ocotillo, of earth wet with summer rain, of firewood, of wildflowers, comes to me . . . and I tell myself that she's close, she hasn't gone, she's still with me. Then I feel like she wraps me up from toes to head with her veil, soft and warm, and then the uncertainties disappear, and I sleep calmly because I know, as soon as I wake, I will hear her voice coming back to me.

MORE ADULT FICTION

¡ÁNDALE, PRIETA!
by Yasmín Ramírez

NOBODY'S PILGRIMS
by Sergio Troncoso

A PECULIAR KIND OF IMMIGRANT'S SON
by Sergio Troncoso

*EVERYTHING BEGINS AND ENDS AT THE
KENTUCKY CLUB*
by Benjamin Alire Sáenz

WHEN A WOMAN RISES
by Christine Eber

. . . and others, from

CINCO PUNTOS PRESS,
an imprint of LEE & LOW BOOKS

ABOUT THE AUTHOR

MARIANA OSORIO GUMÁ is a psychoanalyst and writer. She has published seven books of fiction in Spanish, three of which have been selected by the International Board on Books for Young People for their high quality. In 2014, she was awarded the Premio Literario Lipp La brasserie for her novel *Tal vez vuelvan los pájaros*. Born in Havana, Cuba, in 1967, she has lived in Mexico since 1973.

ABOUT THE TRANSLATOR

CECILIA WEDDELL is a writer, editor, and translator from I Paso, TX. She has a Ph.D. Editorial Studies from Bost University. Her translati from Spanish have appeared *World Literature Today, Lite Imagination, Harvard Review,* and more.